A WHYTE CHRISTMAS

MICHELE BROUDER

This is a work of fiction. Names, characters, places and incidents are either a product of the author's imagination or are used fictitiously, and any resemblance to actual persons, living or dead, events, or locales is entirely coincidental.

Editing by Jessica Peirce

Book Cover Design by Rebecca Ruger

A Whyte Christmas

CHAPTER ONE

December 2009

Kate's eyes widened in horror as the ladder swung out from beneath her. She was no more than three feet above ground level, but that didn't stop all thirty years of her life from flashing before her eyes. Sprucing up the office with a few Christmas decorations should never have been this perilous. She grabbed onto the nearest hand-hold, the edge of the trophy case, but quickly realized it was not meant for the likes of her hanging off of it. The case creaked, buckled and popped off its brackets on the right side. Kate let go and fell, with a thud, to the floor. Flat on her back and showing her big, white spankies was not her preferred way to start off a Monday morning. Or any morning, for that matter.

"Holy—are you all right?" Muttered a deep voice from behind her, with what sounded distinctly like an Irish accent.

Unhurt but horrified, she raised her head in the direction of the voice. Wow. Tall, dark, handsome, and now standing directly over her, making this one of the top five humiliations of her life. She knew she must look a sight: a red and gold 'Merry Christmas' banner draped across her chest, one shoe off, her ponytail all over the place and her glasses crooked on her face. Serious black glasses she had bought because she thought they made her look smarter. She quickly adjusted her navy skirt, but not before the stranger had gotten a blinding eyeful of mother-endorsed cotton underwear.

"Are you hurt?" he asked. He took Kate's hand and helped her up off the floor.

"I'm fine," she said, fixing her ponytail and straightening her glasses in an attempt to recover a shred of professionalism.

He lifted the ladder off the floor and leaned it against the wall.

"Do you always start your day off like this?" he asked, staring at her.

"This is nothing. Wait until you see what I have planned for this afternoon," she said with a nervous laugh.

Men with movie star looks and sexy foreign accents rarely walked through the doors of the Cline & Company advertising agency. In fact, this might be the first time it had ever happened. He ticked all the boxes: height, six feet or so; eyes, to-die-for blue; and hair, thick, wavy, and black. As an added bonus he had a cleft in his chin. Looks like his could be dangerous; if she had passed him on the street she could easily have been distracted enough to step off a curb and into the path of a speeding bus.

She slipped her foot back into her shoe with all the deftness of the ugly stepsister trying to jam her foot into the glass slipper. She looked at the trophy case and assessed the damage. One side of it hung clear off the wall. "Oh boy," she muttered under her breath, hands on her hips.

It was a custom-made case designed to showcase the agency's awards, of which there were plenty. The ADDYs, the CLIOs, and the Golden Lions, as well as the plaques from the mayor and the chamber of commerce, were in one big heap at the end of the case. She groaned inwardly—Mr. Cline, owner and president of the agency, would surely go into orbit over this. But she'd deal with that later.

"Can I help you?" she finally asked.

"Yes, I'm looking for Kate O'Connor," he said.

The last half of his sentence was lost to her as she studied his eyes. Cobalt. They made eyes that color?

"Miss?" he asked.

"Sorry—who?" she asked, coming slowly out of her reverie as if she were swimming up to the surface of a drug-induced stupor.

"Kate O'Connor," he said again.

"Oh, yes, she's here. I mean, I'm here. I'm Kate O'Connor." She was embarrassed by her vocal incontinence.

He raised his eyebrows. Even those were sexy.

"You're Kate O'Connor?" he asked. He leaned closer, frowning. She gulped. "Do you realize you have lights hanging from your ears?"

She smiled weakly and touched her earrings: little Christmas trees with tiny, working lights. Although incongruous with her somber office attire, they were her all-time favorite holiday earrings. She'd worn them to kick off the festive season.

"They reveal a lot about your character," he said. His expression was blank.

She opened her mouth to respond but then shut it, as she wasn't sure if she had been insulted or not.

Who was this man? Lord of the Manor? Assuming an imperial air that rarely worked for her, she asked, "Again, may I help you?"

"Mr. Cline told me to see you when I arrived."

"The office doesn't open until nine," she said loftily.

"Am I disqualified for coming in early?" he asked, without missing a beat.

"And you are...?"

"Gavin Whyte."

Oh. The color drained from her face. Her boss had left her a voicemail on Friday informing her of the expected arrival of Mr. Whyte. He was the vice-president of marketing for Alchemis, one of the top five pharmaceutical companies in the world, presently based in Ireland. Cline & Co. had recently been awarded the US advertising contract for their new diet drug. Kate suspected it might have more to do with the fact that Mr. Cline was related to the president of Alchemis than any actual merit on the company's part, but it was a big deal, regardless. Despite the glorious past commemorated in the trophy case, the agency was on its knees financially.

Rumors about Gavin Whyte had arrived before he did: he was a control freak; he liked to micromanage everything; he had climbed the corporate ladder quickly and his next stop was the presidency of the company. And most of all, he had been against the contract going to Cline & Co., favoring instead an ad agency in Manhattan. Mr. Whyte had come to the US to personally oversee the ad campaign, and Mr. Cline had instructed Kate to give him the corner office. No one had ever used the corner office, not even Mr. Cline himself. This was akin to the Second Coming.

"We weren't expecting you until tomorrow," Kate said weakly.

"Will I come back?" he asked, indicating towards the door.

She couldn't tell if he was joking or not. "Never mind," she mumbled.

Without further delay and with no additional smart aleck comments that might increase her chances of ending up on the unemployment line, she immediately escorted him to his workspace. She opened the door and turned on the lights.

"This will be your office," she said. "During your...um...stay with us."

He walked past her, into the room. One whiff of his expensive cologne nearly made her knees buckle. Drat. She didn't want to have that kind of response to him.

"Can I get you anything?" she offered.

"No thank you." Oh, that Irish accent. He'd have to stop doing that.

Kate watched him as he looked around the room. His expression was blasé and she wondered what he would think of the rest of the clowns who worked there.

Mr. Cline had spared no expense and in one of his smarter moves, he had left the furnishing of the space to an interior decorator rather than his wife, she of the overdone mascara and hair the color of black shoe polish.

Kate walked to the oversized window with its panoramic view of Lake Erie and caught sight of the foamy whitecaps crashing against the breakwater of the marina. Directly across the lake was the hazy shoreline of Canada.

She turned around to face him. "As far as lunch goes, there are a few good restaurants nearby or you could order in, if you're interested," she suggested. "Unless of course, you brown bag it."

He looked at her evenly and said, "I don't brown bag it."

"*That* reveals a lot about your character, Mr. Whyte." She folded her arms across her chest.

"Touché," he answered.

She retreated from his office and closed the door behind her, thinking she'd seen the slightest of smiles on his face.

Gavin Whyte did not want to be here. Buffalo, of all places. He could barely contain his frustration and fury. Cline & Co. had not been his pick to run the biggest ad campaign in the history of Alchemis. He had a vision for Alchemis that couldn't be more far-removed from this nickel-and-dime operation. He resented the fact that he was being forced to babysit.

He stood in the middle of his new office, hands on his hips, and wondered angrily how the hell he'd ended up in the middle of nowhere. This soulless room would be his workspace for the next six to eight weeks. The only positive was the amazing view of Lake Erie. He had done some of his best brainstorming staring out of windows similar to this one: Dublin, New York, London, Tokyo.

He hung his suit jacket over the back of the chair and rolled up his sleeves, trying to resign himself to the fact that for the next one to two months, he was stuck here in this little city five hundred miles west of New York City. Back home, they would have called this the back of beyond.

The current president of Alchemis, Larry Barrett, had asked him as a personal favor to oversee this ad campaign from the ground up. Despite the fact that Barrett's wife and Ed Cline were cousins, he thought that Cline was basically a loose cannon and bore watching. Larry spent more time on the golf course than in the boardroom these days, and it was only a matter of time before he stepped down. Gavin was the number one contender for his position. He'd worked hard for it since joining Alchemis fifteen years ago. He wanted it more than anything, and he wasn't going to allow this sad excuse for a business to blow it for him.

He'd flown in on Saturday and had dinner with Ed Cline and his wife on Sunday. He quickly discovered that the man wasn't so much a loose cannon as he was certifiable. It had been an alarming, eye-opening moment, between the clearing of the appetizers and the serving of the entrees, when he'd realized that the reins of his advertising budget had been given to a buffoon. As much as he didn't want to be here—he hated living out of suitcases and hotels and had hoped his traveling days were over—he knew that if he wanted that promotion, he had to stay. He'd hold everyone's hands if necessary. Whatever it took.

His suspicions about the competence of this ad agency had been confirmed when he arrived to find the receptionist swinging off a ladder. If he hadn't been so tired from travelling or so worried about the future of the campaign, he might have found it funny. But the fact that it only validated his initial impressions robbed him of his sense of humor.

When he'd helped her up, he hadn't missed her pretty face or her shapely figure, especially with her skirt hiked up to her waist. The poor woman had been mortified. No wonder she'd gotten all haughty on him. But then again, he reminded himself, he had no time for humor, or for shapely girls, for that matter.

"O'Connor!"

Kate rolled her eyes. There was only one setting on Mr. Cline's volume control: high. *All I want for Christmas is a remote with a 'mute' button on it*, she thought. She was nearly back at her desk but she picked up her pace, the smell of her boss hitting her before she saw him. It was as if he habitually rolled around in a barrel of Brut.

"What happened here?" he asked. He waved his hand toward the trophy case.

"It kind of fell off the wall," Kate explained, looking down at him. She had to—she had at least five inches on him in her flats. She had to give him credit, though. For a short man, he was not at all intimidated by her height. In fact, he could be a real corker at times.

He stared at her. "No kidding, Sherlock. How?"

"I grabbed onto it as I was falling off the ladder," Kate explained.

"Ladder? What ladder? What were you doing on a ladder? I don't want to know. Get the building super on the phone and see if we can get this fixed today."

"I'm on it, Mr. Cline. Oh, and before I forget, Gavin Whyte has arrived."

The expression on his face made him look as if he were about to blast off.

"Already? And this is how the reception area looked? Remember, Kate, you're the first impression of the company people get when they walk through that door."

She decided against telling him that Mr. Whyte had been front and center when she was hanging off the trophy case.

"First impressions are everything. How you present yourself and the feeling people get when they walk through those doors can make or break our business."

Oh great, she thought. *Maybe I should just pack up my personal belongings in a cardboard box now.*

Mr. Cline went on in the same vein for a few more minutes before disappearing down the hall to his office, a cloud of eye-watering cologne following him.

An hour later, Kate was settled at her desk, almost willing the phone to ring. A ringing phone meant business. She sent memos to staff about the upcoming meetings and appointments for the week. She went through her emails, which didn't take long. The office was unusually quiet for a Monday morning. And that was the problem: the office was too quiet.

The phone lit up—an internal call from the conference room.

"O'Connor! Mandatory meeting. I left it on everyone's voicemail. Do you care to honor us with your presence?"

"I'm on my way," she said. She stood up from her desk and disconnected from her headset. She swore under her breath; she'd made sure everyone else knew about the office meeting but she hadn't realized she was supposed to be there herself.

She hurried down the corridor to the conference room, took a deep breath and went inside. All eyes were on her.

"Nice of you to join us," Mr. Cline said. "I hope we're not keeping you from anything important."

There was a snicker or two from the group.

She scanned the room, looking for an empty seat, until a slight wave from an electric-blue-manicured hand caught her eye. The owner of the hand, Sherrie Santora, indicated a vacant chair next to her. Anxious not to be the center of attention, Kate quickly sat down.

Sherrie was the art director and although barely five feet tall and very thin—as in, Kate-could-pick-her-teeth-with-her thin—she was hard to miss with her jet black hair and fuchsia-colored highlights. Sherrie gave Kate a smile, then returned her attention to the front of the room.

Mr. Cline stood at the podium. He adjusted the microphone downward. Why he needed a microphone in the conference room was beyond Kate. Everyone out on the street would be able to hear his verbal assaults.

Her boss cleared his throat. "Gavin Whyte arrived this morning. I know we weren't expecting him until tomorrow, but we just need to step up to the plate. I don't need to tell any of you how important this account is to us."

There was silence in the room. It was no wonder Cline & Co. looked to Alchemis like a drowning man looked to a lifeline. After the crash of '08, the company's fortunes had taken a nose dive. Jobs were cut and perks were eliminated. Kate, the most junior member of staff, had lost her job as a copywriter back in January. When Mr. Cline had offered her the position of receptionist, she'd taken it in order to avoid the unemployment line. He had said it would only be temporary, and that eventually she'd get her copywriter job back. Almost twelve months later, she needed to pin him down on his definition of 'temporary.'

"Now, listen up," he said loudly. The microphone screeched.

The room quieted. The only noise came from the low hum of the overhead fluorescent lights and the muted sounds of the traffic out the window.

"Kate, what are we doing about an assistant for Gavin Whyte?" he asked.

"I called the temp agency, and someone should be out by the end of the week," she answered.

"Until that temp gets here, you'll do it," Mr. Cline said.

She shifted uneasily in her chair but nodded. *So now I'm an executive assistant*, she thought, which in this office likely translated to coffeemaker extraordinaire.

"Now, people, I want this campaign to be the best advertising product Cline and Company has ever put out," he stated. He ran his hand through his brassy-colored hair.

You'd think he was preparing to do brain surgery, she thought.

"I want this more than I've ever wanted anything in my life," he continued.

He had said that about the last account and the account before that. He needed a new script.

"This account with Alchemis will put us back at the top. It will open doors for us globally." He paused before continuing. "Now, if any one of you doesn't feel up to the task, let me know now as it will save us both the embarrassment of me firing you later. I need all your brain cells and all your attention on this one."

Mr. Cline looked around the room, but everyone remained quiet, except for the occasional cough. "We'll all be under enormous pressure. So let me establish some guidelines." He paused for effect, taking a sip of his coffee.

Sherrie elbowed Kate and giggled softly. "Here it comes."

"Number one. Spend more time at your desk. Skip the office chit chat. Skip the two hour lunches with friends."

Kate knew this was directed at Alexis Winston, Director of Media Relations, who practically carried the whole agency on her back. But she had taken a long holiday weekend to go to New York City and wouldn't be back until the following day, so he had just wasted his breath.

"Number two." He glared at Ben Davidson from IT. "No prowling around the office looking for hook-ups. This is a business, not dating and mating international."

Kate thought Ben looked clueless, as usual. He didn't think these comments were directed at him. Ben hit on every woman who wore a size six and below. Luckily, that left her out, except on those rare company outings when he had too much to drink and his requirements weren't as precise.

"Number three." Mr. Cline inhaled deeply. "Let your families know how important this account is to Cline and Company. Tell them that you want to keep your jobs. So, please, unless they are delirious from a high fever or bleeding from every orifice of their body, no more unnecessary phone calls from your kids asking for permission to watch TV, or surf the Net, or wondering where Mom put their hockey stick." He leveled his gaze at Sherrie.

All glazed-over eyes and catatonic stares were firmly on the boss.

"Lastly. Again, this is a business. Therefore, please leave all hobbies at home. I don't want to see needlework, macramé, or your part-time cosmetic business at the office." He paused, drawing in another deep breath.

Kate wondered if he needed a respiratory treatment.

"Are there any questions?"

There was no response from the group except the coughs and shuffling sounds of people anxious to get back to work.

Mr. Cline pressed on. "On a lighter note, the office Christmas party is coming up. As usual, it will be here at the office, right after work, the Wednesday before Christmas. See Debbie Cjaka about joining the committee. Hopefully, you'll be able to make it." He paused for effect. "If you're still working here."

Kate groaned. The dreaded office Christmas party, and the wild stories the next day about what had transpired: who had rejected Ben Davidson and who'd ended up vomiting behind the bushes outside the lobby. She always wondered if she'd been at the same party or merely in a food coma at the buffet table.

She was grateful that Mr. Cline was a cheapskate and wouldn't pay for a hotel party where everyone had to bring a date and don formalwear. She shuddered at that thought, as memories of her one disastrous prom came flooding back

"Good. On a final note, as you know, Don Anderson, our Creative Director, resigned last week. I'm happy to say that I've found a replacement for him." Kate felt Sherrie tense up beside her. She had been with the agency for over ten years and had been in the running before the position was given to Don. Kate crossed her fingers for her.

He pulled out his phone and dialed an extension. "Come on down and meet the team." Turning back to the group, he smiled. "The guy's been here since seven this morning trying to get a handle on things. How's that for a work ethic?"

She watched as Mr. Cline went over to the door of the conference room, opened it and announced, "May I present the new Creative Director of Cline and Company, Paul Reynolds!"

Kate's mouth dropped open. She felt Sherrie slump beside her.

Paul strolled through the doorway, still as good-looking as ever with his sun-dappled blonde hair and perfect teeth, and totally oblivious that they were sharing the same air.

The last time she'd seen him was five years ago, when he had unceremoniously dumped her right before their wedding.

CHAPTER TWO

Paul, with his hands on his hips and his shirt sleeves rolled up to his forearms, gave a short but inspiring spiel. Kate sank down further into her seat, hoping he wouldn't notice her. She took a peek around the room. He had everyone's attention, but then that was Paul. Men wanted to be him and women wanted to be with him. He knew it and used it to his advantage. It had run her over in the past.

Afterwards, she tried to sneak out of the room, hot on the heels of a crushed Sherrie, avoiding making eye contact with him.

"Kate?"

No such luck.

"Oh, hey Paul," she said, trying to present a nonchalant air while her emotions were roiling inside of her.

"I didn't know you still worked here," he said. She thanked whatever gods were there that he didn't try to hug her, or worse: kiss her.

"Well, yes." With nothing more to say, she walked on.

But he wouldn't let her go that easily. He put a hand on her arm and she looked at it as if it were something distasteful, like a spider. She glanced around quickly, hoping no one would notice that they knew each other.

"Look, I hope we can put all that stuff behind us," he said, smiling with a flash of white teeth.

All 'that stuff' had been her life. She shrugged and slipped out of his grasp. Right now her main concern was how Sherrie was doing, not making Paul comfortable in his new job.

She hoofed it over to the smaller conference room to give Sherrie a hand. One of their newer clients, Epson Bank, would be coming in later that morning and Sherrie needed to set up her presentation.

Sherrie's face looked grim.

"Are you all right?" Kate asked softly, searching her friend's face.

Sherrie nodded quickly. "I'll be fine. I should know better by now than to get my hopes up in this place!"

"It's the company's loss and everyone here knows that," Kate said with conviction. It was true. Sherrie stumped people with her hot pink highlights and her piercings. But anyone who saw her output and artistic talent knew that she was truly brilliant.

"Have you met the international man of mystery?" Sherrie asked, changing the subject. Unlike Kate, who had been mooning over Paul for the last five years, Sherrie wasn't one to dwell.

"Gavin Whyte? Yeah," Kate said, straightening the chairs around the conference table.

"He's nice and he's sooooo hot," Sherrie purred.

Kate stopped what she was doing and looked at her as if she had just grown another head.

"Nice?" Kate asked. Perhaps her humiliation in front of him had biased her impression.

"No?"

She relayed the ladder incident to her friend.

"Ouch. I hate when that happens," Sherrie said, laughing. She didn't mention a word about Paul Reynolds, and Kate was fine with that.

Sherrie placed folders on the table as Kate covered a silver tray with a paper lace doily. She retrieved a tin from the sideboard where she'd left it that morning, opened it, and began unwrapping the pastries she'd made the night before, arranging them on the tray. Sherrie peered over her shoulder.

"You made Danish again! Kate, you're killing me!" she said, and chose a cherry one.

Kate marveled at her. Even with five kids and an incredible sweet tooth, Sherrie didn't weigh more than a hundred pounds soaking wet. While she, on the other hand, worshipped at the altar of the god of elastic waistbands.

"Mr. Cline asked me to make them for the client meeting. I wouldn't look like much of a team player if I refused. Not that I would—he pays me for the supplies, and besides, I love doing it."

"Did you see the ad in the employment section of the newspaper on Sunday?" Sherrie asked.

Kate shook her head. She put the tray on a table at the back of the room, then checked the coffee and tea carafes. They were full. Little white china cups and saucers were laid out beside the bowls of creamer and sugar.

"The IRS is looking for temporary help after the first of the year for the tax season. The only requirement is a four-year college degree."

Kate shrugged her shoulders.

"It might lead to something permanent. Plus, it's a federal job. Good benefits."

Sherrie was always trying to find Kate a better job. She felt that Cline & Co. had been bad for her health. Kate did, too, at times. However, she hoped with the launch of the Alchemis ad campaign she'd find her way back to her copywriting position, a job she had loved.

"You don't want to spend the rest of your life here, listening to his pep talks," Sherrie said, nodding her head in the general direction of Mr. Cline's office.

"I'm holding out for my old copywriting job."

"Sure," Sherrie said then added bitterly: "Besides, there's no room for advancement here."

They left the conference room, agreeing to meet up for lunch, and Kate grabbed a quick cup of coffee from the break room before returning to her post.

Kate rapped on Gavin Whyte's open office door. He looked up at her and smiled. She noticed a dimple in his right cheek. *Oh my God, a cleft in his chin and a dimple in his cheek. What's next? A twinkle in his eye? I'll never go on to lead a normal life. I'll need a twelve step program just to get over his looks.*

"I thought I'd take you around and introduce you to everyone and show you where everything is," she said.

He stood up and took his jacket from the back of his chair and put it on. "That would be grand. I'd love to get a cup of coffee."

She nodded.

"Or do you send out for it?"

She ignored this remark, choosing to prove to him that she was a model of efficiency and not an...idiot. "There should be a fresh pot in the break room." She was surprised he drank coffee as she knew the Irish to be serious tea drinkers. Her father had been right off the boat and had always kept a pot of tea on the stove. She wondered if he'd make coffee or expect her to make it for him. Mr. Cline liked to have his coffee made and poured for him.

The nickel tour she proceeded to take him on turned into an impromptu meet-and-greet with staff as she led him by the various departments: accounting, IT, creative, and production.

First stop was Debbie Cjaka. Gavin extended his hand and Debbie grabbed it, pumping it.

"I'm happy to meet you, Mr. Whyte," she gushed.

"Please call me Gavin," he said.

"I'm the events coordinator here at Cline and Company," she said. "I handle all the events." With this she burst out in a fit of giggles. "It's obvious, I know. Anyway, this is my favorite month of the year. Lots of events planned this month."

This was news to Kate.

Debbie rolled on. "Every Christmas, we do a Kris Kringle, where everyone chooses a name and the gift limit is fifty dollars. I hope you'll join in."

Kate somehow couldn't picture Gavin getting involved in their pokey little Christmas exchange.

"If I'm still here, I'd be delighted," he said diplomatically.

They headed to the next office which belonged to Ann from accounting. Kate was a little nervous as Ann could be surly on the best of days.

She was standing there in the middle of her office with her arms folded across her chest. "So they sent you over to babysit us."

Kate felt the color drain from her face. Ann didn't particularly like men. It was because of her husband at home.

Gavin reached out to shake her hand. She shook his.

"Well, I wouldn't call it babysitting," he said, smiling.

"I would," she said sharply. "And if we don't produce, we'll get the boot."

Kate shot her a look that said 'Back off!'

But Gavin laughed and nodded to her coffee mug with the New York Yankees logo on it.

"Yankees fan?"

"I am," she said evenly.

"I'm a Boston Red Sox fan myself," he announced. A little dangerously, Kate thought.

"Well no one's perfect," Ann said.

Gavin let out a bark of laughter. "No, I guess not."

They talked for a few more minutes about baseball and Kate watched as Ann's face softened which was nothing short of miraculous.

Next, Kate introduced him to Ben Davidson who seemed nervous and all aflutter. They talked briefly about IT related things. Kate tried not to look bored.

"I like the cut of your suit," Gavin said to him.

Ben blushed scarlet. He lifted up the flap of his jacket, revealing the lining. "There's a tailor about six blocks up, Maggio is his name. It's all his own work."

"Really?" Gavin asked.

Ben nodded. "Custom made and reasonable." He took off his jacket and handed it to Gavin. "Here try it on."

Kate raised her eyebrows and prayed he wouldn't remove his pants. Before her very eyes, Gavin Whyte took off his jacket and laid it on Ben's workspace. He shrugged on Ben's jacket but he was too broad in the shoulders. He took it back off. "I don't want to ruin it for you."

"No worries," Ben said.

"Would you have a business card for your tailor?" he asked.

Ben spun around to his desk and grabbed a small metal box. Clumsily, he opened it and all the contents spilled on the floor. Hundreds of business cards.

"Uh, I have it right here," he said, getting down on his knees on the floor and scooping up cards.

Kate didn't think that they could stand there all day watching him sort through stacks and stacks of business cards.

"Ben, when you find it, perhaps you could drop it off to Mr. Whyte," she suggested.

Ben looked up at her and blinked. "Oh, right. Sure. Will do."

He appeared to have developed a man crush on the foreign invader. Kate wondered briefly if he batted for both sides.

They ended up in the break room where he poured himself a coffee.

"Do you know anything about Paul Reynolds, the new creative director?" he asked, spooning quite a bit of sugar into his cup.

Her immediate inclination was to say that Paul was an A-1 jerk who had left her at the altar and run off with one of the bridesmaids. But she didn't want to involve Mr. Whyte in all that drama, or to appear unprofessional by badmouthing her ex. *Say something positive*, she told herself. *He's only looking for information on his ability, not his personality.*

"He's supposed to be very talented. He's worked for some big agencies in New York City." There, she'd said it. It made her want to throw up, but it was done.

"Uh, Kate, could I have a word?" Kate looked up quickly from her computer screen. Paul stood over her, rubbing the back of his head. He always did that when he was nervous.

She took her purse out of her desk drawer and made as if she were heading out the door.

"Now is not a good time, Paul, I've got an errand to run." She gave him a quick, tight smile.

"Maybe later, then," he suggested.

"Maybe." She left the reception area and holed up in the restroom for fifteen minutes, hiding from him.

Gavin couldn't find anything. It had to be the most ill-equipped office he'd ever worked in. Not a pen or paperclip in sight. This was going to be like a prison term, he could feel it. He buzzed Kate to come into his office.

There was a knock on his door and Kate entered, approaching him hesitantly. She smelled lovely: something warm, light and flowery. It reminded him of outdoors. She stood in profile. He wondered what was up with her clothes. She had amazing curves but it was almost like she was hiding them behind her matronly get-up. He tried not to stare.

"There are no pens. No paper for the printer," he said. "And I can't figure out how to set up my voicemail."

"Oh," was her award-winning response. "Well, let's see what you do have and I'll get you whatever you need," she suggested brightly.

"If it's not too much trouble," he said evenly.

"Not at all," she said breezily, waving her hand. She stepped behind the desk and stood next to him.

"May I look in your drawers?" she asked. She immediately reddened.

It took all he had not to laugh. He tried to look stern because someone had to be professional, but it was proving to be difficult with her.

He raised his eyebrows.

"I mean I just want to see what you have. In your drawers. Your desk drawers."

"I'm glad you clarified that for me," he said, suppressing a smile.

He rolled his executive chair back and folded his hands in his lap. She leaned over him and he became acutely aware of her: her scent and the deep, rich brown of her beautiful hair. The way her lips moved as she jotted things down in her notepad. He noticed that the skin revealed in the V of her neckline was quite flushed and he looked away sharply. She finished her inventory and told him she'd be right back.

In no time, she returned with a basket of office supplies, then gave him a brief tutorial on the phone system.

"Thank you, Kate," he said.

"Is there anything else?" she asked, pushing her glasses up on her nose.

"No thank you."

She turned to leave and he wondered why she let out a big sigh as she left his office.

By the time Kate arrived home from work, she was exhausted. She had spent almost the whole day either dodging Paul or helping Irish. She was bow-legged from running back and forth between Mr. Whyte's and Mr. Cline's offices. She'd spent forty-five minutes trying to figure out the three-way phone call conference system so he could 'virtually' attend a meeting in Dublin.

She pulled her car into the narrow driveway and sat for a minute, waiting for one of her favorite Christmas songs to finish playing on the radio before she switched off the key in the ignition.

Her mother's green Chrysler was parked on the road out front. Long ago, Kate had given her a spare key and since then she had spent more time at Kate's home than Kate did. Every so often, she broached the subject about moving in with Kate as if they were two twenty-year-olds instead of thirty and sixty-five. Kate held firm.

Thank God I don't have a boyfriend, she thought. *I'd have absolutely no privacy.*

The brown winter grass was in dire need of snow to cover it up. She walked up the front porch and surveyed the scene, anticipating the delight of putting up exterior holiday decorations. Of course, she'd rethink anything that involved a ladder. A gust of wind blew past, ruffling the shrubs and whistling coldly along her face, stinging her eyes. She'd purchased her home with the little bit of money her father had left her. It was a bungalow with shingled cedar siding, a deep, wide porch, and a sloped roof.

She hung up her coat in the hall closet, walked into the living room and sank down onto the brown suede sofa, closing her eyes and letting out a big sigh. She kicked off her shoes, putting her stockinged-feet up on the glass table and nudging a bayberry candle aside with her big toe. Her cell phone beeped and she glanced at the text from her best friend, Lisa, asking to meet her for dinner the following evening. She quickly texted back an '*ok.*'

She thought of her humiliation on the ladder in front of Gavin Whyte and wondered if anyone would notice if she didn't show up for work the next morning. Probably not. She tried to keep thinking about Irish so she wouldn't have to think about Paul Reynolds and what it meant after all this time to see him, if it meant anything at all.

She opened her eyes as her mother plopped down on the sofa beside her.

"I made pierogi today," her mom said by way of greeting.

Kate's mouth watered. She loved pierogi. And no one made them like her mother.

"C'mon out to the kitchen, and have a bite to eat," she said, patting her on the leg.

Kate knew that her mother would not let up until she gave in and ate. Her dad had spent the last few weeks of his life not eating—he couldn't, and it had driven her mother insane. She still harbored a belief that had he eaten, he would be alive today, despite the fact that he had been riddled with cancer.

She sat down on the stool at the kitchen island and picked up the newspaper. A quick glance told her that it was the same as yesterday and the day before that: blah, blah, blah. She threw it aside.

She loved her kitchen, and not for the obvious reason that it was the room in the house where all the food was kept. Although small in size, the kitchen was warm in appearance with its pale peach walls, pale yellow cabinets, and countertops that looked like grey pebbles. A cinnamon-colored valance hung over the top of the Venetian blinds, providing a nice contrast.

Her mother put a plate down in front of her. Kate's stomach growled and she tucked into the cheese pierogis and the dollop of sour cream.

"I had a call from your Aunt Geraldine today," Mrs. O'Connor said, wiping down the countertop.

Aunt Geraldine was her father's older sister. She still lived on the family farm in Ireland.

"Everything okay?" Kate asked between bites.

"Yes, of course. She asked again about you coming for a visit." Her mother stopped wiping the counter to look at her.

"Mmm."

"You're long overdue, my dear," she said, now turning her full attention to the dishwasher and the task of loading it. "You have to go back sometime. You haven't been there since before your father died."

"I know, Mom," she said. As a kid, Kate had spent all her summers there. She loved Ireland; it was magical and the scenery was breathtaking, especially in the countryside. However, after her father's death, she had become inert, unable to visit the place that reminded her so much of him. "Maybe next year," she mumbled, making a mental note to call her aunt over the weekend.

"I think they call that 'pathological grief,'" Mrs. O'Connor commented. She closed the door of the dishwasher, sat down at the island with her daughter and picked up the newspaper.

"What?"

Before her mother could reply, there was a succession of three distinct raps on the back door.

It could only be Vinnie. Nobody else knocked like he did. Kate opened the door and her neighbor sauntered in. Vinnie Mann was just on the underside of forty. He was six-four, wore his hair in a mullet and passed off a thin, black line of hair above his lip as a mustache. In a good light, on a day when all the planets were in perfect alignment, and from a certain angle, he resembled a B-list celebrity. "Missus, how are you?" he asked Kate's mother. He looked at Kate and smiled. "Hey, babe, how you doin'?"

"Fine."

Vinnie had moved into his mother's house next door after her death a few years back. Until then, Kate had never met him. Since then, she couldn't get rid of him. He worked in the kitchen at the local community college, although rumors circulated that years ago, he had done some time for running a pyramid scheme.

"I was wondering if you're free tomorrow night. I have some business to take care of and I thought you might want to go with me," he said. He drummed his fingers nervously on the countertop. Kate could almost see the little hamster in his head, hard at work on its wheel, going about a hundred miles per hour.

However, she knew from past experience that Vinnie's business was usually nonsense or illegal.

"What about Angie?" Kate asked, referring to his most recent girlfriend. Vinnie's girlfriends ran the gamut of the female species. Angie had been a girl that looked like she'd used volumes of hairspray (you couldn't light a match near her) and applied her make-up with a trowel. Before that there had been Josie, a long-distance truck driver with a fondness for flannel, cargo pants, and truck stops for date nights. And before that there had been Mary Paulette, a woman who had left the convent after twenty-five years. She played a mean accordion. He called them all 'babe.' Kate had asked him once what was up with the variety. He had looked at her strangely and responded, 'It's their loneliness that attracts me.' Saving the world one lonely soul at a time.

"She dumped me," he said. He didn't seem too forlorn. "The problem is they all know I'm holding out for you."

Before she could comment, her mother, who looked on the verge of an apoplectic stroke, butted in. "She can't, Vinnie. She needs to start her holiday baking."

"Aw, Kate, c'mon. Christmas is weeks away, you've got plenty of time," he protested.

"What is it, exactly, that you do for a living, Mr. Mann?" Mrs. O'Connor asked, folding her arms across her chest, trying—and succeeding—at looking high-handed.

"I do a little bit of this and a little bit of that," he grinned, which scored him no points whatsoever with Kate's mother. He continued to drum his fingers on the countertop. To Kate he said, "C'mon, you can bake another night. I can't understand why you won't give me a chance. I'd treat you like a queen. Besides, I need to improve my image and become an upstanding member of the community."

Kate watched her mother pale. She wasn't a fan of Vinnie; she called him a 'shyster' behind his back.

"Maybe another time, Vinnie. Okay?" Kate said softly. Despite the fact that he wasn't her type and that he was a little odd, he was benign. She couldn't help but like him.

Vinnie soon departed to do whatever it was that Vinnie did.

Mrs. O'Connor followed him out the door, as her aqua aerobics class started at seven sharp and she still had to get to the high school and wrestle her bathing suit on.

Alone at last, Kate looked forward to an evening of pajamas, marathon TV, and hot cocoa. But first she wanted to sort through her recipes to see what cookies she would be making this Christmas.

After an hour of compiling Christmas cookie recipes and desserts, she set her list aside, unable to concentrate. She thought of putting on a Christmas movie but she wasn't in the mood. She glanced around the living room: the gleaming hardwood floors, the glass-top coffee table with its assortment of candles and magazines and the non-functioning fireplace with its clutter of framed photographs and sentimental memorabilia. The Christmas decorations made the place look cheery. Except her Christmas stocking, which looked pathetic hanging all by itself from the mantle. Maybe if she got a pet, she could hang its stocking next to hers, but no—she'd managed to kill every houseplant she ever owned, so a live animal was probably not a good idea.

Her thoughts reluctantly turned to Paul. She'd heard he moved out of town but obviously, he was back. It was probably for the best that it hadn't worked out for the two of them; they were so different. He had been voted 'most likely to succeed' while she had been voted 'class clown.' Still, at one time in her life, she had loved him deeply enough to marry him, and since the day he left, she had been unable to move on. She had had a date here and there but nothing serious—she just wasn't interested. A very small ripple of depression rolled over her. What was she waiting for?

And then there was her father. She would never stop missing him. She loved Christmas, everything about the season: all the preparation, the baking, the gift buying, the decorating, all in anticipation of that one big, magical day. But her father's absence was keenly felt, even now, tinging the event with grief. The truth was she was tired of feeling all this sadness over his death, but the thought of enjoying anything made her feel guilty. Her father wouldn't have wanted it that way.

She rolled off the sofa and padded to the bedroom. She opened the closet, flipped on the light switch and was greeted with the blacks, greys, and navy blues that made up her wardrobe. There had been a time when she wouldn't have been caught dead in those morose shades. But everything of color had been packed up and consigned to the charity shop. Now it was time to rethink the dull and the drab. She got a black trash bag from the kitchen and began pulling clothes off hangers and tossing them in the bag. The first to go was the navy skirt she had worn that morning when she went flying off the ladder.

She could forgive herself for not having gotten past the loss of her father or of her fiancé. But it bothered her that Paul had seen it first-hand.

In her fantasies about running into him, she'd always looked fabulous and tanned, often wearing a bikini—which was a bit rich considering she hadn't worn a bikini since she was fifteen. She envisioned herself beaming, with a million and one cutting remarks for him. And most importantly, Paul would always realize what he had lost. It was a sharp contrast from the reality of today's encounter, with her wearing clothes a corrections officer would envy, and spending a good part of the day hiding in the bathroom.

She looked down at her sorry, yellow-flowered flannel pajamas and blue plaid robe. There had been a time in her life when she had taken better care of herself, a time when she had cared.

She took a good long look at herself in the bedroom mirror.

Oh boy. She had her work cut out for her.

First her hair. It was thick and shoulder-length, and chestnut was a good color. She vowed to retire the ponytail and get a proper cut.

Second: lose the glasses, find the contacts.

Nice teeth, straight—of course the four years of braces with the accompanying head gear had helped.

Nice eyes. Everyone always commented on that feature of hers. They were blue to begin with but turned a kind of violet after a lot of crying.

She would start easy with her hair, make-up, and clothes. After all, how hard could it be? And then she would start being her old self again: fun to be with and to be around. These would be the first steps back into the land of the living. She would prove to everyone, to Paul and most especially to herself, that she had moved on with her life.

Because after all, it was time to move on with her life.

CHAPTER THREE

The following morning, retiring the ponytail and paroling the prison matron look, Kate opted for casual: hair down, trousers and turtleneck. When she uncapped the wells that held her contacts, she found two lenses crinkled up like prunes. Sighing, she put them away and put her glasses back on. She was nearly overwhelmed by all the samples of make-up she had collected over the years, but she found something suitable and slapped a little bit on her face. It was like riding a bike; it was all coming back to her.

When Kate walked into the reception area, Gavin almost didn't recognize her. The ponytail was gone. He admired her hair. He had always found a woman with her hair down around her shoulders very appealing. She looked much better than she had yesterday. She wasn't about to set the fashion world on fire, but still, she seemed softer. Prettier.

He watched as she settled at her desk, ignoring Ed Cline. He didn't blame her there. The man was an obnoxious boor.

"Where have you been?" Mr. Cline asked her. He looked red-faced and perturbed. Gavin hoped he wouldn't stroke out on them.

"I was getting a cup of coffee, sir. Would you like me to get you one? Just made a fresh pot," she said smartly, setting her steaming mug on a coaster with the face of Santa Claus on it.

"No, I don't want coffee," he said with emphasis on each word, slapping the folder in his hand against her desk.

She seemed to take her boss' attitude in stride.

"Were you at the meeting, O'Connor? Did you hear anything I said at all?" Mr. Cline asked, his voice full of sarcasm.

She glanced at him, probably embarrassed at his lack of professionalism. Gavin wanted to see how this played out. He'd only been here a day and he was already bored with the place. He wasn't going to get involved.

"Of course I was at the meeting, Mr. Cline. You called me in. Don't you remember? And I hung on your every word," she said, not looking up from the stack of folders she was rifling through. Obviously deciding that she had more important things to do than to listen to his rant.

"This is the reception area and you are the receptionist," he said, exasperated.

"Only temporarily, sir, until the economy picks up or our ship comes in," she looked from her boss to Gavin. She tilted her head a little as if she was challenging him. "Then it's back to copywriting for me."

Gavin was appalled at the way Ed spoke to his staff. He was a boss but he was no leader. Talk about truth being stranger than fiction. This place had a real cast of characters.

As Cline droned on in his ear like an annoying wasp buzzing around, Gavin watched Kate work. At a couple of Ed's self-congratulatory remarks, she rolled her eyes. He had to suppress a laugh.

The double glass doors opened and a statuesque blonde strolled in, decked out in designer heaven. She wore a pink suit and cream accessories. Her platinum blonde hair was long and curly. Gavin suspected that this must be the Alexis Winston he had heard about. Only she would have this much swagger. Ed introduced them and after ten minutes, Gavin knew all he needed to know about her. Number one, she was more glamorous than pretty. Number two, she had Ed Cline wrapped around her finger. And number three, she was a player. Her flirting made that clear. He would seriously give it a thought—it had been six months since Georgina had dumped him. Alexis was the kind of girl he used to date, and her American accent would surely make things interesting.

Kate busied herself at her desk, going through emails and clearing the voicemail, and glanced over at Mr. Cline, watching as he played big man on campus to Gavin Whyte, even though he barely came up to his shoulders. She wondered if they would notice if she tacked up a 'no loitering' sign.

She amused herself with a stack of paperwork that Mr. Cline had left on her desk. Attached to the top of the pile was a sticky note with instructions for the day. She scanned the list; it was much the same as usual, with added instructions to make an appointment with his dentist for a tooth that was bothering him. Her heart sank. A college degree, and this is what she ended up doing—looking after a clown with rotten teeth.

"Kate?" Alexis leaned over her desk.

Kate looked up at her expectantly.

"Ann in Accounting said you'd tried the cabbage soup diet. Could you give me the recipe?"

Both men's eyes were on her and she felt like sliding under the desk. She made a mental note to put 'bitch-slap Alexis Winston' at the top of her own to-do list.

"No problem," she said, plastering on a smile.

"Great. I have a couple of pounds to lose before Christmas," Alexis said, smiling coyly and patting her flat abs.

Kate glanced down at her own abs, or lack thereof, and caught Gavin staring at her. Embarrassed, she looked away.

"Alexis is our in-house media genius. She's spearheaded a lot of our most successful ad campaigns. Nobody knows the TV industry better than she does," Mr. Cline explained to Gavin.

"I'm familiar with her excellent work and I look forward to seeing what she can do for Alchemis," he responded.

If she's such a genius, Kate thought, *why can't she get this diet off the Internet herself?* After a few keystrokes and clicks of the mouse, she hit the print icon.

"If you need anything at all, Gavin, don't hesitate to ask," Alexis said.

"And don't forget, Gavin, Kate is here as well until the temp arrives," Mr. Cline added as an afterthought.

"I think I can manage," he answered. Kate thought he sounded a little dismissive of her, but she couldn't really blame him. After all, he had seen her in action on a ladder; he probably didn't think he could trust her around office equipment.

Alexis turned on her heel to leave.

"Alexis." Kate called after her, pulling a sheet of paper off the printer.

"Yes?"

"Here's a copy of the cabbage soup diet." *And plan on spending a lot of quality time in the bathroom.*

"Thanks, Kate," Alexis said, taking the copy in hand. "By the way, what happened to the trophy case? Look at my awards—they're all over the place."

If one more person asked her about the trophy case, she was going to dive out the window. And where was the carpenter that the building super had promised yesterday? That would be her next call after they walked away from her desk.

"I've got someone coming in to reinforce it," Kate explained.

"Well, how did it happen?" Alexis persisted.

Suppressing a groan, Kate scratched her forehead and raised her eyebrows. "It collapsed under the weight it was trying to hold up."

Surprisingly, this answer seemed to satisfy Alexis.

Mr. Cline and Gavin Whyte started to walk off when Gavin leaned across her desk and whispered, "Don't worry, your secret about the ladder is safe with me."

She looked up at him. He winked at her.

Once she was sure they were out of sight, she pulled out the clothes catalogues and began leafing through them. She flagged things that previously she would only have dreamed of wearing but was never brave enough. She eliminated anything in the colors of black, grey or navy. She also crossed off anything that had elastic, a high neck or the quality of a drape.

With her credit card in hand, she went online and started shopping.

Package in hand, Kate stood at the open door of Gavin Whyte's office. He sat at his desk while Mr. Cline stood at his side. She noticed that he wore reading glasses.

Wow, she thought. *He's the only person I know who can wear glasses and still look sexy.*

She gave a quick rap on the doorframe, then approached his desk and handed him the package. "This just arrived for you, Mr. Whyte."

"Thank-you, Kate," he said, relieving her of the package. He tore across the top of the thick-padded envelope and removed the documents from within. He seemed engrossed in them. At the end of his desk sat a big crystal bowl full of M&Ms. She eyed them up longingly before turning to leave.

Mr. Cline stopped her. "Kate, Gavin is unhappy with his hotel."

What a surprise, she thought.

"Can you book him a more suitable one?" Mr. Cline asked.

"The Ambassador?" she suggested. When her boss nodded, she said, "I'll make the arrangements."

She refused to look at the Irishman, but she felt his eyes were on her. Behind him, out the window, the lake was the color of slate and the sky a dull grey.

"Will that be all?" she asked, but Mr. Cline ignored her. She waited.

"Will you do some sightseeing while you're in town?" Mr. Cline asked the client.

"I don't know if I'll have the time," Gavin replied.

"You should see Niagara Falls while you're here. It's so close," Mr. Cline said.

For once, Kate had to agree with him. It was probably the one and only time she would ever agree with him, so it was worth noting.

"I would love to see Niagara Falls but I'd hate to go alone," Gavin said.

There was only one missed beat of silence when Mr. Cline announced, "That's no problem, Gavin, I'm sure Kate, here, would be glad to take you."

Kate stopped breathing and stared straight ahead, because she thought she had just heard her boss volunteer her to be Gavin Whyte's tour guide.

"In fact, Kate could probably show you all around town. She wouldn't mind, would you, Kate?" He asked, looking at her.

She fantasized about grinding Mr. Cline under her shoe. She was all for doing just about anything to get her old job back, but this really took the cake.

Before she could say anything, Gavin spoke up. "I couldn't ask her to do that on her days off."

See! He doesn't want me squiring him around town.

"Nonsense. We're all team players here at Cline and Company," Mr. Cline said, directing his last comment at Kate.

"I really don't want to impose on your time..." Gavin said to her, his voice trailing off.

"She'd be glad to do it. Isn't that right, Kate?" Mr. Cline said. "Besides, Kate isn't married and doesn't have any kids, so I'm sure she can find some free time on the weekend."

Her chin hit the floor and stayed there. *Why don't you get on the public announcement system and let the whole world know my personal business?* Why was it that people assumed because she was single and childless she didn't have a life? Granted, it was true that she was free on Saturdays and Sundays for the rest of her days, but she didn't want other people making her plans for her.

"Miss O'Connor, are you sure you don't mind?" Gavin asked, looking at her intently.

What was she going to say? She smiled weakly. "No, not at all."

"Really?"

"I'd love to show you around town," her voice squeaked.

"Great, that's all settled. You two can sort out the details yourselves," Mr. Cline said.

Back at her desk, she took a series of deep breaths, trying to calm herself. How could Mr. Cline have volunteered her services like that, to their most important client? What on earth would he want her to do for Paul Reynolds? She couldn't even begin to go there.

A hot Irishman and a former flame. Kate felt combustible.

This was not going to end well—of that much, she was sure.

CHAPTER FOUR

At ten minutes to five, already bundled up in her hat, coat and scarf, Kate sat at her desk, waiting for quitting time to officially arrive. She had relaxed somewhat about being assigned as a tour guide to Gavin Whyte, figuring that by the time Friday rolled around, he would most likely have forgotten all about Mr. Cline's suggestion.

Sherrie appeared, similarly bundled, and the two made their way to the elevator. Kate pressed the 'down' button and they waited to hear the whoosh of the returning lift.

"We're all going out for a few. Want to join us?" Sherrie asked, pulling on her gloves.

Kate shook her head. "I can't, I'm meeting up with Lisa for dinner at Martini's," she explained. She pressed the button again, anxious to get going. "Maybe another time."

Alexis appeared beside them. "Have you seen Gavin?" she asked, checking her reflection in her compact and wiping her pinkie finger along her bottom lip.

Kate looked at her blankly, returning her attention to the illuminated number board above the elevators.

Alexis snapped her compact shut and dropped it into her purse. "We're supposed to go out for dinner and I didn't see him in the office. I wonder if he's already left."

"He hasn't been this way in the past few minutes," Sherrie offered.

"Isn't he just delicious? Isn't his accent to die for?" Alexis asked, not waiting for a reply. "I'll check the office again." She disappeared from view.

The elevator doors finally opened and they stepped inside.

"Boy, she doesn't waste any time," Sherrie said, shaking her head.

"No, she likes a clean kill." Kate pressed the 'L' button on the panel and the doors slid closed.

Down in the lobby, the two women became immediately engulfed in the forward-pressing mass of office workers departing for the day. Once outside, they parted.

"See you in the morning, Kate," Sherrie called, standing on the curb watching traffic before crossing the street to the parking garage.

Kate took one last look in the mirror before turning off
the bedroom light and decided that her outfit would
have to do. The clothes of color wouldn't arrive until
the end of the week. Her look was casual: tailored
pants and a fitted white shirt with pearl buttons down
the front. Living life on the edge, she left a few of
the top buttons on the blouse undone to show a hint
of cleavage. After soaking all day in lens solution, the
contacts had straightened out and she'd managed to get
them in. They seemed all right, but it would probably
be a good idea to get a new pair. No point in risking an
eye injury.

She was already looking forward to coming home,
soaking in the bath, putting on her pajamas and
hunkering down in front of the TV. But she checked
her internal rant and reminded herself that she was
supposed to be having fun. She and Lisa had been best
friends for years, so she was guaranteed a few laughs
tonight, at least.

Martini's was located downtown. Thirty years ago,
the area had been a notorious red-light district, but a
recent renaissance had transformed it from seedy and

disreputable to hip and trendy. There were a number
of restaurants, patio bars, and theatres in the area. It
continued to be a favorite hangout of the college crowd
as well as the downtown after-work set.

Martini's had a downstairs bar of polished mahogany,
burnished brass, and amber lighting. Red brick walls
were covered with all sorts of 1960's memorabilia.
Background music consisted of Christmas songs by
the likes of Frank Sinatra, Wayne Newton, and Judy
Garland. Upstairs there was a cigar bar with a big
fireplace at one end, furnished with leather wing chairs
and low wooden tables.

Kate scanned the room for her best friend, Lisa Green.
She found her seated in a booth near the middle of the
restaurant and made her way through the crowd toward
her.

"Hey, girlfriend!" Lisa said. She stood up and
enveloped Kate in a big hug.

Kate pulled back and studied her. "You look great!
That color really suits you."

They both settled into opposite sides of the booth.
The waiter arrived and they both ordered appletinis

"How's things?" Kate asked, setting her purse down
beside her.

"Okay, I guess." Lisa replied.

"You're not going to believe what he's done now," Lisa
started.

Kate knew without asking that Lisa was referring to her eccentric, long-haired, bicycle-riding boyfriend. She'd been seeing him for almost three months. Kate was surprised it had lasted this long. Lisa didn't usually tolerate nonsense.

"I can only imagine," Kate said.

"He asked me if I wanted to go to dinner and the movies the other night—so far so good. But of course I had to drive. Then he conveniently forgot his wallet and I had to pick up the tab for the evening."

Kate shook her head but she wasn't really surprised. This was the chorus to Lisa's boyfriend's song. The boyfriend before that had major mother issues. And the one before that aspired to unemployment benefits so he could stay home and watch television.

"Lisa, look at the source. He doesn't own a car, and he's not even forty and he's already sporting a comb-over!"

She didn't understand it herself. Lisa was a successful professional with a heart of gold. She was also pretty with her porcelain skin, and eyes and hair the color of midnight.

"You can do so much better!" Kate pointed out, but Lisa didn't look convinced. Kate looked at her, incredulous. She leaned across the table and whispered fiercely, "Do you know what I see when I look at you? I see a beautiful, intelligent, funny, and caring woman. If he doesn't reinforce that about you, then he isn't worth it."

Lisa smiled. "You're a good friend."

"I've got your back." Kate winked. "Now, what are we ordering for dinner?"

As soon as they ordered, Kate leaned back in the booth, sipping her appletini. She heard the distinctive voice of Judy Garland singing a Christmas song in the background and her thoughts immediately turned to her father. Her eyes began to fill up. To take Lisa's mind off of her unworthy boyfriend and her own mind off her late father, she relayed the ladder incident.

"Why is it when you're giving the world an unplanned flash of your underwear, you're always wearing something with holes in it and not leopard print or lace?" she lamented. Although come to think of it, she was no longer in possession of sexy underwear. It was all practical. "It must be some unwritten law of the universe."

Lisa laughed.

The waiter appeared and placed their dinners in front of them. Kate had ordered soup and a sandwich and Lisa had ordered a chicken Caesar salad.

"You're not going to believe who was hired as the new Creative Director," Kate said as she lifted her soup spoon to her mouth.

Lisa looked at her, expectant.

"Paul Reynolds."

Lisa's mouth fell open. Her eyes were as big as saucers. "No. Way."

Kate nodded.

"Have you talked to him yet?" Lisa asked.

"Oh yeah, he said he wanted to put all that 'stuff' behind us," Kate snorted.

"As if!"

"It's going to be awkward working there with him," Kate said quietly. Actually, it felt more like torture. She was pretty sure there was a sub-paragraph in the Geneva Convention about working with ex-fiancés who'd previously dumped you.

"Is he still with Sabrina?" Lisa asked, referring to the infamous bridesmaid he had subsequently married.

Kate shrugged. "I don't know. He wasn't wearing a wedding ring."

"Interesting. Do you still have feelings for him?"

"When I saw him I realized that I don't feel the way I used to, but I don't want to work with him."

She had just pushed her plate away when Alexis Winston and Gavin Whyte walked by their booth in the direction of the exit. Alexis didn't notice Kate but Gavin did. He glanced at her and did a double-take.

Kate panicked. Telepathically, she sent him a message: *Keep moving, Irish, there's nothing to see here.*

He was looking brilliant with his dark wavy hair and serious blue eyes.

Alexis had been giving him subtle signals all evening. He wasn't interested in a relationship—he was too busy and he was still smarting from Georgina's parting comments. Still, Alexis's bed would be a good distraction while he was stuck here. He could think of worse things to do.

By mutual unspoken consent, they finished their drinks and gathered their coats. He paid the bill and they stood to leave, heading for what seemed like the inevitable conclusion: him going home with her. She'd mentioned a loft apartment downtown and he'd agreed he would like to see it.

As they walked away from their table, with his hand on the small of her back, he noticed two attractive women in a booth in an animated conversation. The one looked very familiar. Then it dawned on him; it was Kate from the office. It wouldn't be right not to acknowledge her.

"Kate?"

"It's me, all right." She smiled weakly.

"I almost didn't recognize you without your glasses," he said. He thought she should drop them altogether. She had incredible eyes. Ahead of him, Alexis stopped and backtracked. She smiled tightly.

Kate introduced her friend, who piped up and said, "Join us for a drink."

Gavin saw Kate's eyes widen in horror and was amused.

He slid into the booth next to her, his shoulder brushing up against hers, sending a small jolt through him.

Alexis sat down next to Lisa.

This was going to be interesting, he thought.

"I'll have another," Kate blurted out, when the waiter approached their table.

"Wow, Kate, you're really throwing them back tonight," Alexis said, raising an eyebrow and indicating the empty glasses that littered the table.

Kate ignored her. She couldn't believe she was sitting up close and personal with Gavin Whyte. With his arm pressed up against hers—heat radiated off of him—she couldn't even think straight, much less form coherent sentences. She hadn't felt this way since high school. She watched as he slowly ran his long, tapered fingers up and down the side of his beer bottle; his hands were beautiful.

Lisa saved the day by making small talk. She'd figured out almost immediately that this Irishman was the very man from Kate's story.

"Gavin, I noticed an accent—are you from Ireland?" Lisa asked.

"Yes, I am," he said. "Actually, I was born in New York City, but my parents returned to Ireland when I was still a baby."

Kate had trouble picturing him as a young boy with scraped knees and missing front teeth. He looked like he'd been born wearing a suit and a tie.

"So you have dual citizenship?" Lisa asked.

He nodded. "I went to college here in the States."

"Kate's father came from Ireland," Lisa said.

"Really?" he asked. He turned to look at her.

The close proximity and the intensity of his gaze made her feel hot. She wasn't sure if the flush she felt in her cheeks was from him or the appletinis.

"Where is he from?" Gavin asked.

"He was from Killaloe. His sister still lives there and has the farm," Kate explained.

"We're practically neighbors. I'm from Templemore," he said.

She was familiar with it. It wasn't far at all—just over in County Tipperary. She was pretty sure her aunt had friends there.

"Do you visit often?" he asked.

"I used to spend my summers there as a kid, but it's been a couple of years."

"You should really get back. You won't recognize the place. Ireland has changed."

She thought she detected sadness in his voice but couldn't be sure.

"I've always wanted to go to Ireland. I hear it's a beautiful country," Alexis said.

"It is indeed," Gavin said quietly.

"Maybe someday you could show me around," Alexis suggested.

Kate waited a beat for Gavin's response, but he didn't offer one. "Do you still live in Templemore?" she asked.

"Unfortunately, no. I'm up in Dublin to be closer to work."

There was an awkward silence. Kate stared at her nearly-empty glass, thinking of all the martinis that had gone before.

"Gavin, are you ready? I'm completely exhausted," Alexis said. She put her elbows on the table and rested her chin on her hands. Kate imagined she'd start purring any minute now.

Gavin said nothing; he just slid out of the booth.

First name basis already for Alexis, Kate thought. *Boy, she doesn't let any dust settle.* She had worked with Alexis long enough to know that she would always snare the new man. She just wouldn't have thought it would be so soon with Gavin Whyte. This was only his second day here at Cline & Co. She had mistakenly thought his tastes would be more discriminating, but maybe not. Alexis liked the attention of men. Not just one man, but *all* men. *Share the wealth and throw me one of your crumbs*, Kate thought miserably. *If only I could have that effect on one man. Not all men, just one good one.*

"Goodnight," Alexis said.

"It was nice meeting you," Gavin said to Lisa, and then turned to Kate. "Goodnight, Kate."

"Goodnight."

She watched Alexis walk away with Gavin in her wake. Broad shoulders, narrow waist—she sighed. One couldn't deny his good looks. As they approached the door he held Alexis's coat for her. Kate gazed at him, liking that gesture of solicitousness. At that moment, he turned around and looked at her. Embarrassed at being caught, she quickly looked away.

"Oh boy, you've got a bad case of it," Lisa commented with a whistle once they were out of sight.

"What are you talking about?" Kate asked, draining the remnants of her glass.

"Gavin sat next to you in this booth for the last hour and you couldn't even look at him, much less speak."

"He's too arrogant and vain," Kate protested weakly.

Lisa laughed. "I didn't get that at all. In fact, I would say he was quite friendly."

"Well you don't have to work with him—it's a whole different ball game."

"Whatever you say," Lisa said.

"Besides, it's pretty obvious that Alexis has staked out her claim," Kate pointed out.

"You don't know that for sure. All I saw was him exhibiting great manners."

Kate pressed her lips together and confessed to her friend about being assigned his tour guide while he was in town.

Lisa grabbed her purse and got out of the booth, beaming and said: "That will be interesting."

The server informed them that Mr. Whyte had settled the bill when he left.

"What a gentleman," Lisa said.

"Probably writes it off," Kate muttered.

Once they stepped outside, Alexis pulled her mink coat tightly around her. "I'm sorry we were delayed getting out of there but one has to be polite." She sounded like she was taking a hit for the team.

Gavin could only nod. Something was circling and taking shape at the edges of his brain. Something nagged him like a stone in his shoe but he didn't have a name for it yet.

"Will you come back to my place for a drink?" she asked. The moonlight reflected off her glittery pink lipstick and platinum hair. It was an offer that was hard to refuse. Still.

He hesitated. The truth was he was no longer interested, but it had nothing to do with her. All that talk of Ireland and Tipperary and Clare had made him nostalgic, homesick, and tired. What he really wanted to do was go back to his hotel room, remove this awful tie, pour himself a small glass of whiskey, and sit down with a cigar for a good think. Alone. He wanted to think about Ireland, about home and the farm and his family. With this new ad campaign, he hadn't had any time in the last eight weeks to go home and was beginning to realize how much he missed it.

"I'm going to have to take a rain check, Alexis," he said. "I'm exhausted and I've an early start in the morning."

Her chin lifted slightly. "All right."

He was relieved that she didn't seem too put out or angry or worse, tearful. Women's tears made him weak. He walked her to her car and refused her offer for a lift back to his hotel, preferring instead to walk the eight blocks. The night air was crisp and that was fine—he hoped it would clear his head over whatever was bothering him that he couldn't pinpoint. Yet.

Kate decorated a miniature artificial Christmas tree and set it up on the corner of her desk. The holiday was alive and well in the reception area.

A jeans-and-flannel-shirt-clad fellow strolled in, and Kate wondered if life could get any better. The combination of his dark beard and mustache, his calloused hands and the tool belt around his waist was almost heady. With the current trend of eye candy walking through the doorway, there might be a future in reception after all.

"I'm the carpenter," he announced, smiling. He had a goofy, boyish grin.

Before she could say anything, like, 'I'm free on Saturday, do you want to get married?' he assessed the damaged trophy case and let out a low whistle.

"What the hell happened here?" he asked. "Those rivets are reinforced steel."

"I don't know anything about it. I only work here," Kate answered and put her head down, pretending to be engrossed in a note that Mr. Cline had left on her desk.

After much drilling and pounding, the carpenter left, with the trophy case back in its place. Only now, it was covered in dust. Lots of it.

Kate picked up her keys and headed to the common utility closet near the bank of elevators. Grabbing the paper towels and glass cleaner, she realized that this would involve the stepladder of ill-repute. She decided to face her fears.

Cleaning supplies in one hand and the stepladder over her shoulder, she returned to the trophy case to sort it out once and for all.

Gingerly, she climbed the ladder and began wiping down the glass doors and shelves.

"Do you think that's a good idea?" It was Gavin.

She turned around and the ladder swayed. *Oh no, not again.* But this time, his hand landed on it and the swaying stopped.

"As I was saying..." He grinned at her and nodded to the ladder.

"Well, if you would stop sneaking up on me—" she began, but was distracted by the appearance of Paul.

"Hey, Kate!" Paul said, flashing a smile.

"Paul," Kate said cautiously.

The view was beginning to make her dizzy, so she hurried down the ladder, the rungs rattling noisily beneath her.

Gavin looked at Paul, gave a quick nod to Kate and headed toward his office.

She wished he hadn't gone; it had left her alone with Paul. Awkwardly, she looked up at him. Surely, he must want something, or why would he still be standing there, lingering?

"Would you go to lunch with me?" he asked.

"No," she said flatly, crossing her arms in front of her chest. "I have other plans," she lied. Out of the corner of her eye, she glanced at the clock, delighted to see that it was almost time for lunch.

He looked momentarily stunned but recovered quickly.

She maneuvered around him so she could deal with him from behind the security of her desk. She shuffled some papers to look busy.

"I was hoping to put the past behind us," he said quietly.

"I have," she answered. *And that's where I want it*, she thought. *In the past.*

"Can't we be friends?" he pressed. Paul could be persistent when he wanted something.

"Why?" she asked.

"We were friends once," he said weakly. He ran his hand through his hair and muttered, "We were more than friends once."

"What about Sabrina?" she asked, pulling the bottom drawer open to retrieve her purse.

"We split up over a year ago. Our divorce should be final soon," he said.

She stepped out from behind the desk, purse over her shoulder. He reached for her arm as she walked past.

"Kate, I'm sorry for hurting you," he said quietly.

It had taken him five years to apologize for breaking her heart.

"I've moved on," she said evenly, locking eyes with him.

He was still gripping her arm and she was surprised that it had no effect on her at all. There had been a time when the sight of him had caused her knees to go weak.

"I made a terrible mistake," he said sheepishly. "It took me a while, but I realize that now. I was foolish to ever let you go."

She looked him in the eye and said calmly, "But you didn't let me go, Paul. You dumped me for someone else. Big difference."

Kate pulled her arm away and escaped out the door, making a beeline for the ladies' room. Her cheeks felt hot and her eyes were wet. She wished he'd just leave her alone.

CHAPTER FIVE

Ambush. That was the first word that came into Kate's mind when she returned from lunch and was invited to Mr. Cline's office, only to find Alexis there, as well.

Alexis stood, leaning against the windowsill directly behind Mr. Cline, who sat at his desk. Both looked up when Kate entered and both smiled. Big, broad, generous smiles. It was at that moment that Kate realized it was two to one in their favor.

"Sit down, Kate," her boss said in a suspicious-sounding fatherly tone, indicating the chair in front of his desk.

Alexis continued to smile, her arms folded across her chest and looking ever so chic in a brown herringbone suit, with the city skyline serving as her backdrop.

Somewhat warily, Kate sat. With these two, you needed to have eyes in the back of your head. Nothing was beyond them.

"I think we have something you might be interested in," Mr. Cline said. "Alexis came up with a brilliant idea and we want to run it by you."

Kate's apprehension grew. Mr. Cline was being too nice and solicitous. And anytime Alexis had been brilliant, it had usually been at someone else's expense.

Mr. Cline continued. "Look, Kate, this new diet drug from Alchemis' is going to generate a lot of money. Probably billions. The current research is showing minimal side effects, if any." He paused for a moment and leaned back in his chair. "And of course we, at Cline and Company, want this ad campaign to be successful."

C'mon, get to the point and stop the grandstanding, Kate thought.

"Alexis thought that once the product becomes available to the general public, we could produce a reality TV show following one person during their course on the drug and documenting their success."

Alexis looked pointedly at Kate and spoke for the first time since Kate entered the room. "And we have no farther to look than our own backyard."

Kate felt sick inside.

Alexis continued. "You'd be the ideal candidate for a reality TV show. We'd embed cameras in your house, your car, and here at the office. You're perfect for this, Kate. You're female, you're single, you're in your thirties and you have an attractive face. But most importantly, you have some weight to lose. You've obviously tried everything out there—without success. You probably have dreams of a husband, kids, and the whole lot."

"There is nothing America loves more than an underdog," Mr. Cline injected.

There it was: her whole life encapsulated and flayed open in one speech by Alexis Winston.

"Me?" Kate asked incredulously, still smarting from Alexis' comment about her weight. "You want me to do this?"

"Well, I'd do it myself, just for the national exposure." Alexis smiled, looking down at her designer suit and picking at a piece of imaginary lint, "but to be honest we need someone with a significant amount of extra weight for it to make an impact."

I'd like to show her how I can throw my weight around.

"You'd be well-compensated, kiddo," Mr. Cline said. He leaned forward and rested his elbows on his desk, folding his hands. "Not to mention you'd finally get that beef off."

Ouch. Kate began to feel claustrophobic. She knew she'd never be accused of being waif-like, but what gave them the right to stick their noses into her affairs? And to willingly expose herself on national TV? Not likely!

She flashed back to the ninth grade when the school nurse had decided to do a mass weigh-in during gym class.

"I don't know," Kate mumbled. She was trying to figure out how to exit gracefully. It wasn't beneath her to yell 'Fire' if the need arose.

She focused on Alexis' reaction. There was something intimidating in her eyes that made Kate look away.

Mr. Cline went on. "In fact, Kate, if you could gain a few more pounds before we start filming and really get the numbers up there on the scale, then your weight loss would be even more dramatic."

Kate ignored him and spoke directly to Alexis. "I don't think this is for me."

But Alexis wouldn't take no for an answer. "Well, take a few days and think about it. I have a contact at the Reality Television Network and I'll work up a proposal."

"Why don't you set up a meeting," Mr. Cline suggested to Alexis.

"Wait a minute," Kate protested.

But the two of them carried on their conversation as if she wasn't there.

Kate only half-listened to them. The thought of this highly personal issue being discussed by Alexis (of all women), Mr. Cline, and Gavin Whyte (of all men) was more than she could bear. Not to mention Paul

Reynolds. She shuddered at the thought of humiliation in front of an audience. She spoke loudly to get their attention.

"Thanks, but no thanks."

Both Mr. Cline and Alexis stopped talking and stared at her, as if they hadn't seen her before.

"No, no, Kate," said Alexis. "Please, give this careful consideration. Don't make an on-the-spot decision.

"C'mon, Kate, be a team player," Mr. Cline said.

Wasn't that exactly what she'd been doing since her demotion nearly a year ago? She wanted her old job back and she was certainly willing to do what was asked, but this was off the charts. Kate excused herself, agreeing in theory to at least think it over, but thinking all the while of how she could get out of it. She walked out of the room with tears in her eyes, and bumped right into Sherrie in the corridor.

"What's wrong, Kate? You're as white as a ghost. Your eyes are turning purple. Did he fire you?"

"No. Worse," Kate said, and went on to explain the collective idea of Alexis and Mr. Cline.

"They want you to do what?" Sherrie asked, outraged. "Why, those no-good, scurvy losers!"

Vindicated by her friend's outrage, Kate immediately dismissed the thought that maybe she was being too sensitive.

"You told them no, didn't you?" Sherrie asked.

"Of course I did, but they're not accepting my answer."

"Kate, I'm really sorry about this," Sherrie said softly. "You deserve so much better. Don't let them steamroll over you."

She hugged her and whispered, "It's time for you to get out of this place, honey."

Kate made it back to reception and found a voicemail on her machine from the temp agency, informing her that they couldn't get an assistant out for Gavin Whyte for at least two weeks.

She called her boss immediately to let him know. He thought for a moment and said, "That's all right. Set up a desk outside his office. You can be his assistant."

"But what about reception?" Kate asked, panicking.

"Get one of those interns that just came over from the college to do it," he said airily, and hung up.

After work, Kate bypassed the route home and instead drove toward her mother's house. All sorts of thoughts raced through her head. A reality TV show—out of the question. What were they thinking? A mental picture began to take focus, with her parading across a TV screen in an all-purpose bra and panties, being poked and prodded at by all sorts of scurrilous types. She cringed. What would her mother say? Her relatives? Her friends? Did Alexis and Mr. Cline have no sense of dignity and compassion, or was the bottom line (theirs and definitely not hers) the only goal in sight?

She could feel herself getting worked up into a frenzy. *Calm down*, she told herself. There was a solution to this; she just needed to find it.

She turned onto her mother's street and tried to put all thoughts of work out of her mind. Her mother lived in a small neighborhood of tidy red-brick homes. Her house came into view and the white wrought-iron railing that wrapped around the porch immediately brought back memories of when Kate fell off of it in the third grade and broke her arm.

She was relieved to see the green Chrysler out front. She nosed her car into the driveway and parked behind her mother's car.

Kate walked around the side of the house and went in through the back porch. She took off her coat and draped it over one of the ladder-back kitchen chairs. The house smelled of baked cake and dishwasher detergent. It was very warm; her mother liked the thermostat set at 'tropical.' It was probably the reason her plants did so well.

"Mom?"

No answer.

"Mom?" Kate called out again, a little louder.

Mrs. O'Connor appeared in the kitchen, almost breathless. She was wearing full make-up and a navy twin set, and it looked like she'd just had her hair done. Kate thought she looked surprised to see her.

"Kate, what are you doing here?" she asked.

"Oh, Mom," Kate answered, waving her hand, trying to stifle the tears.

"Actually, I was just on my way out the door..." her mother said. She looked flustered, as if Kate had caught her doing something naughty.

"Geez, Mom, I didn't think this would be a bad time."

"I'm sorry, honey. Can you come back tomorrow?"

Kate noticed that her mother seemed distracted. "Should I make an appointment?" she asked sarcastically.

"Don't be flip, Katharine, it doesn't suit you."

The doorbell rang. They both looked toward the front entrance. Mrs. O'Connor darted a look at her daughter, then back at the door again.

What on earth was going on?

"Oh, it's just the repairman," Kate's mother said breezily, and went to answer the bell.

"You just said you were on your way out," Kate said, more to herself, as her mother disappeared.

She leaned against the kitchen door frame, listening. She heard the front door open and her mother speaking in a hushed tone. This was followed by a very deep, very male voice, answering, "Okay, Rita."

At the sound of footsteps, Kate retreated back into the kitchen.

Her mother reappeared, followed by a short, compact man. His close-cut hair was thick and grey. His glasses made his eyes appear larger than they actually were. He wore a yellow ski jacket over jeans and a navy Buffalo Bills sweatshirt. On his left wrist, he sported a copper bracelet.

Kate's mother did not look at her and instead went to the basement door. She opened it and flipped the wall switch, illuminating the basement steps. In an unusually loud voice, she said, "The hot water tank is to the left at the bottom of the stairs."

The strange man didn't look at Kate, either. He didn't say anything as he disappeared down the stairs. Her mother closed the door behind him.

"Well, I'll see you tomorrow, Kate," she said.

"Mom, who is that man?"

"I told you. He's a repairman. He's going to look at the hot water tank," she said, avoiding eye contact. Kate knew her mother was not a good liar—too many years schooled by nuns.

"That tank is brand new, Mom. It was just installed six months ago," she pointed out. She ought to know, as she'd been the one on her hands and knees wiping up the linoleum floor after the previous tank had leaked all over the place.

Her mother said nothing.

"If he's a repairman, where's his toolbox? He looks a little neat and clean to be repairing anything."

"His name is Hank," her mother blurted out.

"Hank? Okay. But who is he, in the grand scheme of things?" Kate asked, a feeling of dread taking hold in her stomach.

"Hank is my boyfriend," Rita confessed.

"Boyfriend?" Kate repeated, wondering if she'd heard correctly. That couldn't possibly be. Her mother would never betray her father like that.

"You heard me." Her mother studied the floor.

"Mom, you're married," Kate said. "I am a widow, Kate," her mother said firmly, finally looking her in the face.

"But what about Daddy?" Kate hissed.

"What about him, sweetheart? Is he here?"

Her mother had a boyfriend? She couldn't begin to wrap her head around that one.

"How long have you been seeing him?"

"Three months."

"How did you meet?"

"At aqua aerobics," her mother said softly.

Oh, great! Her mother had picked up a boyfriend at age sixty-five, and wearing a bathing suit no less, whereas she, at thirty, couldn't snag one fully clothed.

"Why didn't you tell me?" Kate demanded, trying to keep the hysteria out of her voice.

"Because I knew you would react this way."

"Repairman my ass!" she said in a clipped tone.

"He is a repairman. He's here because of my heart: it's broken but it's still full of hope," her mother insisted.

"Well, don't let me get in the way," Kate said, picking up her coat from the chair. She hated that she sounded like a spoiled brat but she couldn't seem to help herself. She walked to the back door.

"Katharine—" her mother started.

"I'll talk to you later, Mom," Kate said wearily.

On the way home, she cried, thinking of her father and how he had only been dead for a few years. How could her mother just move on like that? Did she not miss him? Kate had sworn she'd never forget her father and she couldn't understand how her mother could have.

Once home, Kate did something she hadn't done since the second grade. She went to bed at seven thirty.

CHAPTER SIX

Kate gave the intern, Krista, a quick tutorial about her duties in reception. It wasn't rocket science; a six-year-old could have handled it.

A laminated desk was set up with a phone and a computer for Kate, directly outside of Gavin's office. Ben Davidson helped her carry some of her personal items over to the new space. When they were finished, Ben nodded toward Gavin's office and gave Kate a lopsided grin. "Good luck."

"Why do you say that?" she asked, setting down her box of belongings. She removed the miniature Christmas tree and placed it on the corner of the desk.

Ben stood a little taller, put his hands in his pockets and lowered his voice. "How long has he been here? Three days? He knows all of us by our first names, where we went to school and probably what we ate for breakfast. Not only has he sat in on all of the meetings, but he's taken them over and run them!"

"Yikes," she mumbled. It gave the term 'micro-manage' a new meaning. She took her favorite coffee mug out of the box and set it down.

Ben laughed. "You should have seen him with that new Creative Director, Paul."

Kate's ears perked up. "Why? What happened?"

He laughed and shook his head. "At the creative meeting, he stood up and told Paul to have a seat. I thought Paul was going to have a stroke!"

Kate would have paid to see that. Paul had never liked to be told what to do. "Whyte proceeds to brief the creative team. Tells them exactly what he wants out of us and what he expects. Paul stands up and says, 'Excuse me, Gavin, I've got this. This isn't my first rodeo.' And Whyte practically takes his head off! 'I don't care if it's your rodeo or your circus, it's my company and my money,' he says. I'll tell you, that shut Paul right up. Serves him right for coming in here and taking the job right out from under Sherrie."

Kate nodded in agreement.

"I mean, what was Cline thinking, bringing him in?" Ben went on. "And when are they moving you back to copywriting?"

"I'm just waiting for the word," Kate said.

"Yeah, like I said, good luck." And he was gone.

She gave a quick rap on Gavin's door.

"Come in," he called, and she peeked inside.

"There's been a slight change in the plans," she announced.

He looked up from his desk. "I can only imagine."

"The temp agency can't send us anyone yet, so I'll be your assistant for, um, the time being," she said.

He nodded. "Well, Kate, nothing you need to do for me involves a ladder, so it should be fine." He held up a pile of papers. "Can you fax these to Dublin for me, please?"

She walked across the room and took the papers from him. Their fingers sparked with an electric shock when they made contact.

"Oh, sorry," she said.

"Are you trying to set me on fire?" he asked, smiling.

She thought the intensity of those blue eyes might just set her clothes on fire. She reddened and pressed her lips together, embarrassed. She cleared her throat. "If you need anything, just let me know." She hoped she didn't sound too eager.

"Anything?" he asked.

Without thinking, she nodded and said, "Yes, anything at all."

"I'll tuck that away for future reference," he remarked. He went back to the paperwork on his desk and without looking up, said, "Leave the door open on your way out."

Kate faxed so many documents to Dublin and London for Mr. Whyte, she could have sworn there was smoke coming out of the back of the machine. When Mr. Cline got the bill, he'd probably blow a head gasket. When all the faxes had been sent and the noise from the machine ceased, Kate became aware of Gavin's voice. He was talking on the phone. She tried not to listen, but that was just about impossible. Served him right for keeping his door open.

"Don't worry about a thing—I'll take care of it," she heard him say. "Now don't cry. I'll be home soon. I miss you, too...okay, good-bye. I'll talk to you tomorrow...I love you, too."

He has a girlfriend back in Dublin! Kate thought. And he loved her and missed her and was going to take care of everything! She couldn't remember Paul ever reassuring her like that. When they'd been engaged, it had been all about what Kate could do for him. Of course, he'd told her that he loved her, but never like that. *From the sounds of it, Irish's girlfriend is one lucky lady.*

At that moment, Mr. Cline appeared, interrupting her reverie, and threw two tickets to that night's hockey game down on her desk.

"Do you have any plans for tonight, O'Connor?" he asked gruffly.

"No, sir, not a one," she said, eyeing up the tickets. Rink level!

"Would you like to go to the game? The Sabres are playing Montreal tonight."

"Thanks Mr. Cline, I really appreciate it," she answered, feeling like her efforts were finally being recognized.

"Great, you can take Gavin—he wants to catch a game while he's in town."

The feeling of appreciation dissolved quickly. "Mr. Cline! I already agreed to take him to the falls," she hissed, hoping Gavin wouldn't hear her. *How could I not know there would be a catch?* He would never just give her a pair of great seats to the hockey game out of the goodness of his heart.

"He's going to be in town for a while. He's going to want to do more than one thing."

"Maybe he would prefer to go with someone else," she suggested, "like Alexis." The woman was practically chasing him all over the office—let her show him the sights.

"No. I already told him you would go," Mr. Cline said.

"You already talked to him—before you asked me?" she fumed.

"Don't go ballistic on me," he said.

She stood up from her desk, hands on her hips, and all but bared her teeth.

"O'Connor, listen. I know it's short notice, so why don't you take the rest of the day off and try to get ready or something..." His voice trailed off and he looked pointedly at her hair and her face. Then he added, "I'll arrange to have a car pick the both of you up."

She grabbed her coat and picked up the tickets off her desk, tucking them into the inside pocket of her purse. At least a hockey game would be easier than the falls. She could watch the game and wouldn't have to worry about the agony of making small talk.

She stood at the door of Gavin's office and peered in. He sat at his desk in front of his laptop, his expression intense, oblivious to her. She watched him for a moment. He rubbed his eyes. He looked tired. Stressed. She rapped on the door.

He looked up.

"Hockey game tonight, Mr. Whyte?" she asked, wrapping her scarf around her neck.

"It's Gavin," he said.

"Okay, Gavin." She tested the name out, but it felt strange.

"Yes, if it isn't too much trouble for you," he said.

"Of course not, I love hockey." She smiled. "Mr. Cline tells me the car will pick you up at seven. I'll see you then."

And before he could respond, she disappeared.

Gavin was anxious to get back to Ireland since the phone call from his mother. A lump in her breast—that was unsettling news. She was to have it biopsied the following week. He was more than anxious; he was alarmed.

Although in their seventies, both his parents had enjoyed relatively good health. They still worked the farm themselves with the help of some local workers. He pitched in as much as he could when he was home. He didn't mind; he loved it. It was how he relaxed—being outdoors, working the land. They had dairy cows, beef cattle, sheep, goats, and hens. His mother grew strawberries and rhubarb that she sold to local grocery stores.

He realized that he had taken them for granted. Just thought they'd always be there. Now his mother was faced with a possible life-threatening illness. It was sobering, to say the least.

He swiveled the chair around, put his feet up on the windowsill and stared at the darkening sky and the vista of the lake spread out before him, thinking of his family and the farm back in Tipperary.

Kate had barely closed her front door behind her when she heard Vinnie knocking at the back.

"Yo, babe, how's it going?" he asked as she let him in. "These came for you today and I signed for them." He indicated the bulky brown packages he carried under his arms.

Her new wardrobe had arrived! She relieved him of the packages and put them down on the kitchen table. She watched as he pulled a small bottle of hand sanitizer from his pocket and gave his hands a good scrub. There was a fine line between his germophobia and a certified psychosis. A line that he jump-roped on quite frequently.

"Where's the Missus?" he asked, looking furtively around.

"I don't know. I haven't had a chance to talk to her today," Kate lied. The truth was, she had avoided calling her. But her mother hadn't called her, either. She was probably out gallivanting with Hank. *Now that she has a boyfriend, she'll probably drop me like a bad habit*, Kate thought.

"Do you have a minute?" Vinnie asked. "I want to show you something."

She followed him outside, across the lawn, and over to his driveway.

Vinnie stopped at the trunk of his car, a souped-up, steel-grey 1982 Pontiac Grand Prix. Kate might have been one of his 'babes,' but this car was his 'baby.'

He unlocked the trunk and she prayed, *Please, dear God, don't let there be a body in there.* Because with Vinnie, you just didn't know. When it popped open, she was surprised to see that it was full of purses. Kate Spade, Prada, Coach, and Gucci, to name a few. There were black ones, brown ones, leather ones, and suede ones. There were stripes and there were polka dots. Her mouth watered. They were beautiful. Accessories like shoes and purses were so much more size-friendly than clothes.

She finally spoke. "Vinnie, where on earth did you get these?"

"NYC."

"You went to New York City?" She eyed him; New York City was five hundred miles away.

He nodded.

"How did you afford them?" she asked, although she wasn't too sure she wanted to know.

"They're not the real deal. They're knockoffs. Imitations," he explained. "They're not genuine." He pronounced 'genuine' as gen-u-wine.

"But they have labels on them." Kate picked one up. It was a black handbag with a 'Gucci' label on it.

"That's what makes them a seller," He paused. "And that, babe, is where you come in."

She looked at him skeptically.

"Now, Kate, remove that look of disdain," Vinnie said. "Listen, it's sweet. These things are selling like hotcakes. Prices between thirty-five and fifty bucks a purse. It's a win-win situation."

"Win-win for whom?" she asked, not looking at him as she was too busy drooling over all the handbags in the trunk. She picked one up for closer inspection. She was still doubtful, but also curious.

"All you have to do is have six or eight of your friends together for a purse party in your home. I'll set out all the bags and the average girl buys two to three. Then you encourage a couple of your friends to book parties, as well. With every hundred bucks in sales you get a free purse. With every party booked, you get twenty bucks."

"What about you?" she asked, stopping momentarily from checking out a blue-striped 'Kate Spade.'

"Don't worry about me. Vinnie Mann always takes care of himself."

"How in the world did you get into this?" she asked, peering up at him.

"A friend of mine..." his voice trailed off.

She left it at that. "I don't know, Vinnie," she said doubtfully. Truth be told, things rarely turned out as easy or sweet as Vinnie said they would.

"Listen, Kate, I did a party last week and sold thirty purses at thirty-five bucks a crack. It was the easiest money I ever made."

Kate said nothing.

Vinnie persisted. "I'll tell you what. Take two purses right now as a gift from me. All I ask is that you use them and take them to work. I'll bet they get a lot of attention. The bags sell themselves."

It sounded reasonable enough. Kate didn't want the girls in the office to feel obligated to come to a home party, like she always did when she got those invitations for make-up, candle, and kitchenware parties. But purses! All women liked purses and shoes. It was programmed into their genes.

"Okay, Vinnie, let's see what happens."

"Your pick, babe," Vinnie said, standing back from the trunk.

She studied the purses. This was better than chocolate. Well, almost. In the end, she picked a 'Coach' knockoff and a 'Chanel.'

"Thank-you, Vinnie." She smiled at him.

"Now how about dinner tonight?" he asked. He looked around the neighborhood and then slammed the trunk shut. "Just me, you, and your double D's." He wiped an imaginary speck off the back of his car.

"Oh, Vinnie," she sighed.

"You're killing me, babe," Vinnie said.

"You know I really like you, but I think of you more like...a brother."

"Well, I don't think of you like a sister," he said. "But I'm going to work on changing your mind about me."

She laughed. "You're too much."

"I'm serious. One night with Vinnie Mann and you'll never leave my side again," he said. He leaned in close and whispered, "the girls don't call me Lance Romance for nothing."

He winked at her and she refrained from rolling her eyes.

"I mean it, babe, once I start my campaign to woo you—"

Woo?

"—you'll be dead in the water."

She laughed again. "Goodnight. And thanks for the purses. I'll let you know how I make out."

She walked back to her house, chuckling to herself. She genuinely liked Vinnie, but there were no sparks there for her. Sometimes, she wished there were, simply because he seemed so interested in her. And at least he wasn't boring.

They had great seats at the Marine Midland Arena, five rows up from center ice. Kate stood for a moment, purse in one hand, a beer in the other, trying to figure out how to get her coat off. Gavin looked up and as if anticipating her needs, relieved her of her beer and purse. *Score one for the Irishman.* She draped her coat over the back of her chair and settled down into it. She had dressed in a cozy cable-knit sweater as it could be quite chilly in the arena, especially closer to the ice.

Gavin wore a brown V-neck over a white T-shirt. He also wore jeans, great smelling cologne, and a five-o'clock shadow. He was smoking hot and despite the chill, she felt herself beginning to melt. She hoped the ice wouldn't turn to slush with him seated so close to it. Slightly agitated, she prayed that she wouldn't get all goofy as she had a tendency to do in these situations. She didn't think he suffered fools.

However, if she was hoping for an in-depth discussion on anything, she was sadly mistaken. He was very quiet, hardly saying a word. Kate attempted conversation but when all she got was one-word answers from him, she quickly abandoned any pretext of small talk. She caught him sporting the fifty-yard stare a few times and she wondered where his thoughts might be. He was probably pining away for the girl he'd left back home, wishing it was her and not Kate sitting beside him.

The Sabres and the Canadiens skated out from their respective dressing rooms as the game was about to start. Everyone in the arena stood for the Canadian and American national anthems. She'd always liked 'O

Canada,' thinking that it was a pretty song and easy to sing. But it was 'The Star-Spangled Banner' that never failed to bring tears to her eyes. Gavin stood next to her, hand over his heart.

They sat back down in their seats for the initial face-off. Gavin leaned forward, resting his elbows on his thighs, watching the play on the ice intently.

His silence continued and Kate became increasingly uncomfortable until she came up with an inspired topic of conversation. She went into a detailed explanation of the game of ice hockey, and the rules and regulations of the NHL. Gavin seemed interested and nodded at appropriate intervals. Once in a while, he would glance at her, give her a quick grin, and then return his attention to the game. When the Sabres scored on a power play, she stopped mid-sentence and waited as the announcer named the goal scorer as well as the man who'd assisted on the play. She then went off on a tangent about the various statistics that were kept.

To include him in the conversation she asked, "Have you ever seen an American hockey game before?"

He turned to her and said, "Yes, I'm actually a big fan of the Flyers. I went to college here on the East coast and I became a hockey fanatic."

He turned his attention back to the game.

Huh. Well, deduct one point, she thought sourly. A Flyers fan—didn't he know that Buffalo had lost the Stanley Cup to the Flyers back in 1975?

"Why did you let me ramble on about hockey if you already knew everything?" she asked, annoyed.

He gave her a small smile. "I like the sound of your voice." He returned his attention to the game.

Oh. She couldn't figure him out, heads or tails. It was quite exasperating, really. She wanted to put him permanently in the box marked 'control freak' but then he'd wink or smile, or say nice things. She wished he'd pick a personality and stick to it.

At the end of the first period, he offered to get some beer. Relief washed over her when he stood up from his seat and headed toward the concession stand. After her Hockey 101 lecture, they hadn't spoken to one another for the rest of the first period, as he was so engrossed in the game. It was probably just as well. They had absolutely nothing in common. She dreaded going to Niagara Falls with him. As uncomfortable as this was, at least the game was a great distraction, not to mention a time killer. But what about Niagara Falls? You could only stare at cascading water for so long. She wondered if he would even find it as awesome as it truly was. With her luck, he'd turn out to be one of the two people in the world that weren't impressed by it.

Gavin returned with a cardboard tray containing two beers and two orders of nachos. Maybe he wasn't so bad after all.

He handed her one of the plastic baskets full of tortilla chips and steaming, hot cheese.

"Thank you," she mumbled. If ever there was a time for comfort food, this was it.

The second period started and they settled into the same uncomfortable silence. It was pretty clear to Kate that he had no interest in being there with her. What was Mr. Cline thinking, forcing her on him?

As soon as the buzzer indicated the end of the second period, Gavin sprang up from his seat, presumably to get away from her.

"Would you like anything?" he asked.

She shook her head. "No thanks."

"Are you sure? A beer? More nachos?"

She shook her head again and folded her arms across her chest. "No thanks, really."

While he was gone, she studied her watch, calculating how long it would be before she would be home and in her pajamas.

The company car headed back downtown to the parking ramp where Kate had left her car.

Gavin climbed out first and offered her his hand to help her out. Kate turned to him and said goodnight. A soft, light rain had started to fall. She wanted to get home before her hair frizzed up so much she wouldn't be able to get her head through the doorway.

"Would you like to go for a drink?" Gavin asked.

He had to be kidding. Go to a bar with him and stand there, saying nothing, like they'd been doing all evening? Trying to make conversation while he thought of the girl he'd left behind? That would be too painful for words. She'd rather stick a knitting needle into the middle of her forehead. Besides, she was no man's consolation prize. Mr. Cline had volunteered her to be his tour guide but she didn't have to make small talk with him. At least not any more.

"No thanks, I have to get home," Kate said civilly, refraining from adding, 'I've got a killer box set waiting for me.'

He sighed heavily.

Oh boy, now what was he unhappy about?

"Listen, Kate, I think perhaps I should apologize..." His voice trailed off.

She said nothing, just raised her eyebrows. The big boss apologizing to her? She looked at his face and something about his expression made her feel sad. She looked away quickly, embarrassed to find tears stinging her eyes. She wanted to kick him for making her feel that way.

"I know I wasn't much company tonight," he said, and looked around to see if anyone was in earshot. "I have a lot on my mind."

She continued to say nothing.

"Not that that's an excuse," he added quickly.

She waited.

"I'm sorry if you were bored, considering you were gracious enough to go with me on your night off."

That was decent enough.

"Mr. Whyte, I am only the receptionist at Cline and Company and I was just doing my job." She gave him a tight smile and bid him goodnight.

She turned around, stumbled off the curb and landed a little too hard on her ankle. She was grateful that her back was to him and he didn't see her wince. She soldiered on, chin up, gritting her teeth through the pain without looking back. She left him standing there on the wet pavement in front of the parking ramp.

Gavin arrived the next morning wanting very much to engage Kate in conversation, especially after his appalling behavior at the hockey game. But she gave him only a tight 'good morning' and returned her attention to the girls from the office, who were huddled around her desk. They were all studying her purse. What was it with women and purses and shoes?

He went into his office. The poor woman had been forced into accompanying him around town when she obviously didn't want to. He couldn't blame her for resenting him. But he was confused as to why he felt so compelled to make things right with her.

"Sherrie, do you know how to use one of these things?" Kate asked, referring to the brand new espresso machine, still in the box, that had been a Christmas gift for the whole office from a client. Gone were the days when boxes of wine, candy, and fresh, exotic fruit had arrived. Sherrie sat in front of her computer, putting together a mock-up of an ad. The walls of her office were covered with framed posters of ads that Sherrie had created as well as artwork done by her children. A chain made up of red and green construction paper hung across the top of the wall. Kate eyeballed it, relieved that there was still plenty of time to get all her baking and shopping done before the big day.

Sherrie stood up and asked, "Where are the instructions?"

Kate waved the manual at her and together, they headed off to the break room.

They hovered over the machine as if preparing to perform delicate surgery. Sherrie read from the brochure about the operation of the machine.

Kate followed her instructions but became distracted when Sherrie steered the conversation to Gavin Whyte.

"Did you know that Gavin is in line for the position of president of Alchemis?" Sherrie said, lowering the instruction manual. "This ad campaign could cost him the presidency."

Kate looked at her. "No pressure there. It explains why he's so demanding." She ground the coffee, wiped off the excess and began to tamp it down.

Sherrie looked at her as if she had an eye in the middle of her forehead. She frowned. "I wouldn't say demanding so much as discerning. He just knows what he wants. If only we could get on the same page with him."

"If anyone can nail this campaign, it's you, Sherrie," Kate said. She turned her attention back to the machine. "Okay, what's next?"

Sherrie read the next part of the instructions. She put the manual down and asked Kate: "How was the hockey game last night?"

Kate shuddered. "Let's just say he's not climbing to the top of the corporate ladder with his personality!"

"Really? I'm surprised," Sherrie said. "I bet you can't wait to show him the rest of the sights."

Kate paused and looked at her. "I'd rather stick something sharp into my ear."

Sherrie's eyes grew wide. Kate heard the door open behind her and continued: "I'd rather get a glue gun and seal my eyelids shut."

Sherrie laughed nervously. "Ok, I get the idea."

Kate heard Paul's voice behind her and didn't bother to turn around. "I'd rather pierce my nipple with a rusty needle than show—"

"Gavin! Paul! We're just making espresso," Sherrie said nervously, her voice high-pitched.

Kate froze, wondering how much of her rant had been heard by Gavin Whyte. She turned and gave both men a weak smile.

"I see the Sabres won last night," Paul said to Kate.

She nodded.

"Kate was gracious enough to take me to the game last night," Gavin said to Sherrie.

Paul shot her a look. "Really? The two of you?"

Kate ignored him, assumed a frosty air and went back to her task. She certainly didn't owe him any explanation. This was the part where she had to froth the milk; she needed to focus.

"Thanks again, Kate, for going with me," Gavin said.

Kate's eyes widened, she didn't want anyone to get the wrong impression. And from the look on Paul's face, he was drawing all sorts of conclusions.

Kate added frothy milk into her espresso. It seemed to have the look and the consistency of old motor oil. Doubtful, she took a tentative sip.

"Gee, it's kind of strong," she said. Her forehead creased.

Sherrie sipped hers, then winced and crossed her eyes, laughing. "Do you think?"

Paul went to pour himself a cup but Sherrie grabbed hold of his arm.

"Oh, don't drink that," she warned. "Kate was just experimenting. It'll corrode your stomach lining."

Kate burst out laughing just as she was attempting another sip, causing her to choke. Coffee spewed forth out of her nose and mouth, and down the front of her white blouse.

"That's classy," Sherrie said in horrified amusement.

Mortified, Kate turned her back to them, grabbed a dish towel and soaked one end under the cold water tap. Her eyes watered as she continued to cough. She furiously dabbed the front of her blouse with the wet towel.

"Are you all right?" Gavin asked.

All she could do was nod, until finally, the coughing subsided.

She turned around from the sink, her horror continuing when she realized the front of her blouse was soaked and clinging to her chest. It afforded both men a view of her big-girl bra—white, industrial-strength and shaped like a Kevlar vest.

There was silence in the room. So much for glacial.

Sherrie buried her face in her hands, trying to stifle a laugh.

Gavin looked at Kate, clearly uncomfortable. He shifted from one foot to the other, unable to take his eyes off of her.

By the time he leaves here he'll probably need to go for some kind of survivor counselling, Kate thought miserably.

Paul chuckled. "Still the class clown, I see. One of the many things I love about you."

"Don't, Paul," she said angrily. The last thing she needed was for anyone to get the impression that they were an item.

"I'd better get back to work," she mumbled. *While I still have a job.*

She made a beeline back to her desk. She grabbed her navy cardigan off the back of her chair, put it on and buttoned it up as high as it would go.

Mr. Cline appeared at her desk.

"How was the game?" he asked.

"Great! We won, so that was good," she said.

Mr. Cline pressed Kate on the next stop of the itinerary.

"Well," she started. "I was thinking of Forest Lawn."

He scowled. "Forest Lawn? Are you nuts? I give you a remit to show our most important client the sights and you want to take him to a graveyard?"

This man has no romance in his soul, which doesn't surprise me. "True, it is a cemetery but may I point out that it is both beautiful and notable?" Kate said.

"If you're into that sort of thing," he challenged, rubbing the back of his head. "So a couple of dead presidents are buried there? Was Gavin a US history major? Doubt it," he said. "No, Kate, you can scratch that from your list."

Kate understood why Mr. Cline's wife had a drinking problem.

Once home, she immediately removed the offending undergarment. "Thank you for your service to the nation," she grumbled, flinging it onto the chair.

She was relieved she was home. A whole weekend away from the office and from Irish. There hadn't been one word said about Niagara Falls or any other sights for that matter. After the debacle in the break room, he had probably had second thoughts about any more sightseeing. She had dodged that bullet.

CHAPTER SEVEN

CHAPTER SEVEN

The phone on the nightstand jarred Kate out of a deep sleep. Without lifting her head from her pillow, she reached for it, fumbling, and put it to her ear.

"Hello?" she said thickly. Her teeth felt like they had socks on them.

"Kate?" asked a male voice. There was something familiar about it that niggled at the back of her mind.

"Yes?" she asked, not yet fully awake. She glanced at the clock. It was a little after eight in the morning.

"Oh no, did I wake you? Ed gave me your number and said it would be okay to ring you at home."

Gavin Whyte.

She immediately sat bolt upright in bed, swept her hair back with her free hand and licked her lips. "No, no, I was up," she said through a groggy haze.

"Will I ring you back later?"

"No, it's all right, what do you need?" she asked. A nightmare began to form in her head of having to go into the office on her day off. These executive types thought nothing of dragging a person into the office on a weekend to do something stupid—like hole-punching.

"I know it's short notice and you probably have plans..." he hesitated.

"Yes?"

"I was wondering if you were up for a little sightseeing today? I had planned to go into work today but I don't feel like it," he let out a nervous laugh. "And I don't feel like hanging around my hotel either."

Oh crap. She didn't even want to go to the corner store with him. Not after the other night.

He spoke before she could answer. "Look, I promise it won't be as bad as the hockey game."

She could beg off and tell him she'd already made plans even though it wasn't true. Other than some baking and shopping, she was free. But then she'd have to worry that it'd get back to Mr. Cline and she had promised him that she'd show Gavin Whyte the area.

"Umm, let me see," she said, wracking her brain, trying to figure out where to take him and if she even wanted to take him there. "Will you leave the details with me and I'll pick you up at noon?

"Sounds good."

They said their goodbyes and hung up.

The phone back in its cradle, she burrowed under her blanket and wondered if she could be trusted to show him the sights. She pushed any self-doubt out of her mind. Sure, she thought, piece of cake. After all, how hard could it be?

Unable to go back to sleep, Kate rolled out of bed and showered. Glancing at the clock, she decided she had some time to make some cookie dough. She began assembling the ingredients and bowls and mixers to make springerle, an anise-flavored German biscuit. It was a recipe that had been handed down to her from her mother's mother, a woman of German and Hungarian heritage who had married a Polish man. Kate had never met her Polish grandfather; he had died when her mother was a child. But she remembered Grandma Baranski, a solid, no-nonsense woman with an unfailingly positive attitude who'd raised a child by herself despite being widowed at a young age, and who always had time for her only grandchild. Kate made springerle cookies every Christmas—it reminded her of her Grandma and it was a way to remain connected to her.

She started with the eggs, beating them until they were light. She added the sugar and let it mix away in the electric mixer. She gradually added the flour, mixing half in the mixer and the remaining half by hand. Kneading the dough, she could hear her late grandmother's voice. 'Remember Kate, don't handle it too much, just enough to take shape or it will end up tough and your cookies will be dry.'

After it chilled, she rolled out the dough, then embossed it using a special springerle rolling pin. She covered the unbaked cookies with a dish towel to let them set for a while. She would put them in the oven tonight when she got home.

Once she tidied up the kitchen, she removed her apron, made herself a hot cup of tea and sat down at her kitchen island to make her Saturday morning phone calls.

She called her mother first, and they spoke of everything but her new boyfriend. He was the biggest, whitest elephant in the room.

Her second call was to her Aunt Geraldine in Ireland.

"What have you been up to, pet?" her aunt asked as soon as she heard Kate's voice.

"Oh, nothing much. Just the usual," Kate answered, shifting in her seat.

"How's your love life?"

"Flatlining."

"What is the matter with those American men? Come to me and I'll find you a nice Irish one."

"Actually, one of our clients comes from Templemore," she volunteered, not understanding why she did so.

"Really? It's a small world," her aunt said.

"His name is Gavin Whyte."

"I'll have to check this out. I have friends in Templemore. Gavin Whyte, is it?"

"And Mom has a boyfriend!" Kate blurted out.

"Oh that's wonderful!"

"It is?" It was not the response Kate had expected. She thought for sure her aunt would join her in raising her fist and railing against the unfairness of it all.

"Of course it is," her aunt said. "Kate, I certainly understand your loyalty to your father, but he's been gone a few years now. He was mad about your mother. He would have wanted her to be happy."

She had a point, Kate had to admit.

"Now, when are you and your mother coming for a visit?" Geraldine asked.

Kate gave her the standard-issue response. "I don't know. We're really busy at work."   Because they really were.

"I'd love to see you, pet. Come any time."

She knew she should get over there. Her aunt was getting older and wouldn't be there forever. Her father had proved that.

She stood at her kitchen sink, looking out the window, and sighed at the fact that there was still no snow. She thought today would be a good time to hang the exterior Christmas lights. If, by the time she arrived home, it was still light out, she'd start the exterior decorations.

She rinsed out her coffee cup and placed it in the top rack of the dishwasher, then grabbed her coat and knockoff purse and headed out the door.

Ignoring Mr. Cline's advice, Kate decided to take Gavin to Forest Lawn Cemetery.

She agonized as she drove downtown to pick him up. Would she have to go up to his hotel room to retrieve him? She hoped not. When she pulled up in front of the hotel at twelve sharp, their agreed-upon time, she saw him waiting outside, looking casual in jeans and a navy coat.

Her anxiety returned. The last time she'd seen him was during that unfortunate incident with the espresso machine. She hoped he wouldn't mention it.

He opened the door on the passenger side and got in the car. He said hello as he buckled his seat belt.

"How's it going with the espresso machine?" he asked, smiling. His eyes were an amazing shade of blue and she had to remind herself that she needed to keep her own eyes on the road.

"I've decided to stick to regular coffee," she said.

"That's a shame. I'd love to see what you could do with a complicated latte order."

She drove north on Delaware Avenue and they settled into an uncomfortable silence.

She watched his expression as they drove through the gates of Forest Lawn but he gave away nothing and Kate would have settled for raised eyebrows, a sigh or even a smirk. It was the final resting place of about one hundred and sixty-thousand people including some presidents and celebrities. The day was gloomy and she had to admit that the overcast sky did not put the cemetery in its best light. A little bit of sun would have been great. Even snow would have been better. She was still hoping for snow for Christmas. There was plenty of time left.

She parked the car on the verge near a small lake. Wordlessly, they got out and headed in the direction of the stone bridge.

"It's so quiet here," Gavin remarked. He reached the edge of the bridge and looked around. There were gentle sloping hills, a variety of leafless trees and memorials, tombstones and graves as far as you could see. Despite being in a heavy populated area, there was no noise. There wasn't even the muted sound of traffic coming from the nearby Scajaquada Expressway.

They strolled across the bridge, heading aimlessly toward the memorials. Barren branches threw a dark silhouette against a dreary sky.

Kate cleared her throat. "The last time I was here, it was fall and the sun was shining and the leaves were spectacular, all red and gold and everything. It's a shame the sun isn't out today." She looked around at the various shades of grey and brown.

"It certainly is atmospheric," he said.

With nothing more to say, they walked on in awkward silence, stopping at different tombs and gravesites until they ended up at a circular memorial. They peered inside the glass of the monument at the sculpture of 19th century parents at the deathbed of their only child.

The scene tugged at Kate, it always had. From the corner of her eye, she looked at Gavin. He placed his palm on the glass and whispered: "All the money it took to build this and yet they couldn't save their child." He turned away quickly and walked on. Kate followed him, hating to admit that maybe Mr. Cline was right and bringing Gavin Whyte here had probably not been the best idea. She had only ended up depressing their most important client.

They started to weave their way through grave markers and headstones. She stopped at one. It was a simple, weathered affair of flat stone with the word *BABY* in block letters. Her breath caught in her throat. Gavin stopped beside her and looked down.

"This was all they could afford," she said. "Not even the child's name."

"Another lost child and yet loved and grieved just the same," Gavin commented. He straightened up and surveyed the cemetery.

"So many grand monuments to the deceased," he said. "They're grand gestures."

There was something there, so Kate pressed on. "You don't approve?"

He shook his head. "Is it a grand gesture or is it guilt or simple ostentatious show of money?"

"When perhaps, smaller kinder gestures during their lifetime would have carried more weight," Kate offered.

Gavin nodded. "Exactly. As beautiful as all this is and it is, if it is meant as a monument for the deceased then what good is that to them when they're not here to appreciate it?"

She bristled, thinking that something as notable as this cemetery, another little Buffalo gem had not instilled the pride that she had thought it would. He either couldn't or wouldn't appreciate it. Discomfort made her neck feel hot. She certainly hadn't meant to upset him.

"Maybe it is an extension of all the little gestures afforded the deceased during their lifetime," she said, challenging him.

He tilted his head to one side as if he were considering it. "Maybe."

"And this is the final, permanent, grand gesture of that life together," she said. She was taking to it. "A sort of closure. A witness of a life lived." The thought of her own father came at her, blinding her and she wondered if grief was something you just had to live with. An unwelcome companion of sorts.

"I see your point."

"I think we should go," she said, lifting her chin a little. Turning her back on him, she picked up her pace, anxious to get out of there. She'd lost interest in the rest of the itinerary she'd planned for the afternoon. She wondered if it would still count if she dropped him back off at his hotel within an hour of picking him up.

He grabbed her arm. "Whoa, wait a minute, Kate. I am so sorry. I didn't mean to sound so rude."

"I've made a mistake," she said. "I thought you'd appreciate the beauty of the place and not look for ulterior motives of grieving family members."

He had the decency to look horrified. "I am truly sorry, Kate."

"Come on, I'll take you back to your hotel."

His eyes widened. "No, really, I'm fine."

Kate looked away. "Well to be honest, there's more grand gestures on the tour this afternoon" And she didn't think she could handle his enthusiasm, it was so underwhelming. She thought of the Albright-Knox Art Gallery that had one of the finest collections of contemporary and modern art in the country, housed in an impressive Greek revival building. Then there was Our Lady of Victory Basilica, the grandest gesture of them all: beauty, grace and splendor in architecture, marble, artwork and gold leaf. She certainly didn't want to show these local treasures to someone who wouldn't appreciate them. Suddenly, she felt protective of her hometown.

He glanced away and then looked back at her. "Do you believe in second chances?" he asked suddenly, running a hand through his hair.

"It depends," she said cautiously. Paul came to mind. And she knew there was no way she was going to be giving him any second chances.

"Can we go back and start at the beginning?" he asked. "I've put a foot wrong here and I want to right it."

"Do you want me to take you back to your hotel and pick you up again?" Kate asked.

He laughed nervously. "No, I don't think we have to go that far back." Gavin Whyte looked around again. "Pay no attention to me." He looked at her and said: "Forgive me."

Kate relaxed a bit, the tension slowly easing out of her body. She put her hands in her pockets as the air felt damp. She watched a large black cloud roll in slowly from the west as if it had all the time in the world and she hoped it wouldn't rain. Her umbrella was in the car.

"Looks like rain," Gavin remarked, following the cloud as well.

"We should head back to the car," she said, worried.

"Probably a good idea," he said. He looked up at the sky and pulled a small, travel-sized umbrella out of his pocket.

Kate laughed. "Do you always carry an umbrella with you?"

He smiled. "I'm from Ireland, I never leave home without it."

At that moment, the sky opened up and the rain fell.

Swiftly, Gavin opened up his umbrella and held it over Kate.

She was horrified to see that it was barely big enough for the two of them and the one side of his coat was getting soaked. He held it more toward her so she wasn't getting wet at all. She stole a glance at him but he was deep in concentration of holding the umbrella over her head as they walked in tandem. It was a small gesture that could be considered very grand on a rainy day.

"Come on, let's get back to the car," she said, picking up her pace. They were so close underneath the umbrella that she could feel his warm, minty breath on the side of her cheek. By the time they reached her car, one side of his coat was soaked.

"Let me take that and lay it on the back seat," she suggested.

He removed it and she had to suppress a shudder at the sight of him in a light knit sweater that hugged his own finely sculpted body. *Why go to an art gallery when I have a work of art right here in front of me,* she wondered.

They climbed into the front seat. Kate turned on the car and blasted the heaters. They sat for a few minutes, waiting for the deluge to peter out.

"Before we head on to our next destination, I think we should get some lunch and a hot cup of coffee."

He nodded his head, rubbing his hands together. "Sounds good."

By Sunday morning, she had embraced the idea of taking Gavin to see the falls. The previous day, they had soldiered on after lunch to the art gallery and the basilica. Gavin had been impressed by both. As they left the basilica, he'd offered to take her to dinner but she declined, saying she had some things to do. Although Gavin's mood had improved as the afternoon wore on, Kate had felt tense trying to make conversation and gauge his reaction and mood and that had been exhausting. She dropped him off at his hotel and they made arrangements to go to the falls the following day.

Now, after a good night's sleep, she was almost looking forward to going to the falls. In the end she decided that it would be good PR for herself. It would show Mr. Cline what a team player she really was. Besides, she was a western New Yorker and everyone knew that there were certain things that were programmed into the genes of western New Yorkers: love of the Bills, the Sabres, and chicken wings; the ability to take a blizzard in stride; and the penchant for dragging every out-of-towner up to Niagara Falls.

It was a good day for the trip. Although the air was cold and crisp, the sun was bright in a cloudless blue sky.

She stole a glance at him as he climbed into her car and said hello. He looked more relaxed than yesterday. Maybe it was the sunshine. Maybe it was the fact that she wasn't dragging him to a cemetery.

"I want to thank you for taking me around yesterday," he started. "I usually work on the weekends, so it was nice to take a day off."

"You work every weekend?" she asked.

"Yes, but only a half day on Sunday, and usually from home. Paperwork. Administrative stuff."

She stared at him. She tried not to be intimidated by his good looks.

"What constitutes a half day in Gavin Whyte's book?"

He looked over at her and smiled. "Finishing early, between two and three o'clock."

She snorted and said: "That's not a half day!"

"What?" He laughed. "I've had this schedule for as long as I can remember."

She shook her head. "I'm sorry but that's not right."

"Why not? I'm trying to get ahead."

"Ahead of what?" she wondered out loud.

When he didn't respond, she continued. "Where's your life? What about hobbies? What do you do in your free time?"

"I go down to Tipperary as often as I can. That's how I relax."

She thought that his girlfriend must be falling down on the job. If Kate had a boyfriend like him, there'd be no way she'd let him work seven days a week.

They made small talk. He mentioned he'd be flying to Dublin the following day.

"Oh," she said. She hadn't expected this. She attempted to make her voice sound as neutral as possible and not betray her surprise. "You're heading back already?" For the life of her she couldn't explain why she felt a little sad at his departure.

"I'll be back in a few days," he said. "I have to report back to the head office in Dublin."

"I thought you were the bigwig," Kate blurted out. She made a mental note to get a filter for her mouth.

He laughed. "Well, I'm one of the bigwigs. But I do have to report what's going on here. We're on a tight schedule."

"Oh no," she said worriedly, biting her lip and mentally reviewing her antics in front of this man. She might single-handedly be responsible for the demise of the biggest account at Cline & Co.

"It's not that bad," he said as if he could read her thoughts.

"What will you tell them?" she asked out of curiosity. *That we're a bunch of idiots? That we're inept at best? That we're not really professionals, we just play them on TV?*

"Now, Miss O'Connor, you're asking me to divulge company secrets," he said lightly. She looked over at him, convinced that this was not the same guy she'd been with at the hockey game or the cemetery. She wondered if she should check for a pod under his bed.

"I am the master secret keeper," she said proudly.

He was quiet for a moment. "I bet a lot of people tell you their secrets."

"Maybe."

"You're easy to talk to," he remarked.

"So is a dog."

He laughed.

She cut over to Elmwood Avenue and then took a few side roads to get to the I-190 North. They circled the edge of downtown and as soon as she saw the sign for Canada, she turned her indicator light on and maneuvered into the far right-hand lane, heading for the exit to the Peace Bridge.

She edged the car into the bottlenecked line for the toll. Customs officers walked among the idle cars in their sunglasses and baseball hats, constantly scanning the steady stream of cars and searching for anything that looked a little suspicious. They randomly approached cars, rapping on the windows and indicating to the drivers to roll them down to answer questions.

They went through the toll and she threw the appropriate amount of change into the basket. With the US in her rearview mirror, she drove over the bridge toward Canada, emerging on the other side into the more orderly line of Canadian customs. A big sign in red and white above the booths said 'Welcome to Canada' in both English and French. They pulled up to the booth and were greeted by a customs official who sat at a computer, his hands flying over his keyboard. Kate turned off the radio and rolled down her window.

"Citizenship?" the officer asked without looking away from his screen.

"US," Kate said.

"Ireland," Gavin answered.

The official looked up then. "Passports please."

They handed him their documents. He studied them. "What is your business in Canada today?"

"We're going to Niagara Falls," Kate answered.

He peered into the car as if trying to discern whether they were the Niagara Falls type. "How long do you plan to spend in Canada?" he asked, starting to look bored.

"A couple of hours."

"Are you bringing anything into the country that needs to be declared?"

"No."

He handed back their passports and said, "Enjoy your visit."

That was relatively pain-free, thought Kate.

She chose the route along the Canadian shore rather than taking the more direct QEW—Queen Elizabeth Way. Although it was longer and a little slower, it was also a lot more scenic. It took almost three quarters of an hour but soon they were driving past the Niagara Gorge and they hit the perpetual mist that indicated the falls were nearby. Despite the fact that it was December, there were still quite a few tourists walking about.

She headed for the closest car park, privately appalled at the fee and grateful when Gavin paid for it.

She clicked the remote on her key ring and listened for the beep, ensuring that the car was locked. She scanned her immediate surroundings, looking for identifiable landmarks so she would be able to locate her vehicle later. She didn't want to end up walking around the parking lot searching for her car and looking like an idiot in front of Gavin. Again. They followed the rest of the tourists and crossed the street to view the mighty Niagara Falls.

Gavin realized that he had gone quiet on her again and he hoped it wouldn't turn into a repeat of the other night at the hockey game or yesterday when he'd become all gloomy and depressed at the cemetery. He'd thought of that memorial of the parents with their dying son. He'd felt similar: he had lots of money but it couldn't buy his mother her health. He felt himself beginning to drift away and he had to force himself back to the present. They had had pleasant conversation on the way up. She was funny and sometimes she didn't even mean to be; she just was. He couldn't remember the last time he had had a good laugh. He'd been surprised at how much he had enjoyed her company yesterday and was equally surprised how disappointed he'd been when she'd declined his dinner invitation. Today, he was determined not to be distracted by work or by his mother's health problems. Internally, he declared the afternoon a 'no problem' zone.

The mist off the falls sprayed them. He didn't mind. In fact, he lifted his face to it, to soak in the whole experience. Kate stood at the rail with him, which was wet and glistening in the winter sun, and they watched as hundreds of thousands of gallons of the heavy, foamy Niagara River thundered over the Canadian horseshoe and crashed to the boulders below. The sight and the sound were marvelous. Across the water was the American falls, comprised of two smaller sets of waterfalls with the smaller of the two being known as 'The Bridal Veil.' The tremendous amount of water and the roaring noise were almost overwhelming.

He leaned forward and then back and then let out a short burst of laughter and shook his head. He almost had to shout to be heard above the roar of the water. "The words magnificent and spectacular come to mind, but they seem so terribly inadequate." He paused before he spoke again. "It's very grand, isn't it?"

Kate pulled her mobile phone out and waved it at him. "Will I get some pictures for you?"

"Good idea. Back home they think I work too hard."

"Well, do you?" she asked.

"Yes, I think I do," he said quietly.

"You know what they say, 'All work and no play makes Jack a dull boy.'"

He laughed. Perhaps he was dull. Georgina's parting shot had been that he'd turned 'boring.' He was still stinging over that one.

Kate instructed him to stand in front of the guardrail with his back to the falls. He leaned against the railing, smiled, and waited while she snapped some pictures.

"Let me take your photo," he said, when she appeared to be finished.

She immediately shook her head no, but he decided that he wasn't going to take no for an answer.

"C'mon, Miss O'Connor," he pleaded, grinning. "You took my picture, now it's only fair that I take yours."

She blushed. She did that a lot. He found it refreshing and oddly arousing. She handed him her mobile but he refused, deciding he wanted to capture the image on his own phone. Again that lingering feeling skated around the back of his mind, yet to be named.

They traded places and she stood against the guardrail while he lined her up in his lens. It was oddly intimate and he wondered if she'd thought the same thing when she had snapped his photo. Once her face came into focus, he thought, *Wow, she's a beautiful girl.* Not glamorous like Alexis or Georgina, but pretty.

As they huddled together comparing shots, she said, "You're very photogenic."

"So are you." He watched as her neck and the top of her chest reddened again. He found her enchanting.

She cleared her throat. "Our hair is getting wet." The spray from the falls settled on them.

"I don't mind," he said absentmindedly, trying to study her photo without looking obvious.

"I do—it'll be frizz city in no time," she said.

He burst out laughing.

An older woman with silver hair and pink lipstick approached them, bundled up in a fuchsia-colored fleece jacket and a purple scarf.

"Here, honey, let me take your picture for you," she said. "Get next to your man, so I can get the two of you together. You're going to want to show your grandchildren these pictures someday."

The woman took the phone from Kate's hand before Kate could protest. Kate looked mortified at the woman's incorrect assumption and Gavin found it amusing. She couldn't look at him.

"Someday when you're older you'll be glad you have a picture of this day," the woman was saying.

Gavin had to admit that he was enjoying the situation. Kate, however, looked as if she wanted to climb over the guardrail and jump.

"C'mon honey, don't keep the man waiting," the woman said impatiently.

"C'mon honey, it's for the grandchildren," he said playfully. "I hope they're all girls just like you."

Kate inched closer to him. They stood shoulder to shoulder like comrades-in-arms.

"Oh, for the love of God. You two look more like college buddies than lovers. Get with it." The old woman shook her head as if they were hopeless. "Young man, put your arm around her."

Good idea. He put his arm around her and felt her stiffen. He wondered what he would have to do to get her to relax. He rested his hand on her upper arm and gave it a little squeeze. She smelled lovely. He felt the tension leaving her body. He lowered his arm and put it around her waist. He pulled her close to him and felt her shiver. She felt wonderfully soft and supple and for a dizzying moment, he got lost in it.

"Is this your idea of fun?" Kate asked out of the side of her mouth.

He looked at her and whispered. "Being with a pretty girl? Yes, I guess it is."

She went quiet. He was thinking of other compliments he could pay her just to see her blush; he'd thought no one did that anymore. But she was no fool—she'd know an insincere compliment a mile away.

"My 'honey' doesn't really go for PDAs," he told the silver-haired woman. "She's more of a private person, if you know what I mean." He heard Kate chuckle. Just a little one. But it was there.

"PDAs? What is that?" the woman asked.

"Public displays of affection," he told her.

She scoffed at this, muttered something inaudible which Gavin was sure was an insult, and shook her head. She looked at Kate with dismay. "What's wrong with you? If my man looked like him, I wouldn't be able to keep my hands off of him!"

She lined up the camera angle. "Young people nowadays, so PC—that's politically correct. You take the fun out of everything. Let's take this picture and get the show on the road. An official royal portrait wouldn't take as long." She held up the phone. "Okay, work with me now, get a little bit closer and pretend you like one another." Her voice dripped with sarcasm.

Unable to resist, Gavin pulled Kate closer to him and she started to shake a little.

"Are you cold, 'honey'?" he asked, winking.

Once the photo shoot was over, the old woman handed the phone back to Kate and walked away, shaking her head and mumbling.

"Will we walk on?" he asked. He could sense that she was heading for the parking lot; she was as skittish as a newborn colt on the farm. He needed to rein her in.

They walked along the falls as far as they could. Although he hated shopping, he went into every shop there was, if only to draw out the day and avoid returning to the hotel and dealing with work. He bought some leaf-shaped maple sugar candy and a lovely scarf for his mother.

By the end of the afternoon, he insisted on taking Kate out to dinner. She agreed and he was delighted that she did.

CHAPTER EIGHT

They headed away from the falls and ended up in Niagara-on-the-Lake, a charming, picturesque town not far from where the Niagara River connected with Lake Ontario. Kate had always loved this place. It was like stepping back in time. It was quaint, with its antique shops, horse-drawn carriages and elegant period homes.

They found a little pub called The Pepper Tree Inn, not far from an original apothecary shop. A bell jingled when Gavin opened the door and he held it for Kate as she stepped across the threshold. The place had a low ceiling and wide-plank floors, and there was a stone fireplace in the center of the room.

A sign hung overhead which read, 'Visit our Homemade Bakery next door.' Kate was greeted with the aroma of freshly-baked cake and tried to suppress a groan.

The hostess, a shapely brunette, approached them with menus in hand and inquired, "Two?" Her gaze locked on Gavin; she ignored Kate.

He turned and asked, "Kate, where would you like to sit?"

"Anywhere is fine."

The brunette led them to a booth against the front window, and they slid in on opposite sides, facing each other. Kate stared out the window, charmed by the sight of old-fashioned lampposts decorated with big green wreaths with red bows, and tiny Christmas lights strung across the streets, twinkling multi-colored lights against the fading daylight. She loved the holiday season. The hostess handed them their menus and spoke directly to Gavin.

"Sightseeing today?" she asked.

Gavin nodded. "Yes, we were at the falls."

"First time?" she asked.

"Yes, and hopefully not the last."

"The first time is always special," she squeaked.

Did she really just say that? Kate wondered, suppressing an eye-roll.

Gavin laughed politely.

"Do I detect an accent?" the hostess asked.

Wow, Sherlock Holmes, Kate thought to herself.

Gavin nodded. Kate felt invisible, and wanted to remain so, her head buried in the laminated menu, studying it as if it was the most interesting thing since the discovery of the Dead Sea Scrolls.

"You're Irish, aren't you? Omigod!" the hostess shrieked, flashing perfect, bleached teeth. She carried on, "Somebody in my family tree came from Ireland."

A tree Kate was pretty sure she didn't want to shake too hard. She turned her attention back out the window and watched a young couple across the street, scarves wrapped around their necks, shopping bags in hand. The man, hands full, leaned over to the woman, laughing, and kissed her. Kate felt a twinge of something—perhaps regret, loss, nostalgia, or perhaps just a wish. A wish for that kind of momentary bliss.

"Can I get you something to drink?" the hostess asked.

"A Guinness," Gavin said.

"Duh, of course," she said, smiling. She turned to Kate and her smile disappeared. "Anything for you?"

What she needed was a stiff drink after having Gavin's arm around her earlier. Him being so close, invading her personal space, had just about been her undoing. But she still had to drive back so she ordered a pot of tea and the hostess scurried off. An unpleasant thought occurred to her—she was actually jealous. Jealous of the small talk this woman made with Gavin. It made her mad at herself. There was nothing to be jealous of; he was the client and she was the employee. And, he had a girlfriend. End of.

He picked up the menu.

"See anything that appeals to you?"

"Oh," she stuttered. "I was just deciding." Everything looked good.

Glancing up, she scanned the restaurant and noticed that a number of people at other tables were staring in their direction. She wondered if she had something unmentionable on her face. Then she realized that they were all women and they were all staring at Gavin. She was intrigued by this phenomenon, to the point that she didn't hear him properly as he went on about something on the menu and gave a little laugh. Cute. He appeared oblivious to the attention from some of the females in the room.

Their beverages arrived and the hostess tried to engage Gavin again. It was like nails on a chalkboard to Kate.

"C'mon, get back to work for Pete's sake and stop harassing the customers," a gravelly voice interjected. An ancient waitress who looked as if she'd been born during the War of 1812 elbowed her way to the table.

The hostess let out a 'hmph' and left.

"Ready to order, folks?" the waitress asked. Her nametag read 'Helen.' She wore squeaky rubber-soled shoes and her eyes were magnified four times their normal size behind Coke-bottle lenses. Her hair was the color of steel wool and permed to kingdom come. It was apparent that she wanted to be anywhere else than here. Preferably, the casinos in Niagara Falls.

"What are the specials today?" Gavin had the nerve to ask.

Helen growled, "Lamb, beef and salmon. And don't ask me specifics, because I don't remember."

They ordered quickly before she had the chance to kick them out and she sighed heavily when Kate asked for her salad dressing on the side.

They waited in silence. Minus the hostess and the waitress, Kate began to wonder if this had been a good idea after all. What were they going to talk about? She had to stifle a yawn. The late afternoon slump descended.

Helen soon returned with their salads. She mixed up the order and placed Kate's salad in front of Gavin. They waited for her to disappear before switching plates, so as to not offend her, and then burst out laughing.

"Thank you, Mr. Whyte."

"Kate, would you please call me Gavin?" he asked.

"But you look like a Mr. Whyte and I look like a Kate O'Connor," she explained. She poured a little bit of dressing onto her salad. "I bet when you were born, your parents took one look at you and said, 'We'll call him Mr. Whyte.'"

"And what does a Kate O'Connor look like?" he asked, picking up his fork and starting to eat his salad.

He had caught her off guard. She looked away. "Well...sensible, efficient, solid. Someone you can depend on."

"That sounds more like a commercial for a truck." He grinned.

She laughed.

"But seriously," he entreated. "I'd like you to call me Gavin."

"Okay...um...Gavin," she said, testing it out, rolling it along her tongue.

He smiled. "See, that wasn't so bad."

Their dinners were set before them with a hard thump by Helen and Kate could have sworn the food bounced on her plate.

She stared out the window, perfectly content to watch the people walking past, and wondered what each of their stories might be. The light was fading early in the winter evening. Big, fat snowflakes fell listlessly to the ground, disappearing on contact with the pavement. *Oh, the first snowfall. How absolutely wonderful!*

"Miss O'Connor, you are a thousand miles away," Gavin said.

She sat up straighter and smiled, picked up her teacup and began sipping it.

He looked out the window and remarked, "It doesn't really snow in Ireland anymore. I remember as a lad, we'd get some decent snow, but not anymore. It just rains. A lot."

"Global warming," she said, laughing. "But I remember the rain. Sometimes, it seemed as if it would never stop." She thought of her summers there—wellies always on hand for mucking around in the mud, riding around in the tractor down the narrow country lanes with Uncle Liam, and the days out at the beach.

"Do you still have family in Templemore?" she asked, shifting in her seat.

"My mother and father."

"Brothers or sisters?"

He shook his head. "No, it's just me."

"You didn't follow in your dad's footsteps?" she asked, curious as to how he'd gone from farming to big-city Dublin and a big pharmaceutical company.

"My father thought I'd be better off with an education, a career..." he explained, his voice trailing off. He looked away.

"What do you think?" Kate asked.

"I don't know. I sometimes wonder about it."

"Do you miss it?" she asked.

"I do," he said, sipping his Guinness. "I miss the countryside. I miss the simplicity of it, the laid-back lifestyle. But I miss the land the most."

This surprised her. Mr. Tall, Dark, Handsome, and Very Successful would also have been content out in the country. Wonders never ceased. Although she had to admit, a picture came to mind of him stepping down from a tractor in jeans, Wellington boots, and an Aran sweater, and that looked pretty good, too. She found it odd that he had not mentioned one word about his girlfriend.

They were both quiet for a moment, each lost in their own thoughts.

"Did you visit Ireland often?" he asked.

"I spent every summer there as a kid on the farm. I loved it. It was a good way of life," she answered. She smiled as the memories came back of things she hadn't thought about in years.

"How long has it been since you were there?"

"It's been a few years." She'd gone to Ireland after Paul had dumped her. When she returned home, she learned that her father had been diagnosed with cancer and she hadn't been back since.

"How come so long?"

She shrugged. "My father passed away a few years ago." She thought of her father— a big man with eyes the color of sapphires, and a practical joker, to boot. It wasn't until he was gone that she'd realized how much she'd been loved and cherished. She cleared her throat and looked down at the table. She decided to go for honesty. "I'm afraid I'm not ready to face the memories head on. Yet." It was the first time since his death she had voiced those reasons.

"I'm sorry, Kate, I didn't know," he said quietly.

She left it at that. She finished her meal and pushed her plate away, comfortably full. Before it could put a total damper on the meal, she changed the topic of conversation.

"So tell me about the farm in Tipperary."

His face lit up. He spoke at length about how the land had been in the Whyte family for almost ten generations, about how he loved being outdoors and about his newest project: beekeeping.

"Beekeeping?" she said in disbelief.

He nodded. "I even took a course through the Irish Beekeepers' Association."

He became downright animated talking about his rural home.

"It sounds lovely," she said, and it did. Irish countryside was some of the most beautiful landscape in the world. Green and lush, it was hard to beat.

"Any dessert?" Helen's bark came out of nowhere, startling Kate.

She shook her head. "No thanks."

"Are you sure, Kate?" Gavin asked.

"I'll pass."

The waitress looked at Gavin and practically dared him to order. Bravely, he nodded and said, "Sure."

She frowned at him and walked away, returning shortly and thrusting a dessert menu into his hands.

He opened it up and scanned it. "I'll have a slice of the chocolate raspberry cake and a cup of black coffee," he said decisively.

Anything but that, Kate thought. Chocolate and raspberries were her favorite combination. Why couldn't he have ordered something with pineapples in it? She hated pineapples.

"Two forks, please," he added.

Helen returned promptly with his dessert and coffee. She also laid the bill on the table to deter them from ordering anything else. The slice of cake was huge. It could have fed an undernourished family of four in a third world country for about a week. It was a deep, rich brown and it looked moist and springy. The frosting was thick and shiny and reminded Kate of silk. It was garnished with a few fresh raspberries and a light dusting of powdered sugar. A raspberry coulis circled around the edge of the plate. Kate could feel her blood sugar levels rising just looking at it. She tried not to whimper.

He handed her the other fork and put the plate in the middle of the table between them, with a look that encouraged her to dig in. She did, and it was divine; the chocolate was velvety and the raspberries sweet.

She was dying to ask him about his girlfriend but that felt too much like fishing.

After a few mouthfuls, he sat back in his chair and let out a big sigh, signaling the meal had come to an end for him.

As they headed out of the restaurant, the hostess ambushed them and gushed out a goodbye to Gavin, bidding him to come back real soon. He smiled and placed his hand on the small of Kate's back and followed her out the door. The sun had set and the sky had gone dark.

They headed toward the parking lot in silence. It had turned out to be a lovely day. Other than that nosy woman who insisted on taking their picture, she couldn't believe how well it had gone. In fact, if it had been any other man than Gavin Whyte, Kate would have thought of it as the perfect date. Surely this would score big points with Mr. Cline. She was proud of herself.

They ran into trouble at US Customs trying to get back into the country. The man at the booth must have been having a bad day. Or maybe he had a quota to make. But Gavin, despite having handed over his Irish passport, could not answer any of the questions to the customs officer's satisfaction.

It was his accent. Kate had to admit that she loved the sound of it. It was lyrical and beautiful. She would love to close her eyes and just listen to him talk. The customs officer was intrigued as well, but for very different reasons.

Gavin explained patiently to him that he had been born in the US, which made him an American, but he had been raised in Ireland and currently resided there, thus the accent and the Irish passport.

These facts didn't seem to impress the guy. He looked at Kate, studying her. She wished she could read his expression.

"Are you his wife?" he asked her.

She shook her head. The customs officer wasn't smiling. It must be like working for the Department of Motor Vehicles, where having no sense of humor seemed to be a prerequisite. Kate explained to him who she was and that she was simply showing Gavin the sights.

"You're going to have to pull over for further interrogation."

Oh crap. She'd heard about people being detained at the border and being stuck for hours, and that had been before 9/11.

The officer gave them directions to the bay where they could park, and then they were to go inside the building and wait to be called. He took Gavin's passport from him.

Wordlessly, they followed his instructions.

The customs office looked like the inside of a bank, except with a waiting room. On the left were rows of institutional brown plastic chairs and to the right was a long counter with a glass window with customs officers behind it, like tellers.

They found a pair of seats in the middle row.

Kate offered a quick smile to the woman sitting next to her. She was one of those women whose age was indeterminate. She could have been twenty. Or forty. She was diminutive and wrapped in a maroon-patterned sari. She had liquid brown eyes and a tentative smile.

The woman said, "I was taken from my tour bus and told to wait here."

"How long ago was that?" Kate asked.

"Almost four hours," she said sadly. "And the bus left without me."

Yikes!

Gavin looked at Kate and said, "Don't worry, this shouldn't take long."

Boy, was he optimistic!

The foreign woman stood up when her name was called, and an officer escorted her to a private room.

As they waited, they drank several cups of vending machine coffee that was both scalding and tasteless and gave Kate the jitters. By the time Gavin's name was finally called, three hours later, she was practically bouncing off the walls. She felt awful. She remained seated but watched him up at the counter, trying to explain things. *Why didn't I just take him to the American side of the falls?* She thought miserably. *Why did I have to drag him to Canada just to impress him?*

After half an hour, he returned to her. She stood up immediately.

"Well, that's all sorted out," he said. It was late and he looked tired. *Nice way to spend a weekend,* Kate thought. *Crossing your fingers and hoping your host country doesn't give you a one-way ticket to Guantanamo Bay.*

"Oh Mr. Whyte, I am really sorry. I never thought they would hassle you at the border."

"Well, after 9/11, I guess they're just doing their jobs," he said wearily.

"You hardly fit the profile of a terrorist," she pointed out.

He shrugged and headed toward the exit and Kate followed in his wake.

He held the door open for her and as she passed in front of him, he said, "I thought you weren't going to call me 'Mr. Whyte' anymore."

"I must have regressed." They stepped outside into a black, starless night.

The sari-clad woman stood outside, clutching her bag in front of her with a nervous expression on her face. Kate approached her and Gavin followed.

"Are you all right?" Kate asked.

The woman nodded but tears welled up in her eyes. Kate reached out and touched her arm.

"Yes, they have let me go, everything is in order, but my bus left hours ago and I don't know how to get back to my hotel," she said, trembling.

"That's no problem, we'll get you back to your hotel," Gavin said firmly.

The woman lowered her head and Kate realized that it was because she was crying.

"It's all right, we'll help you," she said softly.

"Perhaps we could call a cab for her?" he suggested.

"What hotel are you staying at?" Kate asked.

The woman mentioned the name and Kate nodded. "Actually, that's not far from yours," she said to Gavin. "We could drop her off, if you don't mind."

He smiled and shrugged. "Of course not. Whatever she feels most comfortable doing."

Kate gave the woman the option of traveling with them, or they would hire a cab for her.

The woman smiled and grasped their hands. "You are so kind to me. Thank-you. Thank-you."

She opted to drive with them and Gavin took her bag from her and put it into the back seat of Kate's car.

They were back in downtown Buffalo in fifteen minutes. Kate broke all sorts of speed limits and may even have sailed through a stop sign. Her passengers were mute but Gavin did raise an eyebrow on occasion. They arrived at the woman's hotel and Kate accompanied her into the lobby to make sure she re-connected with her tour group. As they approached the front desk, a large man wearing a sport coat with a lanyard hanging around his neck called out. They both turned.

"You've made it back!"

The woman turned to Kate and embraced her and thanked her profusely.

Kate said goodbye and rejoined Gavin in the car. She started it up and pulled out into traffic.

"Would you like to go for a drink?" Gavin asked as she slowed to the curb in front of his hotel.

Boy, this guy was some kind of masochist. And a polite one, too. For the world, she couldn't figure him out.

"We'd better call it a day. I think I've gotten you into enough trouble," she said, unable to make eye contact with him. Not to mention that her nerves were shot.

"Are you sure?" he asked, rubbing his hand along his chin.

She nodded.

"Well, thank you for showing me the falls," he said as he got out of the car.

And US Homeland Security in action, she thought.

Once he shut the car door, she peeled away from the curb, anxious to get away.

CHAPTER NINE

All the way home, Kate couldn't stop thinking of the fiasco at the border and she felt as if she was starting to unravel because of it. She had created a vicious cycle of constantly humiliating herself in front of Gavin.

By the time she arrived at her house it was almost bedtime, but she was practically spinning from all the vending machine coffee. To distract herself, she went through all the brand new clothes that had arrived the other day. She took them out of their plastic bags, cut off the tags and laid them out along the sofa and the living room chairs. It looked like color and style had arrived and exploded in her home. She fingered all the fabrics, and held the items up one by one against herself as she stood in front of the mirror.

She wasn't ready for too much color yet, so she a chose a pencil skirt and a ribbed cream turtleneck along with a pair of knee-high boots for Monday morning.

Feeling inspired, she drove up to the drugstore and bought a box of wash-out blonde highlights. What was not to love about a place that was open twenty-four hours? It was nice to know that if the mood hit her at two in the morning and she was thinking of living life on the edge, she could drive over and pick out lipstick or mascara.

She looked around the aisles, wanting something else, but not sure what. After twenty minutes of browsing, she found it. False eyelashes. It was Sunday night—there was no salon open to apply eyelash extensions, so these would have to do.

Once home she put on the coloring cap, and using what looked suspiciously like a knitting needle, she pulled strands of her hair through the holes. She read the instructions, pausing once and rereading the part about not getting the product in her eyes as it may cause eye injury. She put on the dye and waited the allotted time, watching bits of a holiday movie.

Pleased with the thick, sunny highlights, she went to bed, thinking of her new hair, her new clothes and pushing her continuing saga of embarrassments to the outer recesses of her mind.

Kate managed to get the false eyelashes on without incident as she got ready for work on Monday morning. She wore her newly colored hair loose. She went for a smoky look with her make-up, hoping it wasn't too much for daytime. Then she shrugged, figuring no one would notice anyway. She put on the outfit she had picked out last night.

She looked in the mirror. *Wow!*

She walked into the office, feeling so good about herself she was swinging her imitation 'Chanel' purse. She had decided to put the border incident out of her mind. Anyway, Gavin was on his way to Dublin today, so she wouldn't have to face him. By the time he came back next week, perhaps he would have forgotten about it.

"Oh my God, you look so different!" Ann said.

"Kate, you're gorgeous," gushed Sherrie.

This went on for a few minutes and Kate was delighted. Then they noticed her purse.

"C'mon, O'Connor, give it up. Friday, you brought in a 'Coach' and today a 'Chanel.' I, for one, am dying to know how you are affording all these purses," Amy Mohr said.

"Yeah, Kate, spill it," said Debbie Cjaka.

"This must have cost hundreds of dollars," Ann observed. "Nobody here makes enough money to afford designer accessories. Except Alexis, of course."

Kate told the girls about the imitation bags and the party concept. They were all eager to be invited to a gathering at her house.

"It's going to be my Christmas present to myself. The good Lord knows that husband of mine would never think to buy me a gift," Ann said as she walked away from Kate's desk.

The girls dispersed, heading back to their cubicles. Kate settled down at her desk, feeling good about things and even a little self-confident. She had a new-and-improved look and was looking forward to making a few extra dollars at her purse party.

For the first time in a long time, she was happy to be at her job.

That feeling lasted about two minutes.

Mr. Cline appeared with Gavin at his side. They were deep in conversation. Kate stared at Gavin, her mouth practically hanging open. What was he doing here? He was supposed to be on a plane to Dublin.

Mr. Cline took one look at her, shook his head and muttered, "Well if it isn't the swinging sixties."

Gavin blinked hard and said nothing. He continued to stare at her and appeared almost agitated. A sensation traveled down Kate's spine. Despite the fact that she was almost six feet tall in her boots, she felt almost kittenish towards him. She suspected it had something to do with her sultry make-up.

"Oh, I thought you were going to Dublin today," she said as nonchalantly as she could. He didn't look so bad considering his ordeal at the border yesterday afternoon. She wondered if he had mentioned it to her boss. She hoped not.

"I am. But my flight to JFK doesn't leave until late this afternoon," he explained, not taking his eyes off her.

Oh.

Both men walked away together toward Mr. Cline's office, returning to their conversation. Gavin glanced back at her several times before disappearing down the hall.

Paul did a double-take when he saw Kate. He slowed down and stopped in front of her desk. She wished he'd keep moving.

"You are smoking today!" He grinned. "I love the new look."

There had been a time, not too long ago, when she had been dependent on what Paul thought of her. His opinion had served to validate her self-worth. But not anymore. The only opinion she cared about was her own.

"You're absolutely beautiful, Kate," he said.

"Thank you," she said politely.

He gave a quick look around to make sure they were alone and he bent over, placing his hands on the edge of her desk, so they were facing each other, eye to eye.

"Will you please forgive me?" he said.

"I do forgive you, Paul," she said evenly.

"Then why won't you give me a second chance?" he asked, with a pleading look in his eyes.

"Because I don't want to," she said. After he'd left with Sabrina, she had put her life on hold for two years, waiting for him to change his mind so she could forgive him and they could go back to the way they used to be. But then her dad had gotten sick and died, and it had taken what little wind she had left out of her sails.

"You loved me once," he pressed on.

"Yes, that's true," she said. "But then you chose Sabrina."

He stood up and sighed. "I made a colossal mistake and I regret hurting you." He sounded sincere and she wanted to believe him, but she just wasn't interested in revisiting the past.

"What do I have to do to get you back?" he asked.

"Paul, it's over," she said. "I don't trust you anymore. There can be no relationship if there is no trust."

He leaned over again and whispered, "Remember how happy we used to be together?" She noticed he'd skipped over her comment about trust.

"You couldn't have been too happy as you did leave me for Sabrina," she pointed out. She wished that Gavin had left her more to do.

"Everything all right, Kate?"

Irish.

Paul straightened himself up and shot Gavin a look. But Gavin did not back down. He stared evenly at Paul.

"All's well." Kate smiled weakly, refusing to look at Paul. He finally got the hint and walked away, and Gavin disappeared into his office without another word.

Gavin felt restless. Kate's new look had left him full of desire. For her. The feeling had both caught him off guard and unsettled him. He loosened his tie, feeling constricted though it wasn't even nine in the morning.

He reminded himself that Kate O'Connor wasn't his type. She wasn't the type of girl he would have pursued in the past, anyway. A series of former girlfriends paraded across his mind: Georgina, Miriam, Chloe from Quebec, and Ekaterina from Prague. They'd all had poise and intelligence, and had been career-minded. Not one of them had had a sense of fun. Everything they did was a means to an end. They all had been quite serious. Like him.

Yesterday at Niagara Falls had been more than pleasant—it had been downright enjoyable. As for Saturday, once he got over himself at the cemetery, he'd been impressed by both the art gallery and the basilica. In fact, he couldn't remember when he had had such a great weekend. Kate had been as enthusiastic as he was when he'd gone on about the farm over dinner. She was a good listener, and she made him laugh.

Georgina had left him because she said he was 'too boring.' That had come as a shock to him. He thought himself many things, but boring wasn't one of them. She had complained that all he ever wanted to do was go home to Tipperary on the weekends. He'd taken her a few times, but she hadn't gotten on well with his mother—his mother referred to her as 'The Georgina'—and she'd hated the rural lifestyle. Everything had bothered her: the cows, the mud, the quiet. She was more interested in glamorous and exciting Dublin, in clubbing and dining on the weekends, seeing other important people and being seen. It had been that way for him, once, as well. But as he got older and nearer to forty, wild weekends no longer held an appeal for him. But Kate...he shook his head. There was no way he could start falling for the local girl. Impossible. Out of the question. He was three thousand miles away from home. He was lonesome. That's what this was all about. As soon as he set foot on Irish soil he'd forget all about her. He was certain of it.

And what was up with Kate and Paul? There always seemed to be a lot of tension buzzing around them.

No, the sooner he got out of here, the better.

Kate was pouring black coffee into a Santa Claus mug when Sherrie walked into the break room.

"What's this I hear about you and Gavin Whyte?" she asked, smiling.

Kate could feel her face color beneath all the make-up. "What did you hear and who did you hear it from?"

"Gavin himself. He told me that you and he practically spent the whole weekend together. Going all around western New York. The cemetery, the art gallery, the basilica and the falls. How romantic! Oh, Kate, he's quite a catch," Sherrie was beaming like she was the mother of a poor, bedraggled girl who was about to marry the richest duke in the land.

"No, Sherrie, it's nothing like that," Kate said quickly, hoping to dispel any rumors. The last thing she needed was for Gavin to think she was telling everyone at the office they were an item. "Mr. Cline was kind enough to volunteer me to show him the local sights. Everything was going smoothly, until we tried to get back into the US last night." She explained their four-hour stint as the guests of US Customs.

"He never mentioned that."

"He's probably blocked it out." Kate stirred her coffee vigorously, dumping a load of creamer and sugar into it.

"His manners are impeccable," Sherrie said dreamily. "He opens doors for women, he says thank you and means it..."

Kate looked at her friend like she'd just grown a second head. Who was she, Miss Manners?

"He's so nice and he's handsome, too, and to have all of that wrapped up in one package? Wow!"

"Easy now, you're married with a slew of kids," Kate reminded her.

"Yes, but I'm not dead. You should make a play for him," Sherrie said.

"He's a little out of my league."

"That's ridiculous."

Kate chose not to respond; she didn't want to have this conversation. She had had it a thousand times with various girlfriends, all encouraging her and making her believe that boys A-Z were just as interested in her as she was in them. She stopped herself. *Am I interested in him?* She shook her head, warning herself not to even tread that path.

"The Gavin Whytes of the world do not choose the Kate O'Connors of the world."

As that little gem was coming out of Kate's mouth, Gavin walked in, carrying an empty coffee mug.

She wanted to die.

"Ladies." He smiled, but his expression was otherwise blank. He had to have heard her. And he probably agreed with her, she thought.

She made a hasty exit from the room with Sherrie hot on her heels, giggling.

"Stop trying to fix me up." Kate admonished. Although, admittedly she needed some help in that department. A lot of help.

"We better get to the conference room. The Monday morning meeting is about to start."

Kate groaned. "Great. Another pep talk about how we're 'falling down on the job and falling asleep at the wheel.'"

"Basically."

They'd no sooner taken their seats in the conference room when Mr. Cline appeared behind the podium. He gripped the sides of it, white-knuckled, like he was hanging onto a midway ride.

"I want to bring you up to date on the current progress of the Alchemis campaign and let you know what I think about it."

Uh oh, here it comes, Kate thought.

"To sum it up—it stinks." He paused for effect. "In all my years of advertising, I have never seen such lame ideas in my life. You call yourselves professionals? The second-grade class down at PS 61 could do a better job."

He paused again to make eye contact with all those present.

Okay, everyone all together, Kate thought, as Mr. Cline said, "You people are falling down on the job and falling asleep at the wheel."

He paused and looked over at Paul. "Paul, perhaps you'd care to take over."

Paul walked to the front of the room as Mr. Cline sat down. Paul did not stand behind the podium. He stood to the side of it with his hands on his hips.

"For whatever reason, we have an unhappy client. Obviously, we are not on the same page as Alchemis."

Mr. Cline piped in from his seat, "This is ours to lose. This is our last chance or we'll all be having our Christmas dinner at the local homeless shelter."

Paul went on. "Let's go back to the creative brief to remind ourselves again as to the objective of this campaign. I want the research department to go over their report and see if we can glean anything else out of it."

"Excuse me, Paul," Mr. Cline interrupted. "The research department was dissolved with the layoffs last year. Everyone chips in and does research around here."

Paul looked at him in disbelief. "Well that could be the problem. The research isn't right."

Kate bristled at this. She had done some of the research herself, one of the many projects that Mr. Cline had assigned her. Typical of Paul to pass the blame on to someone else.

"Blah, blah, blah," Sherrie whispered to her.

"I want the account team to rethink the strategy. You've got two days to sort that out and re-brief creative. Now, that doesn't mean I want creative sitting around and waiting for accounts to spoon feed them..."

Kate started to mentally doze off while keeping her eyes open.

"One great idea has come forth from Alexis and she can fill you in on it as she hammers out the details," Mr. Cline said, standing up, an indication to Paul that he could take a seat.

Kate hoped he wouldn't tell the rapt audience present that Alexis' idea involved her and a bout of televised public humiliation.

"Santora!" he directed. "I'm putting you in charge of problem-solving and I want you to figure out what is wrong with creative in regard to this account. Report personally to me tomorrow morning."

Sherrie muttered under her breath and whispered. "What about Paul? Isn't that his job?"

"Before we adjourn this meeting," Mr. Cline continued, "it has come to my attention that no one has signed up for the committee to organize the Christmas party."

Kate looked up to the ceiling, wishing for the meeting to be over.

"Can't anyone here take initiative? It's bad enough that you can't think for yourselves as far as the job goes—but this? How hard is it to decide who brings the beer and the chips? Therefore, I will assign a committee. Pay attention. Reese, O'Connor, Winston. See Debbie at some point today regarding the Christmas party. That's it. Now get back to work."

Oh great! I don't even want to go to the stupid thing and now I have to plan it.

Kate sat at her desk, wondering how she was going to get out of this Christmas party committee. She could tell them that she really didn't do Christmas, but that probably wouldn't work as she was sitting at her desk in a sea of red and green decorations of her own doing.

Alexis sashayed down the corridor and hesitated in front of Kate as if she didn't really want to stop and be forced to engage her in conversation. She could keep right on stepping, as far as Kate was concerned. But these types always stopped, if only to screw up your day.

"Debbie said there's a meeting at three in the conference room to discuss the Christmas party," Alexis said.

"Sure," Kate agreed meekly.

"I'll be at Joseph's for lunch, but I should be back in time."

Must be nice. Joseph's was a swank, tony place. They used real linen napkins, they didn't print the prices on the menus, and the maître d' spoke only French. They wouldn't be seeing the likes of her for a few hours, and so soon after Mr. Cline's pep talk. That was Alexis for you—always assuming that the rules didn't apply to her. It wouldn't be funny someday when she was doing five to ten. She probably ran with scissors in kindergarten, too.

Gavin and Paul appeared and joined Alexis. Gavin had his phone in the palm of his hand and it had his undivided attention.

He spoke to Paul and Alexis. "It's Dublin—I have to deal with this right now. I'll catch up with you and Alexis as soon as I can."

Paul walked past Kate, smiling, and she ignored him.

Gavin headed back into his office. As he passed her, he grinned and winked at her. He closed the door behind him.

Now what was that all about? she wondered.

Kate had a panicky thought that the three of them would discuss Alexis' idea of a reality TV series over lunch. The mere thought of it made her physically sick.

"O'Connor!"

Kate's head snapped up. It was Sherrie doing an impression of Mr. Cline.

"Are you ready to go to lunch?" she asked. Her hot-pink winter coat complimented her hair with its fuchsia highlights.

Kate stood up, reaching for her coat and purse.

"Hey, do you know that you have a package here, leaning against the side of the desk?" Sherrie asked. She bent over and retrieved an odd shaped parcel that was wedged between the desk and the potted plant. She handed it to Kate.

They studied it. It was irregular, covered in basic brown wrap and sealed with duct tape. It was addressed to 'Kate O'Connor at Cline & Co.' in permanent black marker.

"Are you expecting anything?" Sherrie asked, her brow furrowed.

Kate shook her head.

Ann and Debbie walked by, on their way out to lunch as well.

"Oooh, what did you order for yourself?" Ann asked. She was a catalogue shopper and had her purchases and credit card bills sent to the office so her husband couldn't track her spending.

"Nothing, absolutely nothing," Kate answered, puzzled. "I don't know what it is."

Ann picked up the package and examined it. "Definitely homemade. No return address. And no stamps, which means it was dropped off." She paused and eyed Kate suspiciously. "And you're sure you're not expecting anything?"

"No," Kate said again.

"Well, c'mon, open it up," prompted Sherrie.

"Let's see if you have a secret admirer," Debbie chimed in.

Kate retrieved a letter opener from her desk, worked her way through the tape and opened the box to reveal layers of red tissue paper. Curious, she began to dig through them. The other ladies waited expectantly. Out of the corner of her eye, Kate caught sight of Gavin standing nearby with a stack of paperwork in his hand that would keep her busy until her retirement. He was watching them with an amused expression.

A small piece of lined paper was lodged in between the sheets of tissue. Kate drew it out, unfolded it and read it aloud. "Babe, you make my heart tick."

Vinnie. Kate squeezed her eyes shut and groaned.

Sherrie and Debbie took her hesitation as permission to sift through the package themselves. Debbie pulled out a red plastic clock in the shape of a heart. On the face of the clock were drawn eyes, a nose and mouth. One of the eyes was winking as if to say, 'Joke's on you, Kate O'Connor.'

"Oh my goodness, what do we have here?" Sherrie hooted. She held up a scarlet lace bra and panties with strategically placed bows.

Kate felt the heat creep up her neck and flood her face. She was going to kill Vinnie with her bare hands. She stole a look at Gavin, who seemed mesmerized by the lingerie.

"Oh wow, Kate has an admirer!" Ann howled.

If ever there was a time that Kate wished the floor would open up and swallow her, this was definitely it. The other girls were passing the items around, examining them. She tried to grab for them as she wanted to shove them back into the box and burn them, but they kept them out of her reach.

"Are they from your boyfriend?" Ann asked.

"No, they're from her neighbor," Sherrie said.

Mortified, Kate looked up to see that the bra and panties had landed in Gavin's hands.

This is not happening, she thought.

He was quiet for a moment and then he handed them back to her, his fingertips brushing hers as he did. "The color would suit you."

This made Sherrie, Debbie and Ann howl louder.

Quickly Kate jammed them back into the box and shoved it under her desk. She pulled herself upright and relieved Gavin of the stack of paperwork, pretending that what had just happened, hadn't happened.

"When you get a moment—" he started.

But she cut him off and said briskly, "Consider it done."

"I'm heading off to—"

"Fine," she answered, bundling herself quickly into her coat. She slung her purse over her shoulder and stole a glance up at him, her face still burning.

By mid-afternoon Gavin had left for the airport. He had to catch a flight from Buffalo to JFK where his Dublin flight would be leaving at ten that night. He wouldn't be back until the following Tuesday.

Kate was glad to see the back of him. As hot as he was, her nerves were shot. She was looking forward to a week free of humiliating moments. And a weekend free of sightseeing. She'd thought the past weekend's itinerary had been enough, but then Mr. Cline pressed her for the next stop on the tour. She'd pawned him off with a vague statement. "I'm working on it."

His response was a little less vague. "You'd better be if you want to continue working here."

Kate waited in the conference room with Ann and Debbie for the Christmas party committee meeting to start. By now, they had stopped laughing at Kate's gift from Vinnie.

Debbie talked about the get-together at Kate's house the following week. It would be a good excuse to have a few drinks and eat hot appetizers, all the while engaging in a bitch-fest about Mr. Cline. Sherrie volunteered to bring a couple bottles of wine, and Kate thought of how she'd like to down a bottle right at that moment.

Alexis finally joined them. Kate made a show of looking at her watch but she ignored her.

Alexis spoke directly to Kate. "I heard about all the fun I missed while I was at lunch. It's very romantic of your boyfriend to send you sexy underwear."

Ann and Debbie burst out laughing.

When was this day going to be over? Kate wondered.

Once they regained their composure, Debbie started the meeting. "Ok, let's get going. We need to assign tasks of who is bringing what."

Alexis interrupted her. "Oh forget about that, ladies. I have a better idea." Her eyes shone with excitement. "Instead of the usual Christmas party in the conference room, let's do it up big. Let's have it at a hotel ballroom—dinner, champagne, dancing, Christmas trees, Christmas music. The works! Let's have a party befitting of Cline and Company."

Hmph! A party befitting Cline & Co.? *That's a good one*, Kate thought. The ensuing silence was deafening. They stared at Alexis as if she had lost her mind.

It was Ann from accounting who spoke first. "Alexis, what are you smoking?"

"Only one thing, Alexis. Mr. Cline has given me a budget and it will barely cover a party here at the office," Debbie pointed out.

Kate said nothing, because she couldn't have cared less. It was highly unlikely that Mr. Cline would foot the bill for this. The conversation seemed pointless to her. Besides, she had more important things to think about. She was still doing a slow burn over Vinnie's present and was thinking of ways to dispose of his body.

"Yeah, Alexis, how would we pay for it? Charge by the plate? No one will come, much less bring a date," Ann said, her voice rising. Hysteria was setting in. Ann always dealt with the bottom line. She had the precarious position of having to report profit and loss to Mr. Cline. So naturally something like this would surely send her right over the edge.

"We'd have to bring a date?" Kate asked, horrified.

"Well, of course, silly. Dining and dancing," Alexis said in a sing-song voice, like she was eight years old.

Kate wanted to smack her.

"What about the gift exchange?" Debbie asked. This was Debbie's baby. She organized it every year, painstakingly writing names on pieces of scrap paper and putting them in a jar so that each person could draw the name of their recipient. She lived and died by it.

Kate remembered with a shudder the gift exchanges of the past. One year, she didn't get a gift, another year she was given a low-fat cookbook, and last year, Mr. Cline had chosen her name. He'd given her a bottle of drugstore perfume. The thought of her boss buying her perfume, drugstore or otherwise, made her skin crawl.

"Deb, we'll still do the gift exchange," Alexis said.

"Alexis, you still haven't said how we're going to pay for this," Ann persisted. She sat there, sour-faced, her arms folded across her chest.

"Oh, that's easy," Alexis said with a dismissive wave of her hand. Her diamond bracelet glittered in the harsh fluorescent light. "We'll get Mr. Cline to pick up the tab."

They all stared at her in astonishment. She was definitely high on something. Everyone who worked at Cline & Co. knew that Mr. Cline was pretty tight with money.

"What are you talking about?" Debbie asked.

"Listen, when we sew up this Alchemis account, Mr. Cline will give us anything we want on a silver platter. Guaranteed," Alexis said.

Kate thought she sounded kind of smug. Did she not know Mr. Cline the way they did?

"By the sounds of Mr. Cline's meeting this morning, things don't look so good," Ann pointed out, ever the voice of reason.

Good point.

"Don't worry about that," Alexis said.

"It sounds a little dicey," Kate finally said.

"Oh will you live a little?" Alexis snapped.

Kate shut her mouth. Why have a committee when Alexis was going to do what she wanted? *Doesn't play well with others, either.*

"Let's put some feelers out there and see what everyone thinks about it. In the meantime, I'll talk to Sherrie and the rest of them at the meeting and see if I can light a fire under their collective asses," Alexis said.

The meeting broke up and Kate left, more depressed than ever. A fancy Christmas party meant bringing a date. It would be like flying solo at a wedding, or like high school all over again with the dread of the upcoming prom and no date in sight. She would rather stay home.

She hadn't gone to her junior prom as she'd been too shy to ask anyone. She did go to her senior prom with an acne-scarred kid who was a year younger and half a foot shorter than she was. He gave 'surly' a new meaning. She later found out that her mother had paid him. The flashback of that memory made Kate want to hurl, or worse—quit her job so she wouldn't have to go to the stupid Christmas party.

Gavin sat back in his seat in business class. He loosened his tie and rubbed his eyes. He declined the flight attendant's offer of coffee and asked for a glass of whiskey, neat. The first sip burned going down and then he settled into the burning sensation that caught in the middle of his chest and soon fanned out to his arms.

He looked forward to meeting with the company president and letting him know in no uncertain terms that Cline & Co. were certainly not up to the task of Alchemis' biggest-ever marketing campaign. The sooner they distanced themselves from this second-rate wannabe ad agency the better. He could feel himself getting tense again and he finished off his whiskey, forcing himself to push Cline & Co. out of his mind.

He turned his thoughts instead to the farm back home. He'd give anything to be up in the tractor in the field, or driving slowly down one of the narrow country lanes with a great view of what Ireland was best known for: scenery. He'd try to squeeze in a visit home this trip back. He wanted to talk to his father about purchasing the neighboring farm. The Crowleys had been their neighbors for generations, as long as anyone could remember, but with Mae's death last summer, the line had died out. It had been left to some distant cousin in London who had no intention of moving to Ireland to farm the land, and who'd made it known that he'd be willing to sell. Now Gavin was thinking they should buy it. He wanted to expand the growing aspect of their farm despite the unpredictable, uncooperative, and oftentimes rainy weather. He was no artisan or crafter, but he couldn't deny that farming was in his blood.

Relaxed now, his thoughts wandered and he found himself thinking about Kate O'Connor. This surprised him.

When Kate arrived home, after a day that she'd begun to believe would never be over, she marched directly over to Vinnie's house, package in hand.

Kate stepped onto his front porch and banged on the door with her fist. There was no answer but his car was in the driveway, so she kept right on pounding. And she would keep it up until either he answered or she was arrested for disturbing the peace.

It took a while, but he eventually opened the door.

He appeared looking bleary-eyed as if he had been in the middle of a deep sleep. She seriously wondered about him. Why couldn't he work a normal nine-to-five job like everyone else?

"You're still in bed?" she asked, incredulous.

"I was napping. If you must know, I was up half the night, cleaning the grout in the bathroom. You've got to stay one step ahead of the mold and mildew," he said defensively.

She shook her head.

"Hey, babe, I like the look. You're looking hot—like Raquel Welch in her heyday," he said.

She ignored him. "Vinnie, what is this?" She thrust the package at him.

He took it and a lazy smile emerged across his face. "I see you got my little gift. Do you see how serious I am, babe? You and me. Together."

"This arrived at the office by some unknown means—"

He cut her off. "That was me. I snuck in when no one was around and put it by your desk." He smiled, apparently proud of his subterfuge.

She was tired and frustrated and he wasn't getting it. She wanted to cry but she wasn't too sure about the eyelash glue she'd used that morning.

"So, do you think you'll model this for me tonight?" he asked, holding up the bra and panties.

"Ugh!" She grabbed them out of his hands and stormed off his porch.

"C'mon, Kate," Vinnie said. "Lighten up."

She stopped. Why couldn't he see that she wasn't interested? Why did he continue to pursue her? What is it about me that he finds so attractive? What is it about me that makes him think I'm his dream girl? She wished she could return those feelings, as it would really simplify her life.

"I didn't think you'd be angry," Vinnie said. He sounded hurt.

Kate felt bad and attempted a smile. "No, Vin. I'm not really. It was just a little embarrassing, that's all."

"What's so embarrassing about a man being interested in a woman?" Vinnie asked sincerely.

She sighed and couldn't figure out why she felt like crying.

"Does this mean that the purse party is off?" he asked. "Because what am I going to do with a trunk full of purses?"

She could sense him starting to get hyper. "No, Vinnie, the purse party is still on. Next week. For sure." She said. She looked around, wanting to make her exit.

"Come in babe, out of the cold," he said.

"I have to get home. Thanks anyway. I'll be talking to you," she said, walking back over to her place without looking back, all the time aware of him standing there watching her.

CHAPTER TEN

The office buzzed with the talk of a black-tie Christmas gala. Everybody was excited. Everybody, that is, except Kate. She knew that if anyone could pull it off, it would be Alexis. For the first time since she didn't know when, the employees at Cline & Co. were running at full throttle.

This did not go unnoticed by Mr. Cline when he strolled by a few minutes before noon. He paused at Kate's desk and looked up, like a retriever trying to get a scent off the wind.

There was no one at the water cooler. No one was milling about. No one was draped over a cubicle wall talking to their neighbor. No raucous laughter drifted out from the break room.

"What's going on here?" he asked, scanning the office. "It seems like there is actually work being done."

"Yes sir, it does," Kate said, not looking up from her computer screen.

"Humph. There must be delirium going around. Check for high fevers among the staff."

And with that, he stomped off to his office.

Kate was rinsing out the coffee pot in the break room when the door opened and Alexis popped her head in.

"Kate, if you're not busy, could you come down to Mr. Cline's office for a few minutes?"

Behind her back, Kate lifted her eyes to heaven. "I'll be along shortly." What could he possibly want now?

She poured the water through the top of the coffee maker, placed a filter in the basket and added a few scoops of coffee. She turned it on and as it started to bubble and brew, she left the break room.

She gave a light rap on Mr. Cline's door before walking in.

He sat behind his desk wearing a black pinstripe suit and a horrendous tie. Mentally, she shook her head, thinking he was hopeless.

Alexis stood behind him with her ass perched on the window sill, wearing a black suit with a pink blouse. On her feet were a pair of black Chanel boots that had everyone in the office talking.

There wasn't only Mr. Cline and Alexis to contend with, but another man, as well. He was tall, corpulent, and wore too much styling gel—his hair looked as if it had the consistency of cement. His face was pockmarked and puffy, either from too much alcohol consumption or the over-ingestion of large quantities of air. However, he presented a much better suit and choice of tie than did Kate's boss. The newcomer stared at Kate. Immediately, she was leery.

Mr. Cline stood up and indicated with his hand that she was to sit in the empty seat next to the stranger.

Kate sat down, not saying a word.

"Nick, this is Kate O'Connor, our receptionist. She's our person of interest for this project," Mr. Cline said, smiling broadly.

The man called Nick turned to Kate, held out his hand for her to shake, and said, "Nick Sommers, RTN. Reality Television Network."

Kate nodded and said nothing. She wanted to squirm as she felt Sommers assessing her.

"Oh yeah, Ed, I think this could work," Nick said. "This could be really good. She's got beautiful hair and a pretty face."

Sommers practically licked his lips. Kate felt like she was being thrown to the big bad wolf.

Her boss rubbed his hands together, pleased with himself.

Alexis smiled pleasantly.

"Mr. Cline, I have no intention of being involved in this project," Kate said. It was time she asserted herself. How many ways did she have to spell it out for them?

"Our Kate here is a little excitable," Mr. Cline explained to Sommers, half-laughing and half-giving her the stink eye. He wanted her to play nice.

Sommers waved him off. "Don't worry about it. I like a little vinegar with my greens."

"What do you think, Nick? Of our proposal?" Alexis asked, moving on.

Kate thought that she might as well be talking to a brick wall.

"I like it. And she has the personality for it."

He looked Kate up and down again and then turned back to Mr. Cline and Alexis. "We'll start off the show with her walking around without make-up, in glasses and frumpy clothes, like grey sweat suits and flannel robes," Sommers mused, his face contorting in disgust.

Hey, wait a minute! Kate's at-home uniform consisted of grey sweat suits and flannel robes and it was an attire she would highly recommend.

Sommers continued. "She'll metamorphose into a beautiful swan. Of course, we'll have to get in a personal trainer to put her through her paces and tighten her up. In the end, we'll do laser surgery to get rid of the glasses and we'll bring in a hair and make-up expert to update her look. And voila, she can parade around in something skimpy and sexy."

The three of them were in self-congratulatory moods, nodding and smiling at each other.

Sommers concluded, "Uh-huh, it'll be a real Cinderella story." He leaned back in his chair and folded his hands in his lap, smiling at Kate.

"I'm not doing it," Kate snapped. The conversation was finished for her.

"Oh wow, she's real spunky," Sommers laughed, slapping his thigh.

"Yeah, that's our Kate," said Mr. Cline. He gave her a look that told her to start acting like a team player and stop being so surly and uncooperative.

"Mr. Cline!" Kate said through gritted teeth.

It was no use. She stood up from her chair, turned, and without another word, headed toward the door.

As she stormed out she heard Mr. Cline say, "Don't worry about her, Nick. I can handle her. I have a way with Kate O'Connor."

"Hey, Kate, wait up," Nick Sommers called after her, having followed her out of the room.

She stopped and turned to him, looking him straight in the eye. "Look, I'm not doing this. Plain and simple."

"But you'll be famous," he said and he placed his hand on the wall, blocking her way. He leaned in close to her and whispered, "I can make you a star."

"Listen very carefully," she said. "I don't want to be famous. I don't want to be a star."

"Of course you do. Everyone wants to be a star."

She rolled her eyes. "Excuse me—I have to get back to work." She turned and started walking away.

"Just one question—" he said.

She stopped and faced him again.

"Are those real?" Sommers asked her.

"What's that?" she asked, not having a clue as to what he might be talking about.

He nodded to Kate's chest, his hand reaching across the divide as if he were going in for a squeeze.

Outraged, Kate slapped his hand away, quickly looking around to see if anyone else was present in the corridor. They were alone. "If you so much as reach for me like that again, you'll be taking your meals through a tube!" Fuming, she turned on her heel and walked away, with the sound of his laughter echoing in her ears.

On Thursday night, she met up with Lisa for a hockey game. The Sabres were playing the Ottawa Senators. They found their seats and settled down into them, the chill of the ice pervading the arena.

They nursed their beers, talked about their jobs and watched the game. Their eyes went back and forth between each other and the action playing out below them. A shout echoed from the rink and their conversation was momentarily diverted as they watched and waited to see the outcome of the slugfest in the corner. Once the penalties had been assessed and a player from each team skated to his own penalty box, they resumed their conversation.

Kate explained to her what had happened with Nick Sommers.

Lisa was taken aback. A dark cloud passed over her face. "He actually made a grab for you?" When Kate nodded, she continued, "Boy, if that isn't sexual harassment, I don't know what is." She thought for a moment. "Did anybody see this? Kate, you need to do something about it. This needs to be reported."

The Sabres won and afterward, they went over to Martini's for a drink.

They stood at the bar with their drinks in their hands. A man walked by, and a look of recognition appeared on his face when he saw Lisa. He gave a shy smile and waved at her. He was tall, whippet thin, and possessed the biggest hands Kate had ever seen. They looked like baseball mitts.

Lisa smiled at him and waved back. "That's Nate. He's the computer consultant who was hired by the firm to tighten up our security after the hack last summer. He came in from Boston. Apparently, he used to be a hacker himself in a previous life."

"Very interesting."

They ordered another round of drinks.

"How's it going with Tim?" Kate inquired, referring to Lisa's chemistry professor boyfriend.

Lisa shook her head and sighed. "Mercifully, that died a quiet death over the weekend."

"Why? What happened?"

"I learned that he's so out there, he's never coming back," she said. "You know what he said to me last week?"

She didn't wait for Kate to answer and carried on. "He said that he wasn't attracted to me because I was fat, however..." She put her finger up in the air. "He thought that I looked like a breeder and he was definitely interested in me becoming the mother of his children."

Kate raised her eyebrows. Lisa wore a size twenty-four and had basically been big since kindergarten. To Kate she was beautiful. Her skin was like porcelain, her hair was very thick and was such a rich brown it was almost black. Her eyes were a deep brown with a hint of mischief. The contrast of her milky skin with the dark coloring was stunning. She always wore scarlet lipstick and the effect was deadly. Five years ago, she had gone on a medically supervised liquid fast and in one year had slimmed down to a size four. But the ensuing misery of trying to maintain that weight along with the drastic change in her appearance was too much for her. She'd decided she was happier heavier. It was who she was. She'd made peace with it. Kate envied her that.

"What did you say?"

"I could have said a lot. Like, for instance, that people with only five strands of hair on their heads shouldn't wear it long. Or, I could have mentioned the fact that he was limited with the bike. Kids are one thing, but managing car seats on a bike is something else. And where would I sit? The handlebars? Obstructing his view?"

"So what did you say to him?"

Here, Lisa smiled. "I told him that I understood. That I wasn't attracted to him, either. And that I didn't want him to be the father of my kids."

She laughed. "And do you know what? He was offended. He had just insulted me, yet apparently what I said was out of line."

They shook their heads, laughing.

Saturday finally rolled around and Kate spent it at home, baking thumbprint cookies and peanut butter blossoms. She stored them in tins she had saved; they kept freshest in these. Later on, she went out to put up the exterior Christmas decorations. In her front yard, she eyed the ladder nervously, said a few prayers to anyone who would listen, then climbed up and hung icicle lights off the gutter. She placed a lighted plastic snowman and Santa in front of her garden, wondering how long it would take before a gust of wind drove them into someone else's yard.

As Kate walked through the kitchen, she heard her phone ringing. She saw her mother's number flash across the screen.

"Hi, Mom, what's new?"

"Not too much. How about you?"

They spoke about generalities for a while. They spoke of the baking and gift buying they had done. Then they discussed what would be on the menu for Christmas dinner. It would be some form of beef. It always had been. Turkey for Thanksgiving, ham for Easter and beef for Christmas.

Kate got the sense that her mother was hesitant to hang up the phone.

"Is there anything else, Mom?"

Her mother cleared her throat. "Would you come over for lunch on Sunday?"

"Sure," Kate said, dreaming of her mother's homemade cooking.

"Hank is going to be there. I'd like you both to meet properly."

"Oh."

Kate thought about backpedaling, wracking her brain to come up with some excuse. But her mother's disappointment traveled down the telephone line. She caved in.

"I'll be there. What time?"

"One."

Saturday evening, she shopped for a Christmas tree. She went up to the gas station nearby as she had seen a stall of Christmas trees on the side lot. The combination of her nearsightedness and driving by at a high rate of speed had made them appear Christmas-card perfect. However, up close they looked like North Pole rejects. It would have to do. Once home, she managed to get her tree up the front porch and into the house. She struggled to get it into the tree stand, but finally managed to get it standing, though it was listing to the right. After an hour of trying to right it, she gave up.

She collapsed on the sofa and poured herself a glass of wine.

Aunt Geraldine rang Sunday morning.

"Good morning, pet," she said.

"Hello there," Kate said thickly as she was just waking up. What was it about all these early morning callers on the weekend? She looked at the clock. It was nine-thirty, but Ireland was five hours ahead. Her aunt had probably just finished her midday dinner.

"Did I wake you?" Geraldine asked.

"No, no," Kate lied, stifling a yawn.

"I rang my friend, Bridie, over in Tipperary. You remember Bridie, don't you?"

"Yes, I think so," Kate said, remembering the name but unable to put a face to it. She adjusted her pillow and sank her head back down into it, flinging her free arm over her forehead.

"She's the one in Templemore. Been there more than twenty years since she married Tom."

Kate sat up. She knew where this was going.

Her aunt continued. "I asked her if she knew your man, Gavin Whyte."

"And?"

Her aunt laughed. "She knows the whole family. In fact, they're related to Tom. Far out relations, of course. Can you imagine that?"

"What did she say?" Kate asked, her curiosity rising.

"Well, apparently, he's been in Dublin the past fifteen years. He's an only child. The parents are farmers."

"Girlfriend?" Kate asked.

"The last Bridie heard, he was going out with a girl named Georgina—you know, one of those model types."

Her heart sank. She knew all too well.

"Why all the interest? Oh, Kate, are you falling in love with him?"

It was just like her aunt not to beat around the bush.

"No. No. Nothing like that. You know gossip is currency in the office," she answered. Although she would never tell anyone that she was digging into Gavin Whyte's past. She wouldn't even tell Sherrie.

She hung up the phone determined to put Irish out of her mind. At the same time, she wondered why she was so curious about his private life.

Kate approached the lunch with her mother and Hank with some trepidation. She was determined not to be a spoilsport, or at least fake it well enough so as not to be labelled one.

At the very least, she would be well fed. She wondered what her mother would whip up for them. Would it be pierogis, or stuffed peppers or—dare she dream it—chicken paprikash? Her mouth watered in anticipation.

She arrived a few minutes before one, carrying a bottle of wine and a box of soft cream centers from the candy shop around the corner, which she knew to be a favorite indulgence of her mother's. When she entered her mom's kitchen, a spicy aroma floated out to greet her. Lunch was going to be good. It wasn't a scent she recognized or one that was familiar in her mother's kitchen, but it smelled good nonetheless.

Kate found her mother in the dining room, folding linen napkins that Aunt Geraldine had sent over from Ireland. The linen napkins were never set out when she came over. She was about to make a smart remark to that effect but she bit her tongue instead, and secretly promised to behave and keep all comments to herself.

"Oh hello, Kate," her mother said, looking up from her task. She had had her hair done and her make-up was subtle. And she was wearing a pair of jeans! Kate's mouth fell open. She had never seen her mother in anything other than polyester twin-sets.

"What's with the jeans?" she asked, grinning.

Her mother shrugged and smiled coyly.

"Need some help?" Kate asked.

"No, honey, we're just about ready." She glanced at her watch. "Hank will be back any minute. He ran up to the bakery."

"The bakery?" Kate liked him already. She loved any kind of baked goods: home-made, store bought, or church raffle. She wasn't fussy.

"I hope you brought your appetite," her mother remarked, removing three plates from the china cabinet and setting them on the table.

"I sure did," she said. "It smells good."

"Hank insisted on making lunch today. He wouldn't let me help out at all," Rita said.

Kate raised her eyebrows. Her mother was dating a man who cooked? Wonders never ceased. Her own father, God bless him, couldn't have boiled water. And her mother had prepared him a hot breakfast and a hot dinner every day of their married life.

"So what's on the menu, anyway?" Kate asked. She wanted to ask, 'and when is it going to be served because I'm starting to see wavy lines in front of my eyes?'

Her mother gave a little chuckle. "It's chicken curry."

Oh no. Anything but that. Kate loved the taste of it but it didn't agree with her, making her violently ill more often than not. Within one hour she could guarantee that she would be clammy and doubled over at the waist from severe pain. She wanted to eat any curry-based dish like she wanted to be infected with the black plague.

She didn't know what to do. If she ate it, she was in for a miserable night. And if she didn't, her mother would think she was being nothing more than a pain in the neck, especially after all the trouble Hank obviously went through to make the lunch.

Hank arrived with a bulging bakery bag. Kate consoled herself with the fact that at least if she ate the curry she would have earned the right to eat dessert.

He handed Rita the bag and she broke into a generous smile. The years, especially the last few, seemed to melt away from her face. And then it dawned on Kate. Her mother was in love. With a sinking heart, she bit her lip. And then she knew; she would have to eat the curry.

Her mother introduced them properly, as the last time they'd met, he'd been heading down into the basement pretending to be a repairman. Kate realized he must care for her mother, too.

He pulled a small box out of the bakery bag.

"Your mother said that birthday cake was one of your favorite desserts," he said. He sliced the tape open on the sides of the box and lifted the lid. Inside was a small cake with buttercream frosting and pink flowers. *Yummy.* "Who says it has to be your birthday to eat birthday cake?"

She bit her lip again. He was making an effort on her behalf. She gave him a smile. Just a little one. She didn't want to encourage him so much that by the end of lunch he would be insisting she call him 'Dad.'

Kate said nothing when Hank sat in her father's chair at the dining room table. Nobody had sat in that chair since her father had died. She looked over at her mother to see if this was all right with her, but she was too busy serving the curry. Hank poured the wine.

The meal was delicious and against Kate's better judgement, she had a second serving—to hell with GI distress. She figured that since she was going to be sick anyway, she might as well load up. They made small talk.

Hank's first wife had died of a heart attack six years ago and he had two sons who lived out of state. This, Kate mused, presented possibilities. Although realistically, Hank was a few inches shorter than her and she could just about guarantee that the same was probably true of his sons, as well. Hank had retired from the auto plant ten years ago. In all honesty, she couldn't find anything wrong with him. But she still felt that she was being disloyal to her father.

Kate insisted on doing the wash-up. She quickly rinsed the plates and stacked them in the dishwasher. She put on the kettle and took the teapot from the top cabinet to make tea. She hesitated, wondering if Hank drank tea. She'd better ask. She headed back to the dining room, hoping not to interrupt them in the middle of something unseemly, like her mother sitting on his lap. They were chatting and laughing, and she asked Hank if he'd prefer tea or coffee. He said tea would be fine.

She finished the cleanup and made the tea. She brought dessert plates and forks to the dining room and then carried in the cake. Her mother cut and served the cake while she poured the tea. She pushed the tray with the sugar and creamer toward Hank's side of the table and he looked up and smiled at her.

Her mother didn't seem to fuss over him the way she used to fuss over her father. At the beginning of lunch, Kate thought it odd and perhaps telling and that maybe this wouldn't go anywhere. If there was one thing her mother liked to do, it was make a fuss over people. But by the end of the meal, Kate realized a small shift had taken place. Hank actually fussed over her mother and her mother seemed to enjoy it! After all the years of taking care of everyone and everything, she now found herself on the receiving end.

It wasn't long before the curry kicked in. It happened just as Kate shoveled the first bit of cake into her mouth. A sharp stabbing pain jutted across her lower abdomen and she felt a fine sheen of sweat spread out across her forehead. She tried to be discreet about it and not jump up out of her chair like she wanted to. Instead, she slumped slightly forward, hoping no one would notice.

"Kate, what is it?" her mother asked.

She waved her hand as if to dismiss the question and tried to stand up from the table, but pain gutted her again and she couldn't help but moan.

Rita immediately came to her side. Kate was relieved—her mother wasn't about to stop fussing over her.

"Mom, I don't feel so good."

"Honey, you look awful," Rita said, putting her arm around her daughter.

Hank stood. "Should we take her to the emergency room?"

"No, no, it's not that bad." Kate protested. Another sharp pain sliced across her lower belly. Instinctively, she folded her arms across her lower abdomen. At some point, she would have to get to the bathroom. Any bathroom.

"Honey, go lie down on my bed," her mother said.

No way. If Hank hadn't been there, she probably would. But she couldn't allow Hank to witness her gastrointestinal distress. That would be too embarrassing. The pain subsided momentarily, as she knew it would, and she gradually straightened herself up. She needed to get home, as it would return, and probably with a vengeance.

"Mom, I think I'll just get going," she said weakly.

"Oh, honey, I don't think you should be alone," her mother protested. "Stay here. Or I'll go home with you."

"No, Mom, really, I'm starting to feel better," Kate lied. "I'll just go home and sleep it off."

"I hope it wasn't the chicken curry," Hank said worriedly.

"Oh no," she lied. "I felt a little off this morning. I must be coming down with something."

The pain rushed back and gripped her. She headed to the bathroom as there was no way she could put it off. She eventually came out, temporarily relieved, but she knew that she was in for a long day.

She put on her coat, thanked Hank for the dinner, and apologized profusely.

Her mother was still adamant about coming to Kate's house to look after her, and expressed her fear of Kate driving herself home. Kate tried to reassure her without success. Hank suggested that Rita drive Kate's car and he would follow in his. This compromise seemed acceptable to Kate. Frankly, she didn't care who drove what. She just needed to get home to her own bed and bathroom.

As soon as they pulled up in front of Kate's house, her hands went clammy and a spasm grabbed her. She ran inside with her mother hot on her heels. They must have looked a sight to Hank. Kate was sure Hank must think she was some kind of freak of nature. She wondered if her mother would ever hear from him again.

After spending some quality time in the bathroom, Kate collapsed on her bed. Her mother tucked her in and placed a cup of weak tea at her bedside. Kate assured her that she would be all right and insisted that her mother go home.

CHAPTER ELEVEN

Kate retired the false eyelashes on Monday morning and opted for a simpler look. She wasn't in her best form after Sunday's curry disaster, but the worst had passed and she knew she was on the mend. Hot rollers helped her hair achieve a natural-looking curl. Toning down the make-up, she put on a little eye shadow, mascara, and lip gloss. She wore a wrap dress in block colors of blue, green and black.

Mr. Cline took one look at her when he strolled by her desk, murmured something about the 1970's wanting their style back and threw back his head and laughed. Kate wanted to smack him.

"What's next, O'Connor? The '80s? Big hair and shoulder pads?" he asked. He slapped his thigh, guffawed, and carried on down the hall, talking and laughing to himself.

She ignored him and consoled herself with the thought that she suspected he wore lifts in his shoes.

At the weekly meeting, Mr. Cline refrained from his usual quota of verbal abuse.

"Well, I don't see any one thing that stands out for me but I have to admit that a lot of the ideas that have come forth are not all that bad." He paused as if searching for just the right phrase. "Granted, some of them downright stink, but at least you have on your thinking caps. Remember, what is the one thing we are trying to get across to our target audience? You're straying too much, trying to say too much, and in the end it only confuses people. Keep it simple and keep it basic. Paul assures me that our team will have something substantial by the end of the week. Hopefully, they won't let us down. And Alexis tells me that the plans for this year's Christmas party are well under way. Any questions?"

The meeting broke up much earlier than expected and Kate headed to her desk.

To her surprise, Gavin walked in late that afternoon. What was he doing here?

"I thought you weren't due in until tomorrow," Kate said to him, looking up from her desk. He was so unpredictable; he was never where he said he was going to be. It was quite discombobulating.

"We wrapped things up on Friday and I flew back over the weekend," he explained.

She noticed him taking in her hair, her lip gloss and her dress.

Cline & Co. is probably getting the axe, she thought. Good. Hopefully, it would be before Nick Sommers had his way with her. She involuntarily shuddered.

"Cold?" Gavin asked.

She shook her head. *Boy, he doesn't miss a trick.*

"Uh, Kate, do you have multiple personalities or something?" he asked, the corners of his mouth twitching.

"Excuse me?" She wasn't sure if she'd heard him correctly.

"Well, every time I come in here, you've got a new look or your hair is totally different or something. Some days, I don't even recognize you. I walk in here and I'm not sure I'm in the right place." He was grinning now. Kate was not.

She stood up and put her hands on her hips, trying to stare him down, which was just about impossible because he was a head taller than her and his eyes were twinkling. Just what Cline & Co. needed—another comedian when the place was already full of clowns.

He walked into his office, chuckling to himself. He looked back at her once, shaking his head and smiling.

When Gavin sat down at his desk, still chuckling to himself over Kate, he realized that despite the fact that he wanted to pull the account from Cline & Co., he had been looking forward to seeing her again. In fact, to his surprise and consternation, he had found his thoughts drifting toward her a lot while he had been in Ireland.

He had been unable to convince his boss that Alchemis would be better off without Cline & Co. Larry Barrett wouldn't budge. He'd told him to make it work— 'do whatever you have to do,' he had said, as there'd be no peace in his home or marriage if he dumped his wife's cousin from the campaign. He had said all this while he played on a putting green that had been installed in his office.

To Gavin's surprise, he hadn't been as angry or frustrated as he would have expected to be with Larry's answer. At least he'd still see Kate. That was the only bright light on a very dark horizon.

He hadn't had time to go to the farm as he had hoped and that had upset him. Especially with his mother's health being questionable. They were just waiting on the biopsy results. He wasn't a praying man, but now seemed as good a time as any. He promised himself that as soon as this drug launch was over, he would take an extended vacation and spend it at home on the farm.

His thoughts drifted back to Kate. She was obviously experimenting with a new look. He thought they all looked good. She had amazing eyes and skin. More than once, he'd wished he could reach out and brush his hand across her cheek, just to see if it felt as soft as it looked.

Kate's mother had left two messages on her home answering machine inquiring about her state of health. She would never ring her on her cell phone or call her at work because she didn't want to disturb her. *If she only knew how truly busy I wasn't*, Kate thought.

She called her back first thing and informed her that she was definitely on the mend.

"I wonder if you picked up some sort of bug," her mother said. Kate could hear the worry in her voice. She knew how older people were about their bowel habits and picking up germs. This would have been a double whammy.

"No, Mom, it's definitely not a bug," she said.

"You don't know that, Kate. Maybe you shouldn't have gone to work. You might have infected all those people."

Kate sighed and confessed. "It wasn't a bug. It was the curry."

"But it couldn't have been! Hank and I are fine."

"I'm sure you are. It's just that curry doesn't agree with me. At all. This same sort of thing has happened in the past," Kate explained, then added, "That's why I don't eat it."

"Honey, why didn't you say something yesterday? I could have made you something else," her mother cried.

"Because I didn't want to be a stinker and ruin lunch. And I didn't want to hurt your feelings."

"Oh, Kate," Rita said.

"It's okay, Mom. I'm fine now. And for the record, the curry was delicious—it just doesn't agree with me."

"Is there anything else you don't like? Hank likes to cook Mexican, Italian, and some Asian dishes."

"Sushi. I absolutely hate it," Kate told her. "But I love Mexican and Italian."

She thought of her father, who had been a simple man with simple tastes. He'd preferred meat and potatoes every night and wouldn't have dreamed of eating something as exotic as pizza for dinner.

They chatted for a few more minutes before hanging up. Kate assured her mother that she would talk to her soon.

She left a message on Vinnie's cell, informing him that the girls were coming over the following evening.

She pulled a frozen dinner out of the freezer and popped it into the microwave. Standing at the counter, fork in hand, she wolfed it down. She looked at the picture on the box. The portion seemed bigger and tastier-looking on the cover of the carton.

She put on holiday music and turned on the Christmas lights. She felt restless.

Back into the kitchen she went, where she pulled out cookbooks, mixing bowls and baking trays. She tied on her apron, found the cookie cutters in the back of the cabinet, and after washing them in warm soapy water, she got right down to it. She made the dough for butterhorns and put it in the fridge for an hour to chill. Then she got on with the cutouts, rolling out the dough, cutting the festive shapes and baking them. While they cooled, she took out the three balls of dough and rolled each one out in the shape of a pizza, cutting it up like a pie. She brushed them with butter and sprinkled them with a cinnamon-walnut mixture before rolling each segment into a crescent and placing it on a cookie sheet. While they baked in the oven, she made the frosting for the cutouts.

Once done, she made herself a cup of tea and sampled a few of her creations.

At midnight, exhausted, she donned her flannel pajamas, crawled under her blankets, and fell fast asleep.

Kate brought a huge plate of her homemade Christmas cookies to work the following morning. She removed the cling wrap and placed them on the table in the break room. She had to admit, they looked quite appealing—magazine picture-perfect. She wrote 'enjoy' on a piece of paper and set it in front of the plate.

Alexis stood at the refrigerator getting her water bottle from the top shelf. "Those look wonderful," she said. "What bakery did you get them from?"

"I baked them myself," Kate said proudly.

"I didn't think anyone did that anymore," Alexis said. "Baking, that is."

Kate shrugged. She wasn't interested in debating the merits of home cooking versus store bought with Alexis.

Gavin walked in. Kate balled up the cling wrap and threw it in the trash.

"Good morning, ladies," he smiled. He headed toward the coffee pot. He had that crisp, freshly showered look. His dark hair was still damp and he smelled wonderful. Kate felt the room closing in on her.

"Hmm. What do we have here?" he asked, eyeing up the home-baked cookies.

"Christmas cookies, made by our very own little Miss Suzy Homemaker here," Alexis said, not breaking eye contact with him, but indicating Kate with a nod of her head.

"I love home-made baked goods," he said, studying the variety of cookies before choosing a butterhorn.

"I'm glad I don't bake," Alexis said. "I'd weigh two hundred pounds."

I'm looking forward to beating the crap out of you someday, Kate thought.

She watched as Gavin bit into the butterhorn. A smile broke out on his face. "These are amazing," he said of the rich, buttery cookie. "Is it okay if I take a plate?"

"Sure," Kate said, secretly delighted. She shot Alexis a dirty look.

As Gavin made his selections, Paul walked in and bid them all good morning. He went straight for the coffee pot, not noticing the cookies on the table. Kate remembered that he had never been big on sweets.

Gavin left with cookies piled high on a small plate and Paul started to say something to her but she ignored him, scooting out the door. She followed Gavin down the hall and watched him, secretly amused. He had the plate in one hand and a coffee cup in the other. There was nothing nicer than cooking and baking for someone who appreciated it.

Mentally, she planned what she needed to do once she got out of work. She needed to pick up a few bottles of wine, do a little light housecleaning and make some hot appetizers. Her mother called and invited her over, but Kate suggested she come and join them at the purse party, instead. Her mother hesitated only briefly before declaring she'd get there early to help Kate set up.

Kate rang up Lisa over at the law firm and invited her, as well.

"I can't," Lisa answered, giggling. "I've got a date."

"With who?"

"Nate, the security expert."

"Is this the guy we ran into the other night?" Kate asked.

"Yes—he's the security consultant in from Boston."

"He's the guy with big hands," Kate said, remembering the size of his mitts.

"That's him. And you know what they say about men with big hands..." Lisa was laughing.

Kate started laughing, too. "Yeah, yeah I know what they say about men with big hands—" Swiveling around in her seat, Kate caught Gavin standing in front of her desk. *Oh crap!* She blushed and whispered into the phone, "Gotta go." She hung up before Lisa could answer.

Kate tried hard not to look at Gavin's hands.

He raised an eyebrow, tapping his fingers on her desk. "Conducting scientific research? I like someone who shows initiative."

She opened her mouth, but she wasn't sure how to respond.

He had his coat on and appeared to be heading out the door. He glanced quickly at his watch.

"I'm late for an appointment," he said. "I'll be back before the day is out."

"Okay," she said feebly.

He looked over his shoulder. "Good luck with your research." He winked at her and was gone.

She didn't have to look in the mirror to know that her face had gone the color of puce.

Sherrie appeared at Kate's desk.

"I have bad news," she said. "Alexis heard about the purse party and invited herself."

"Oh no," Kate groaned. "Now we won't be able to talk about her behind her back."

"Tell me about it," Sherrie said. "Boy, I could use a night out. We are finally making headway with this Alchemis account. And it looked like it would never happen."

"Really?"

"We've been brainstorming all day and night lately and it seems like it finally might be coming together." Sherrie sighed. "And not a moment too soon."

"Why do you say that?" Kate asked.

"Initially, Gavin didn't like any of our ideas. He felt we were missing the point as to what this drug is all about."

Kate looked at her.

"But our output now seems to be more in line with his way of thinking. So maybe we're on the same page after all."

"Were we in danger of losing the account?"

"Nepotism can only carry you so far," Sherrie explained. "It also looks like Alexis is going to get her Christmas gala. Word is out that she booked the Towne Royale."

Kate's mouth fell open. "The Towne Royale?"

It was a brand new hotel downtown that gave luxury a new meaning.

"How she managed that, I don't know," Sherrie said. "How does one manage to book one of the ballrooms at the most expensive hotel in the city at the last minute during the holidays?"

The Towne Royale definitely meant a black tie affair.

"I suppose this means I can't wear my black pantsuit," Kate griped, referring to the all-purpose outfit she wore to every occasion: weddings, funerals, and job interviews.

Sherrie shook her head and said, "No, I don't think so."

"Hello," Kate said, answering her cell phone for what she hoped would be the last time today. She had just shut down her computer and was reaching for her coat.

"Kate, it's Gavin."

She wondered where he'd obtained her number. But then she remembered he had called her at home once. Mr. Cline must have given him both her landline and cell numbers. "Yes?"

"Could you do me a favor? I left my laptop in my office and I'm held up here. I won't make it back to the office tonight. Can you lock it up in the safe?"

"We don't have a safe," she said.

"Can you lock it up somewhere else?" he asked.

"There isn't anywhere else. Mr. Cline's office is the only one that has a lock and he's already left for the day," she explained.

She heard him sigh on the other end.

"May I ask a favor of you?" he asked.

"Yes," she said, tentatively.

"Would you mind taking my laptop home with you?" he asked. "And if it's not too much of an inconvenience, could I pick it up from you later?"

"No, that's no trouble at all," she said. She thought about all the company coming to her house that evening. She crossed her fingers. "What time were you thinking of picking it up?"

"I'll be there before seven," he said.

"That's perfect." He'd be gone before the company arrived. She gave him her address and the directions to her house before hanging up the phone.

It was five after five and that was the end of that. She retrieved the laptop and headed for home.

Kate arrived home after stopping on the way to pick up a few groceries. Her mother, true to form, had come over, cleaned up, and baked a pan of brownies. She was now sitting on the sofa, mesmerized by a game show.

Kate put Gavin's laptop in the kitchen closet and promptly forgot about it.

She prepared appetizers: spinach and artichoke dip, stuffed banana peppers, and a taco spread. Her mother joined her when her show was over and busied herself putting together a platter of cheese and crackers. Kate looked at the clock and realized she had some time, so she made a quick batch of meringue kisses, a light cookie made of baked meringue and chocolate chips. She set out an assortment of Christmas cookies.

Her mother sat at her kitchen island, reading articles aloud from the newspaper while Kate half-listened. She was a little worried about Vinnie. She hoped that he wouldn't come on too strong.

After a quick bath, she freshened up her make-up and started rummaging through her closet, finally choosing a cobalt blue turtleneck.

She lit the candles on the mantle, turned on the Christmas lights on her sorry-looking tree and put on the holiday music very low.

A few minutes before eight, making one final check of everything, she noticed her mother putting on her coat.

"Where are you going?" she asked, putting gold hoop earrings in her ears.

"I'm going home. Your friends will be here soon."

"Mom. You cleaned my house. You baked. And now you won't stay for the party?"

"I'd only be in the way."

"Oh, please. You like my friends and they like you. Don't leave now. Besides, Vinnie should be here shortly. I want to treat you to a purse."

Rita hesitated. Kate held out her hand for her coat and she thought her mother looked secretly pleased.

CHAPTER TWELVE

Kate's co-workers started trickling in shortly after eight o'clock. She laid their coats on her bed while they maneuvered around the living room, looking at Christmas decorations, inspecting the lopsided tree, and admiring the photos on the mantle. Kate and her mother set out appetizers and baked goods on the glass-topped coffee table, along with snack-sized plates and napkins. Sherrie brought out wine glasses from the kitchen.

"I like your hat. It suits you," Ann said, referring to the Santa Claus hat perched on top of Kate's head.

"Thanks."

Alexis arrived and Kate was shocked; she had Paul with her. Kate looked at the two of them uneasily. She hadn't invited either one of them, but here they were. She could hardly refuse them entry.

"I hope you don't mind that I invited Paul," Alexis cooed. "We were all talking about it at work and I didn't want him to feel left out." She turned to him and gave him her high-wattage smile.

Kate hoped Alexis hadn't invited Mr. Cline under the same pretense. She kept her mouth shut, because what could she say? The truth was, she didn't want Paul and their co-mingled past in her home. He had never been here before. She had bought the house after her father had died and Paul had been long gone by then.

Kate's mother stood up and the smile disappeared from her face as soon as she saw Paul.

"Mrs. O'Connor, how are you?" Paul asked, stepping forward to shake her hand. She looked over at Kate who could only shrug. Reluctantly, she took his hand.

"How is Mr. O'Connor?" he asked her politely.

"He's dead," she said, and she walked out of the room.

He turned to Kate and had the decency to look sheepish. "I'm sorry, I didn't know."

The doorbell rang and it broke the tension. Kate opened the front door to Vinnie Mann, loaded down with a box full of purses. She held the door wide open for him.

The box was big and unwieldy. Vinnie stumbled in. "Hey, babe—" He looked at the crowd of people and his mouth fell open and stayed there.

Affectionately, she popped up his chin, shutting his mouth. "You'll catch flies like that, Vin."

'Babe?' Sherrie mouthed behind Vinnie's back.

Kate shrugged, having no idea how to explain the inexplicable.

Vinnie's eyes narrowed when he caught sight of Paul. Kate could sense his testosterone levels getting the better of him. She hoped he wouldn't start marking his territory.

To distract him, she called to the group, "The purses have arrived."

She didn't expect what happened next. Everyone except for Paul lunged at Vinnie. They were all shouting at once and trying to step over one another in a bid to get at a certain handbag. At one point, the dodgy Christmas tree swayed a little.

"Gimme that one!"

"I want the 'Kate Spade'!"

"Get your hands off that 'Coach,' it's mine!"

Paul stood back and watched with an amused look on his face. A scuffle ensued.

Kate was surprised at how quickly Vinnie gained control of the situation.

"Ladies! Ladies! Please," Vinnie pleaded, gathering the purses, throwing them back into the box and clutching it awkwardly to his chest. "If you don't get a grip, I'll take my purses and go home."

That quieted them down. Then, looking at Alexis, Vinnie said, "Hey, you, Blondie. Give me a hand here. This thing is heavy."

Alexis stared at Vinnie, mute, unmoving, and clearly offended. She didn't do manual labor.

Vinnie repeated, "C'mon, Blondie."

But Alexis remained silent, her eyes like daggers. Vinnie, of course, was clueless.

"What's wrong? Afraid of a little manual labor?" he pressed on, bending over to deposit the box on the floor.

"I am not the hired help," Alexis said tartly.

"Well, excuse me," he riposted, straightening up.

"Let me help you, Vinnie," Kate said, heading off an argument as she could see they would both want to have the last word. She helped him carry the box over to the center of the living room. They took the purses out and began to set them up around the perimeter of the room.

As Kate helped him position the purses, Vinnie whispered, "Would it hurt you to run a dust mop around here once in a while?"

Paul distracted everyone by topping up their wine glasses.

Everyone started milling around, admiring the bags. There was a lot of oohing and aahing.

In the midst of all of this, the doorbell rang once again.

Kate answered it to find Gavin standing out on her porch. She had forgotten about him. Immediately, she took off her Santa hat, feeling foolish.

"Uh, hi."

"I'm sorry I'm so late. I was detained."

She noticed that Gavin still wore his suit and tie; he looked tired.

Raucous laughter came from inside and he looked up at the sound of it.

"If this is a bad time..." he started, taking a step back.

"Of course not." She smiled and opened the door wider, reaching for his arm and pulling him inside. "Come on in, Gavin."

He followed her into the living room. A hush descended when everyone saw him standing there. Vinnie scowled at him. The presence of a third alpha male in her house would probably send him right over the edge. Gavin was busy taking everything in: the tree, the scented candles, the music playing in the background. He glanced at the wine and the food on the coffee table. He regarded the purses with curiosity.

"It's very Christmassy," he said. "It reminds me of home."

"We're just having a little work get-together," she explained.

He nodded. "It looks like a lot of fun."

Everyone yelled hello.

"Gavin, here's a seat. Have a glass of wine," Sherrie said, patting the cushion on the sofa next to her.

He put up his hand. "No, thanks, Sherrie. I'm not staying."

Vinnie came barreling over like an angry bull. He thrust out his hand. "I'm Vinnie Mann."

Gavin shook his hand. "Gavin Whyte."

"Vinnie is my neighbor," Kate added.

Gavin looked at her for a moment as if piecing something together. "Is this the neighbor who sent you—"

She cut him off, her face reddening. "Yes, it is."

"What are your intentions toward Kate?" Vinnie asked, getting in Gavin's face.

"Sorry?" Gavin asked.

"Vinnie!" Kate wanted to die on the spot. "He intends to pick up his laptop—that is his intention. Now go over there, sell your purses, and behave yourself."

Vinnie skulked away like an errant seven-year-old child.

"Let me get your laptop for you," she said, heading off to the kitchen with Gavin in tow.

Kate's mother was sitting at the island, drinking a cup of tea and doing a crossword puzzle. She peered over the rim of her glasses at Gavin when he walked in behind Kate.

"Mom, this is Gavin Whyte, from Alchemis," she said. To him she said, "This is my mother, Rita O'Connor."

Her mother put down the crossword puzzle and took off her glasses. "Is this the Irishman?"

"It is indeed, ma'am," he smiled.

"I've heard good things about you."

"Really?" he raised his eyebrows in a genuine look of surprise.

Kate wondered, herself; she couldn't remember ever mentioning Gavin Whyte to her mother. *Aunt Geraldine.*

"My late husband, John, was from County Clare. He was a mighty fine man," she said proudly. It always made Kate feel warm inside when her father was remembered like that.

Kate retrieved Gavin's laptop from the kitchen closet and handed it to him.

"Are you sure you won't have a glass of wine or something to eat?" she asked.

He put his hands up. She noticed his long, tapered fingers and smooth oval nails.

"No, thank you. Really. I appreciate it, but I want to grab some dinner before I head back to the hotel."

Mrs. O'Connor pounced on this last statement like a cat on a mouse. "It's eight o'clock at night and you haven't had dinner yet?"

Oh no, Kate thought.

Her mother swung into action, practically jumping down off the stool. "Sit down there. Give me your coat. I'll fix you something to eat."

"Oh no, Mrs. O'Connor, that's quite all right," he protested.

"Listen, you may be a big shot at Alchemis, but in the kitchen, I'm the big shot," she said.

"Don't fight it. She won't take no for an answer," Kate whispered to him.

He laughed and said, "Very well then." He set down his laptop and removed his overcoat. She took both the coat and laptop and put them in the closet. He took a seat and she watched as he lifted his chin to get at his tie. He loosened it, and unbuttoned the collar on his shirt. He removed his cufflinks and rolled up his sleeves. Oddly, she felt voyeuristic—watching him loosening his tie had her nerve endings buzzing. She shook her head. *I really need to get out of the house more*, she thought.

To distract herself, she poured him a glass of wine.

"Thank you, Kate," he said. He lifted his glass to both women and said, "Cheers."

Kate excused herself and went back to the living room. "Is he gone?" Someone asked.

"My mother is feeding him in the kitchen," she said.

Paul had taken a seat next to Alexis. She watched as Alexis leaned over, her blonde hair brushing Paul's shoulder, and whispered something into his ear. Kate thought they looked awfully chummy, and she decided Alexis was welcome to him. But she had thought Alexis had set her cap on Gavin. Kate wished Alexis would make up her mind, once and for all.

Kate settled down next to Sherrie and eyed up the food and the purses. She took a big gulp from her wine glass—it was going to be a long night.

Later, when she took some empty plates back into the kitchen, she saw that her mother was in a friendly debate with Gavin over the merits of dieting and diet pills.

Kate placed the dirty dishes in the sink. She noticed Gavin's empty dinner plate on the countertop. Next to it was a freezer container with the label 'PIGS' on it. Her mother had made pigs in the blanket and they were wonderful—minced beef and pork, mixed with cooked rice and wrapped up in a cabbage leaf with a tomato gravy. They were hard work to make, but worth it. Kate's mother usually made a big pan and would always put some in Kate's freezer. And Gavin had just eaten her last three.

He was drinking a cup of tea and working on a plate of Christmas cookies.

"Now take a look at my daughter," her mother was saying.

"Mom!" Kate groaned. However, she noticed that Gavin was indeed taking a look. Suddenly, she felt self-conscious.

"That's her build. It would be far better for her to eat right and exercise than to diet," Rita said to him.

"I agree," he said, not taking his eyes off of Kate.

"I can't believe that every man out there wants a flat chest and a bony butt," Rita opined.

"Mom!"

"Gavin, what do you prefer?" Rita asked, ignoring Kate's warning looks.

"Funny you should ask. I've always gone out with girls who were tall and thin but recently, I've changed my preference," he said, looking intently at Kate. "I definitely prefer the curves."

"Look at my Kate," Mrs. O'Connor said, continuing to ignore her daughter's dirty looks. "She has a beautiful shape with womanly curves. She isn't a size zero, but I think she is absolutely lovely. Don't you?"

"Mom! Stop it. You're embarrassing him and me," Kate hissed. She turned to Gavin. "Dieting is the only thing where losing is everything. Would you like more tea?"

He sat straight up and blinked. "What did you say, Kate?"

"Mom, stop it, you're embarrassing him?" she repeated.

He laughed. "No, the thing about dieting," he said, helping himself to another cookie off the platter.

"Oh, you know. They say winning is everything. Except in dieting, losing is everything," she said, shrugging her shoulders.

He drained his teacup. "Kate O'Connor, you're brilliant. And yes, I would love more tea."

She filled his cup, feeling confused.

"What you just said, about losing being everything. That's very catchy." He was reflective for a moment. Then he looked at Kate's mother and explained. "This is a big thing. This drug is not a gimmick—it's going to revolutionize the weight-loss industry. Alchemis doesn't want just one ad. Our campaign is going to be multi-phasic. We have different demographics to reach, not just the eighteen to thirty-four year olds, not only women, and not only chronic dieters. This drug is for anyone who needs it. And our ad campaign has to be reflective of that. It has to be inclusive, not exclusive."

"Would you recommend it for Kate?" Rita asked.

"Mom!" Kate said, horrified.

But her mother pressed on. "Do you think Kate needs the drug?"

"You don't need to answer that," Kate said quickly, waiting for the humiliation that was coming.

He looked surprised at the question. "No, I don't think she needs it at all."

He stood up from his seat. Kate thought he looked less weary than before.

"I really should go," he said, looking at Kate.

Something stirred within her.

Gavin turned to Kate's mother. "Mrs. O'Connor, thank you for dinner, dessert, and the conversation."

"Any time, Gavin."

He took his teacup over to the sink and set it down.

Kate pulled out his coat from the closet, acutely aware that he was right behind her. Turning around quickly, she realized they were up close and personal. He looked into her face and their eyes locked. Kate swallowed hard.

For a moment, everything fell away: the presence of her mother, the voices and laughter from the other room, even the kitchen itself. For a wonderful, long moment, neither looked away.

He cleared his throat suddenly and turned away. "I should get going."

Unable to look at him for fear that he might see the flush in her face, Kate led the way as he said goodbye to her mother. He followed her out of the kitchen. Everyone yelled goodnight, except Vinnie.

Alone on the front porch, Gavin cast a glance at her and rooted in his pocket for his keys. "Thank you again. It turned out to be a very pleasurable evening."

"You didn't have to stay in the kitchen," she said, her breath coming out in wisps in the cold. "You could've joined us in the living room."

"I enjoyed your mother's company. She's a very intelligent woman." He paused. "Plus, she's a brilliant cook."

"Yes, she is. She likes to feed people."

"I gathered that." He smiled.

The air between them felt charged.

She folded her arms across her chest to stave off the dampness of the winter night. He looked out into the darkness and then back at her. He inhaled deeply and let out a sigh. "You should go inside, Miss O'Connor, before you catch a chill." His gaze lingered a moment, but then abruptly, he said, "Goodnight, Kate." He stepped off the porch and walked down the driveway. The snow crunched under his feet.

Kate watched him walk off into the night. It bothered her that he was leaving—there was no escaping that fact.

She took a minute before re-joining the others inside.

The party was winding down. Everyone sat around with their selection of purses at their feet, drinking wine and picking at what was left of the appetizers.

"These are the best knock-off purses I have ever seen," Amy Mohr said.

"Vinnie Mann always delivers," Vinnie said, smiling as he licked his thumb and counted the wad of bills in his hand.

"Why are they the best?" Kate asked. She wasn't really interested; she couldn't get her mind off of Gavin Whyte.

"There's an actual designer label inside," Amy explained. She opened her imitation 'Coach' bag to show everyone the inside label.

"Mine has a business card with care instructions," Debbie said.

Pretty soon, they were all checking the insides of the purses.

"Wow, these are great—you can't tell the difference," Ann said.

Kate's mother appeared in the doorway, coat on and purse on her arm.

Kate got up and walked her to the door.

"Honey, I'd stay, but I'm exhausted," she said.

"That's okay, Mom. Pick out a purse or two before you go," she said.

"Ask Mr. Mann to leave them here, and I'll stop by tomorrow to pick one out."

"Okay, Mom."

Everyone yelled goodbye to Mrs. O'Connor. Kate kissed her mother on the cheek and told her she would talk to her the following day.

Kate surveyed the remaining purses on the floor. There was still a variety. She mulled over which ones she was going to choose for herself.

The doorbell rang. She wondered who it could be, as it was getting late. She was surprised to see Gavin standing there.

"Hello again," she said, inviting him to step inside. Secretly, she was happy to see him.

He laughed. "I forgot my laptop."

"Oh, of course," she said, disappointed.

They walked back to the kitchen; Kate retrieved his laptop and handed it to him.

As she escorted him back to the front door, she noticed everyone was standing, picking up their plates and glasses, and getting ready to depart.

The doorbell rang. Again.

Who could it possibly be? She wondered. It seemed nearly everyone in western New York was already standing in her living room.

She threw open the front door to find two men in suits and overcoats. Immediately, she assumed they were at the wrong address.

The tall man on the left pulled something out of his breast pocket. He flashed her a badge. Police officers? They were definitely at the wrong address. He introduced himself as Detective O'Grady and presented the other man, a much shorter man with the most amazing green eyes, as Detective Pratt.

"Are you Katharine O'Connor?" Detective O'Grady asked.

"Yes," she said.

"May we come in for a few minutes and ask you a few questions?"

"About what?"

"We'd like to ask you a few questions about your neighbor." Detective Pratt with the incredible green eyes stared at her with a frown. She felt like a specimen under his microscope.

She invited them in. Why not? Everybody else was here. She offered to take their coats but they informed her that they wouldn't be staying long; they just wanted to ask her a few questions about her neighbor, Vinnie Mann. When she informed them that Vinnie was there in her house, they exchanged a quick glance between themselves. Kate highly doubted they would ask her questions with Vinnie standing right there. But she couldn't help but wonder about what Vinnie had done now. They pushed past her and went through to the living room.

Chaos ensued when the detectives walked in and saw Vinnie stuffing a big wad of cash into his pocket.

They pushed Kate aside and she went flying into Gavin, who dropped his laptop. Everyone started screaming at once. Alexis and Paul jumped up on the sofa and Kate thought she'd kill Alexis if she put a hole in the suede fabric with her stiletto shoes. Ann, Amy, and Debbie clung to each other and screamed. Sherrie quickly scarfed down the two meringue kisses left on the plate, obviously worried the police might beat her to it.

Kate put her hand up, stepped forward and said, "Wait just a minute—you can't barge in here like this!" She was indignant.

"Get over there, miss, with the rest of them," Detective Pratt said.

"This is my house!" she protested.

"Miss, I'm not going to tell you again," he said, warning her.

She went and stood next to Sherrie. Gavin stood beside her.

Detective O'Grady picked up one of the knock-off handbags and began to inspect it. *Suddenly, he has a desire for a knock-off purse?* He pulled his cell phone from his coat pocket, made a call, and requested back up. That part Kate didn't understand, but she became distracted by the other detective. Detective Pratt removed the wad of cash from Vinnie's hand and bagged it. Then he handcuffed Vinnie. She heard the detective say to Vinnie, "We've been watching you, Mann."

Kate watched Vinnie's shoulders sag. He seemed to deflate before her very eyes. Despite her fear and confusion, she felt the hair stand up on the back of her neck. "Hey, wait a minute—you can't do that to him. Leave him alone." She took a step forward, but Gavin took a firm hold of her forearm and quickly pulled her back. She looked up to him but he shook his head slightly. He held onto her arm.

The girls started protesting about the purses.

Detective Pratt escorted a handcuffed Vinnie out the front door. As he walked past her, she whispered, "Oh, Vinnie."

Detective O'Grady put up his hands. When they all quieted down, he spoke. "Let's see some ID, ladies."

Soon uniformed officers poured into the house and, taking instruction from Detective O' Grady, began to bag up all the purses, including the ones the girls from the office had paid for. Kate groaned so loud she was sure they heard it in the next state.

"Hey wait a minute, we paid for those purses," Ann yelled.

Voices rose. Kate thought for sure there must be some mistake.

The detective put up his hand again. "These purses are stolen goods."

"What?" Kate asked.

"The purses are stolen goods."

"But they're not real, they're imitation," she countered, immediately wondering if she should have. "They're knock-offs."

"I'm afraid these are real. They are not imitation."

The chatter picked up amongst the group as this information settled in.

Detective Pratt returned with more officers. He approached Paul, took him aside and asked for some ID. When Paul handed it to him, he started asking him some questions which Kate couldn't hear.

Detective O'Grady did the same with Gavin and at one point he gestured toward Gavin's laptop. Kate became alarmed. She imagined Gavin was probably explaining that he had been in the wrong place at the wrong time. Again. She noticed that he had handed the detective his passport when asked for ID. She was surprised he hadn't had it tattooed to his forehead.

Simultaneously, the detectives indicated to Paul and Gavin that they were free to go. Gavin pulled Kate aside.

"Kate, what can I do to help?" he asked. He searched her face.

She felt like crying. She quickly shook her head no. She had gotten him into enough trouble already. Besides, what could he do? Take the stand and give a character witness? He'd be obliged to tell them the truth—that she was nothing but a troublemaker. "Thank-you, but you should go."

After several reassurances from her, he finally left the house. She noticed that Paul had high-tailed it out of there without so much as a goodbye.

Detective O'Grady turned to the rest of them and said, "I'm going to ask you all to come down to the police station to answer some further questions."

"Wait a minute—we all have to go?" Alexis asked, pouting.

"Yes, everyone present," he answered.

"But it was her party and it's her house," Alexis said, pointing a finger at Kate.

"Thanks a lot," Kate said. She wanted to point out to her that she hadn't even been invited, but she didn't think now was the time to split hairs.

"I can't go down to the station. I've got kids home with the chicken pox," Debbie said.

Every man for himself, Kate thought, raising her eyes to heaven.

Somebody suggested, "Yeah, Kate can go for all of us. She's single and has no kids."

"What does that have to do with anything?" Kate asked, searching for the owner of the voice and strongly suspecting it was Alexis again. Alexis was also single with no kids. If Kate found her, she might just ask her to step outside and deal with her once and for all on the front lawn. Right now, she was in the mood to clean up a parking lot with her.

"Well, um, nothing. It's just that you're in a better position to go and sort this out than those of us with families," Ann said.

Wow, tough crowd.

"Hey, wait a minute," Sherrie said. "I'm pregnant."

"Again?" They all yelled in unison.

"What can I say? I'm fertile." She smiled sheepishly. "Anyway, officer, do I have to go to the station?"

"Look, you're all going. I don't care if you have notes from your mothers."

Gavin hadn't wanted to leave Kate and he felt like a coward for doing so. He'd wanted to remain at her side.

He walked to his rental car and locked his laptop in the trunk. He sat in the car, turned it on, and waited for it to warm up and for the windows to defrost. Earlier, when he had approached Kate's house, he'd been taken by the glittering multi-colored Christmas lights and the muted laughter and music coming from inside. Something tugged inside him. The dinner, the conversation, everything—it had all been so inviting. He thought of his own hotel room, silent, with not a decoration in sight, and it depressed him. Then he realized that his own apartment in Dublin was much the same as his hotel room—cold and unwelcoming.

He watched Paul get into his car and drive away. He'd known there had been something between Paul and Kate, the way there was always tension buzzing around them. As he'd eaten dinner in Kate's kitchen, Mrs. O'Connor had told him how Paul had literally left Kate standing at the altar. She'd been furious that he'd shown up at Kate's house uninvited. "Of all the nerve!" she'd said.

The police brought out Vinnie first, in handcuffs, and bundled him into the back of a squad car. Gavin wondered what kind of trouble the man had gotten Kate into. He'd help if he could. He admired Kate's loyalty to her friend—Gavin hoped he was just a friend—even if it was misguided.

He watched as the women from Cline & Co. filed out of Kate's house and piled into waiting police cars. He blew on his hands to warm them up; it was damp and frigid outside. Somewhere along the way, he had misplaced his gloves.

The windshield clear, and warm air blowing out of the vents, he fell in line behind the police cars and followed them to the station. More than once he thought himself crazy, but he kept coming back to that moment in the kitchen when something had happened between the two of them. He knew—he was sure of it—that Kate had felt it, too. The attraction and desire was so strong and palpable that, had her mother not been there, he would have pushed Kate up against the wall and, at the very least, kissed her.

CHAPTER THIRTEEN

After much questioning, the five of them—Sherrie, Ann, Debbie, Alexis and Kate—sat together in a small interrogation room at the back of the station, saying nothing. They were all bone-tired. There was no sign of Vinnie, and Kate had no idea what had happened to him.

A very somber, professional-looking man entered the room. He introduced himself as Captain So-and-So. Kate didn't get his name as it was late and her eyes were at half-mast. She assumed he was there to give them a little slap on the wrist and warn them to stay out of trouble or something like that. She looked at her watch, anxious to get home to bed. She hoped it wouldn't be much longer. She couldn't stop yawning, and was starting to think of her bed the way a man in the desert would think of water.

"I want to give you ladies something to think about." The captain paused, making sure he had their attention. "I understand you ladies were under the misguided assumption that you were purchasing 'knock-off' purses. Yet, they were actually the real deal. I'd like to say one thing about these imitation handbags. I know these purse parties are very popular and all the rage. What you don't realize is that selling these counterfeits is illegal, it's a violation of federal law, and a crime that is handled by both the FBI and the Department of US Homeland Security."

Oh great, US Homeland Security again—I'm practically on a first name basis with them, Kate thought sadly. *Pretty soon we'll be exchanging Christmas cards.*

He continued. "These laws do not extend to the buyers of these purses. But did you know that when you buy a counterfeit purse, you are supporting organized crime and terrorism?"

A lot of 'ohs' rumbled through the group as if he had just given them a tip on how to make their mashed potatoes starchier. None of them wanted to be responsible for aiding and abetting the enemy.

"Just something to think about. That'll be all." With that, he departed the room.

He had used the weapon of choice of mothers everywhere: guilt. They'd never go near another knock-off purse again.

Kate could see her mother sitting on a plastic chair in the waiting room as she approached. Kate had called her for a lift home. She was surprised, though, to see Gavin sitting next to her. They appeared to be deep in conversation; at one point her mother laughed, slapping him on his thigh. However, as soon as she saw Kate, her laughter evaporated and the smile disappeared from her face.

They both stood.

"I can go home now," Kate announced.

"Thank God!" her mother cried. "I was afraid they'd keep you overnight."

Kate looked questioningly at Gavin.

"I just wanted to make sure you got on all right," he explained.

"I'm fine. We're all fine," she said, watching the others leaving the station. They looked like she felt—weary.

"Well, I guess I'd better get going," he said. He bid them both goodnight. As she watched him depart, a feeling for him developed within her. Interest? Definitely. Longing? Yes. Affection? Fondness? That alarmed her. She didn't want to acknowledge what she was feeling about him. It just couldn't be. She blamed it on his good looks. She blamed it on her fatigue. She blamed it on the Christmas season. People felt and did all sorts of foolish things during the holidays. She couldn't fall for him. She would only end up disappointed in love again. There was no way he'd ever be interested in someone like her. He probably thought she was an idiot. She gave her head a good shake, hoping she could physically dislodge her emotions. In the meantime, once home, she'd start scouring the internet for a cat-lady starter kit.

Kate's mother didn't say one word until they got into the car. Her lips had practically disappeared, she had them pressed so tightly together. Once she started the car, she said quietly, "I thought I raised you better than this, Katharine. I know I did."

Kate said nothing. She closed her eyes and leaned her head against the window.

"If your father were alive—" her mother started.

Kate cut her off. "Mom, I thought they were knock-off purses. Everyone has a knock-off purse party. It's like going to a Tupperware party."

"But Tupperware isn't illegal. Besides, just because everyone else is doing it..." Mrs. O'Connor's voice trailed off.

They rode in silence the rest of the way home. She was trying to sort things in her head. How had everything gone so horribly wrong? And Gavin Whyte—she'd bet he never left his laptop behind anywhere again. He'd been kind to her when he left her house, but what must he think of her? *There goes the big account with Alchemis.* All that money had been confiscated by the police, probably never to be seen again. She was going to have to offer some kind of reimbursement to the girls. Her paltry savings account was going to take a big hit. Poor Vinnie! He was waiting to be arraigned. She would call Lisa first thing in the morning to see if she could do something.

They walked into Kate's house and were greeted by the ruins of the party. Half empty lipstick-smudged wine glasses and cold, congealed appetizers littered the coffee table. There were muddy footprints all over the hardwood floor from the police entrance. Kate wanted to cry at the sight of it. She looked at the clock and tried to figure out how many hours' sleep she would get if she went to bed right at that moment. She'd love to call in sick tomorrow, but she knew that that wasn't an option.

Her mother draped her coat on the arm of the sofa and started picking up plates and glasses.

"Aw, Mom. Leave it. I'll get it tomorrow."

"C'mon. There's not much here to clean up," Rita said, walking off with an armful of dirty dishes. "Trust me. You're not going to want to look at this mess in the morning."

What did she know? Kate thought. Her life was turning into one big mess that she had to look at square in the face every day.

Her mother loaded the dishwasher while Kate scraped the plates off into the trash can.

"I'm really worried about Vinnie," Kate said.

"Vinnie's troubles are of his own doing," her mother pointed out.

"He's all right, Mom. He's harmless," she said. She dared not reveal that Vinnie had already done time.

"That Gavin Whyte is a very nice man," her mother said as she squirted liquid dish soap into a pan in the sink.

"I guess," Kate said, only half paying attention.

"I think he likes you."

Kate stopped scraping the last plate and looked at her mother. "Have you lost your mind?"

Rita shrugged in response. "I know what I see."

"Mom." Kate said wearily. "He's one of the bigwigs at work. The mother of all bigwigs. He's the biggest wig of them all."

"I don't care what he is," Rita said. "At the end of the day, he's just a man."

"The Gavin Whytes of the world don't pick girls like me," Kate explained. "Besides, I've been the cause of a lot of his troubles since he arrived."

"I don't think so, honey. I saw the way he looked at you tonight," Kate's mother smiled knowingly. "The same way your father used to look at me."

"Well, you didn't see how he looked at me when the police showed up."

"You're imagining things."

"No, Mom, you are. He's been cooped up in a hotel room for weeks. At this point, I'm probably starting to look like Jennifer Aniston."

"It's true that he's a lonely man. He told me that himself," Rita said, putting dirty cutlery into the silverware basket.

"He told you he was lonely?" As hard as Kate tried, she couldn't visualize Gavin having a heart-to-heart with her mother.

"Well, not in those exact words. He said he was sick and tired of traveling all over the world, of all those nights spent in hotel rooms and late-night business meetings."

Kate said nothing.

"Do you know that he has an apartment in Dublin where he's lived for a year, and he's never used his stove?" To Rita O'Connor, this was blasphemous.

"Maybe he doesn't like to cook," Kate said.

"You know what I told him?" Rita asked.

Kate was afraid to ask.

"I told him that it is not good for a man to be alone."

"Gee, where have I heard that before?"

Rita ignored Kate and continued on. "I told him that people are basically pack animals."

"Oh, Mom, you didn't," Kate groaned. "Now he's going to think we're both idiots."

"You've misread him. How could you live with me all your life and not be able to read people?"

"I don't know," Kate answered. Misreading people was the least of her problems right now.

"Anyway, I invited him for Christmas dinner."

"What? That's a family day!" Kate stared at her mother in disbelief. Nightmarish images of having to buy Gavin a Christmas present flooded her mind. What did a person buy for a guy who already had everything?

"Don't worry—he's going home to Ireland for Christmas to spend it with his parents."

And probably with his girlfriend, Kate thought miserably.

Gavin, exhausted, arrived at the office early the following morning. He was relieved that Kate had showed up, as well, as many of the girls had called off. The place was abandoned. She looked as tired as he felt, but she was still lovely. She sat behind her desk, looking wilted.

"Good morning, Kate."

"Good morning."

Unconsciously, he tapped his finger against her desk. He still wore his trench coat with a cashmere scarf draped around his neck. There had been a little more snow overnight and the morning had started damp and grey.

"Kate, you used to be a copywriter here, am I right?"

She brightened up, nodding.

"Listen, about last night—what you said about losing being everything as far as dieting goes, would you be willing to play around with that for me?"

"Seriously?" she asked.

"Yes," he answered. "Keep it between us for now until I get it sorted out with everyone else."

"All right."

He hovered, but he had nothing more to say. He wanted to stay at her desk and talk to her. But he couldn't come up with anything interesting. He thought dismally, *I can't even make inane conversation. Perhaps Georgina is right. Perhaps I am boring.*

He turned to walk away but Kate stood up.

"Uh, Gavin...um...I'm really sorry about last night."

"Don't apologize," he said. Then he added. "Things are never dull when you're around, are they?"

"I admit that things do seem to go wrong. A lot," she said weakly. "But it's not intentional."

He chuckled. "I know—that's the beauty of it." He shook his head and laughed. For whatever reason, he liked this girl, really liked her. By no means was she his type but he was beginning to wonder if he needed to think outside the box. She made him laugh, and laughter had been absent from his life for a long time. He found that he wanted to be around her. He wanted to see what happened next, what would come out of her mouth. He didn't want to miss a thing.

Kate planned to keep a low profile for the rest of the morning. She had done the right thing and apologized to Gavin. He seemed to have taken the whole thing in stride. She got busy working on the ad copy, grateful to be flexing her copywriting muscles again. She worked it out from all angles. She didn't want to disappoint him.

Sherrie called her at ten o'clock.

"I tried calling you at home and when I got no answer I figured you'd gone into work," she said.

"Alexis and I are the only ones who came in. Everyone else called in sick."

"How upset is Mr. Cline?" Sherrie asked.

"I don't know," Kate said. Mr. Cline, in his perpetual fog, hadn't even noticed that his team was down several people that morning.

"I can't believe I had my hands on a real Coach for only fifty dollars. If only I had left when I was supposed to, I'd still have it," Sherry complained.

"Tell me about it," Kate said. "Vinnie is in big trouble."

"Oh no," Sherrie said, making sympathetic noises.

"I'm very worried about him."

"Something tells me that Vinnie always lands on his feet," Sherrie said.

"I hope so," Kate said. "Hey, by the way—why didn't you tell me you were pregnant?"

Sherrie laughed. "Because I only just took a pregnancy test yesterday morning. I hadn't even told Nick yet. I was trying to get out of going to the police station."

"When are you due?"

"Next summer."

"Well, congratulations."

"Thank you. This is definitely the last one," Sherrie said firmly.

Kate laughed. "Sherrie, you said that about baby number four and baby number five."

"Yeah, but I'm hoping that if I keep saying it, it might stick."

Later that morning, Kate called Lisa at work and was told by the receptionist at Crump, McKenna and Stack that she was gone for the day. There was no sense in leaving a message on her voicemail if she wouldn't be back. Kate dug her cell phone from the bottom of her purse and sent Lisa a text asking her to call as soon as she could.

Lisa called after lunch. Kate filled her in on what had happened the previous night and, more to the point, what had happened with Vinnie.

"I have some friends over at the DA's office. Let me put out some feelers to see what's going on. It may take a while as I've got back-to-back meetings today, but I'll call you back as soon as I can," she said.

Kate thanked her and hung up.

Shortly after lunch, Kate was summoned to Mr. Cline's office, dashing her hopes for minimal contact with him that day. She wasn't up for Mr. Cline right now. She'd hoped that the one good thing that might come out of this purse party fiasco was that the reality TV show would probably be nixed.

The meeting with him and Alexis went downhill as soon as Kate stepped into his office.

"Let me state, first of all, that we are distressed by your illegal activities outside Cline and Company—especially the fact that you insisted on dragging Gavin Whyte through the mud with you," Mr. Cline started.

Kate hoped this was the part where he fired her, severing all ties with Cline & Co. She practically rubbed her hands together.

"However, Alexis and I feel that we may be able to use the situation to our advantage."

Kate's heart sank to her knees. *Of course. Why would it be any other way?*

"I guess this ruins the reality TV show," she ventured, wanting to test the waters.

Alexis broke in. "On the contrary. Negative publicity is a good thing."

"Alexis and I discussed this and we decided that we're going to put on a show of suppressing your criminal record, when in fact what we'll do is secretly leak it to the press beforehand," Mr. Cline explained.

"Of course, we'll issue a denial," Alexis said. "And only when confronted with the facts by the press will we issue a statement."

Mr. Cline chimed in. "By then the controversy will have attracted a lot of attention to the show."

Kate couldn't believe it. They were going to suppress a criminal record that she didn't have. All in the name of ratings. Only Ed Cline and Alexis Winston would find a way to capitalize on her bad luck.

As if he were reading her thoughts, Mr. Cline plowed on. "Not only does America like an underdog, they love an underdog who makes mistakes. Alexis, call Nick over at RTN and run this by him."

"Oh, I'm sure he'll love it," Alexis gushed.

I'm sure he'll love it, too, Kate thought miserably.

It was pointless to tell them, yet again, that she had no interest in their TV show. As they congratulated each other on their brilliance, Kate slipped out.

It was time to put this brainchild of theirs to bed once and for all.

Gavin sat in his chair with his back to the desk and his feet stretched out on the windowsill, staring at the lake. He was thinking of being at Kate's the previous night. She had a lovely home. It made him nostalgic for Christmases past in his own family home. He thought of his chrome-and-black-lacquer penthouse apartment in Dublin and shook his head. He didn't feel nostalgic for that at all. Certainly nothing had ever been baked there. It was cold looking and cold feeling.

He was startled when Kate came storming into his office, furious. He had been playing around with the catch phrase she had suggested the other night, doodling 'Losing is everything' over and over on a scratch pad. It just might work.

But suddenly she stood before him, all volcanic fury. He took his feet off the windowsill and sat straight up, anxious to hear what had put her in such a state and suspecting that it had something to do with Ed Cline.

"Look, this is your diet drug. Not mine. You market it. I used to be a copywriter here, but now I'm just the receptionist making a receptionist's pay."

She had her hands on her hips and his immediate thought was that she was very sexy when she was angry. Her eyes were practically glittering.

"This has gone too far," she continued. "I've said no right from the beginning and I mean no. I won't have any part in it."

"It's only a bit of copywriting," he said, beginning to wonder about her mental health.

She shook her head. "I'm not talking about the copywriting. I mean, really, Gavin, to use the misfortune of last night for Alchemis' own economic gain is really the lowest of the low. And to top it all off, you throw me to the likes of that clown, Nick Sommers."

Nick Sommers? Who the hell was he? Gavin wondered, but he let her continue with her rant.

"I am able to humiliate myself without any help from anybody. But I will not humiliate myself on national TV for Cline and Company or Alchemis, or anyone else for that matter."

She folded her arms across her chest and looked at him defiantly.

He had steepled his fingers together and rested his index fingers against his bottom lip. He looked intently at her and said, "Kate, would you have a seat, please?"

She hesitated at first but then plopped down in the chair across from him.

He looked straight at her and said, "I have no idea what you're talking about."

"Oh please," she said, smirking. "The reality TV show? You know the one—with me parading around in my underwear, transforming myself in front of the nation using your wonder drug? Does that ring any bells?"

"To be honest, it doesn't," he said quietly. He couldn't wait to get his hands around Ed Cline's neck.

"C'mon. The brainchild of Alexis and Mr. Cline?"

"Really, Kate, I know nothing about this." He was lost. Something had clearly upset her and she had assumed he was behind it. He'd rectify it immediately.

She stared at him, incredulous, and then suddenly she looked embarrassed. She stood up quickly, almost knocking the chair over, and stammered what sounded like an apology. She headed for the door. Just as quickly, he was out of his own chair to head her off at the pass. He couldn't let her leave without getting to the bottom of it.

"Hold on—" he started.

She had managed to turn the doorknob and open the door slightly, when he came up behind her, reached quickly over her shoulder, his arm brushing past her hair and closed the door with the palm of his hand.

"Kate, don't run off like that," he entreated behind her. She was trembling and he wanted to touch her, to comfort her, but he balled up his hands into fists to fight off the urge.

"Come back, sit down, and start at the beginning," he said softly. "Tell me everything."

She sighed and turned around. Big, fat, hot tears formed and fell down her cheeks. She wiped them away quickly with the back of her hand.

The tears undid him and he placed his hands on her upper arms, transfixed. "It's all right," he murmured, rubbing her arms soothingly.

His face was inches from hers.

"They can fire me over this. I don't care. And if they try to force me to do it, I'll quit." She sobbed harder and before he realized what was happening, she had buried her face in his shoulder.

He put his hands on her hair and whispered, "Shh. Kate O'Connor, you don't have to do anything you don't want to do."

He led her back to the chair and she sat down. He went into the little half-bath off his office and emerged carrying a box of tissues, which he handed to her. Then he offered her the bowl of M&M's from his desk. She picked out a couple of red ones and popped them into her mouth. He sat down behind his desk and leaned forward, giving her his undivided attention. He could hardly wait to hear what Ed had put her up to.

"Now tell me," he instructed.

She relayed the story of the reality TV show and that eel, Nick Sommers, with his ideas of what she would be wearing on national TV. By the time she finished, she had stopped crying.

Gavin didn't say anything at first. He tapped his pen on the desk. Of all the low down, dirty tricks. Of all the gimmicks! He had given this agency the benefit of the doubt—a nagging doubt—but even he hadn't thought they would do something as underhanded as this. The girl was very upset and rightly so. And to make matters worse, she'd thought he had put his stamp of approval on it.

He made his voice as emotionless as possible. "First of all, I would never have gone along with such a charade." He paused to search her face for a reaction. She seemed to be registering what he was saying. "Second, I want to apologize for the distress this has caused you." He was trying to get his own emotions under control. "And lastly, I will personally put an end to it."

Her shoulders sagged and he watched the tension leave her body.

She stood up and nodded toward the bathroom. "May I use your..."

"Of course."

She emerged a few minutes later, dabbing at her eyes with a tissue.

"Are you all right?" he asked softly. He stood up and walked over to her.

She nodded.

"Can I get you a cup of tea?" he asked.

She shook her head.

Against his better judgement, he took her face in his hands and said softly, "Do you believe me when I tell you that I will take care of it? That you don't have to do anything you don't want to do?"

She nodded. Her skin was softer than he had imagined. It would have been so easy to close the gap and lean in and kiss her. But she was vulnerable right now and he wasn't one to take advantage.

"Kate, believe me when I say I had nothing to do with this. I knew nothing about it," he said. "I would never have gone for this."

She nodded.

He walked her to his door. "Would you like to stay in here for a while?"

She managed a weak laugh. "I'd like to stay in here for the rest of the week." He wondered fleetingly if he could manage that.

Something caught her eye. "Oh, your shirt! Look what I've done to it," she said, mortified. "I've ruined it!"

He laughed. "Don't worry about it. It's only a shirt."

"I'll wash it for you. I'll even hand-wash it." She was rambling. When he shook his head, she said, "At least let me pay for the dry-cleaning bill."

"Your eyes are...purple," he said, frowning.

"It happens when I cry," she said in a matter-of-fact tone.

"That is very interesting, and somehow, Kate, not the least bit surprising," he said, grinning. "I would expect nothing less from you."

"I'd better get back to work."

After she left, he sat back down at his desk and grabbed a handful of M&Ms, popping them into his mouth. He was so fed up. Tempted to walk out, pull everything. Take the Alchemis account with him. He had every right to do so. They had certainly breached some aspect of the contract. It wouldn't take long to read the fine print to be able to come up with something. It would probably cost him the presidency of the company, and the worst-case scenario was that he would lose his job. But that wasn't what kept him from walking out that door, never to return. The reason he remained was her. Kate.

If he left, he'd almost certainly never see her again. With her here and him in Ireland it was highly unlikely that their paths would ever cross. He wasn't ready to say goodbye to this girl, who was always closely followed by trouble, and who used wit as her weapon of choice. No, as much as he knew he should, he couldn't leave Cline & Co. just yet.

He needed to sort out this mess with Ed about the reality TV show. The thought of her being forced to expose herself against her will awakened something primitive in him. He wanted to protect her. Nobody was going to hurt Kate O'Connor while he was around.

CHAPTER FOURTEEN

Kate pulled herself together and made a beeline for the break room for a cup of strong coffee. She felt she had earned a bottle of whiskey but coffee was all there was, so it would have to do. Crying in Irish's office—it didn't even bear thinking about. She had truly lost her mind. She was brooding over this when raised voices drifted through the heating vent near the ceiling. They were coming from Mr. Cline's office next door. She leaned against the counter, sipping her coffee, listening.

"I can explain everything," said Mr. Cline nervously.

"You'd better start, Ed." It was Gavin. "You need to give me one good reason why I shouldn't pull this account from you."

Kate raised her eyebrows; Gavin sounded absolutely furious. It was good to hear the boss getting a tongue-lashing from someone. Anyone.

"Of all the low-down perverted tactics," Gavin yelled. "I don't know if I want Alchemis mixed up with a company that resorts to such tacky measures."

"Now Gavin, don't be hasty, it was a little mistake on Alexis' part," Mr. Cline said.

Kate snorted at how quickly he'd thrown Alexis under the bus.

"This nonsense about a reality television show ends now!" Gavin said angrily. "And then I want you to give me one good reason why I shouldn't pack my bags and my money and head back to Dublin." That ultimatum was followed by the slamming of Mr. Cline's office door.

It went quiet just as Paul walked into the break room. He was like a bad odor—he lingered. He stood next to Kate, holding out his empty mug. If he was waiting for her to pour, he had another thing coming. She set the coffeepot back on its stand.

"I was wondering if you'd like to go to the Christmas party with me," he said casually.

She shook her head.

"Are you seeing someone?" he asked.

She shook her head again. "No, Paul. I'm going alone."

"Then we might as well go together," he offered.

"I'd rather go alone," she said sharply.

"I've changed, Kate. I've learned my lesson. And I want you back. We were happy and I didn't realize it until I lost you."

"Paul, we've already had this conversation," she pointed out evenly. He was getting tiresome.

He sighed. "I need you." He paused. "You're like a comfy pair of old slippers that's welcoming and always there and so dependable."

"Well, that makes me want to run straight back into your arms!" Her laugh was brittle. "You're the creative director, Paul! That's the best line you could come up with? 'Like a comfy pair of old slippers?'"

"Kate, please," he implored.

"I'm not interested. Leave me alone." She just couldn't make him see that she had moved on. She began walking away, but he grabbed her by the wrist and pushed her up against the wall. She dropped her mug and it shattered, splashing hot coffee everywhere.

"We used to be so good together." He pressed his lips to hers, hard. She shoved him away, then hauled back and slapped him across the face. He looked stunned.

Angrily, she said, "You made that mess, so you can clean it up!" She stormed off and left him alone to deal with the coffee running down the wall and the broken pieces of her mug scattered across the floor.

Kate listened to a radio station that played non-stop Christmas music in the car on the way home. The snow was falling lightly. She tried to take her mind off of Paul and what he'd done that day. She hadn't seen him again for the rest of the day which was just as well, as she might have hurled a stapler at him. He was starting to get a little too pushy and presumptuous, thinking that now that he was free they were automatically going to pick up where they'd left off. Puh-leese! She realized that what she'd said to him was true—she'd rather be alone.

Vinnie emerged from an unknown car in front of his house just as Kate arrived home.

Her relief, which was palpable, was quickly replaced with concern when she saw his face. He looked awful. He still wore yesterday's clothes and they were badly rumpled. He had big, black circles under his eyes.

"Oh, Vinnie! Are you all right? I've been worried sick about you," she said, hugging him hard.

"Vinnie always takes care of Vinnie," he said, although his voice lacked conviction.

She followed close behind him as he climbed his front steps. She huddled up in her coat against the bitter cold as he fumbled for the keys in his pocket. Once he unlocked and opened the door, she followed him inside.

The house was, Kate suspected, just as his mother had left it. All the furniture was covered in plastic and there were plastic runners over the gold sculpted carpet. There were two armchairs with doilies resting on the backs and arms and there were knickknacks and figurines of all sorts of animals: bunnies, squirrels, and kittens. Snow White would have had a field day in here. But Vinnie had added his own touch—the co-mingled scents of bleach and pine-based disinfectant.

"Boy, your mother must have liked animals," Kate noted.

"She loved them. But her allergies were so severe she couldn't go near them. This was the closest she ever got to her beloved animals." He sounded almost maudlin. She seriously began to wonder about his state of mind.

They went into the kitchen where the late Mrs. Mann's decorating style continued. The cabinets were of a dark brown laminate with black wrought-iron handles. All the appliances were avocado green and the wallpaper was an explosion of oranges and green leaves on a background of bamboo. Kate found that if she stared at the wallpaper too long it made her dizzy.

"Have you eaten, Vinnie?" she asked. She was her mother's daughter, after all.

"Yeah, on the way home. We stopped for lunch," he said.

What alarmed her was that the 'Vinnie-ness' was missing from his eyes.

"Will I make some tea?" she asked softly.

"No, actually, I'll have a beer," he answered. He sat down at his kitchen table and stared at the wall.

Kate grabbed a cold one from his fridge and pulled back the tab. She set it down in front of him.

"Will you join me, babe?" he asked, sipping foam off the top of the can.

"As a matter of fact, I think I will." She took another can of beer out of the fridge and opened it up. She sat down across from him at the Formica-topped table.

"What's going to happen, Vin?" she asked gently.

He shrugged. "I dunno, babe. Might go to the big house for this one."

"Oh no," she said softly, reaching across the table to place her hand over his.

"Well, I was able to post bail finally, once they tallied up all the charges against me. My lawyer said I might get off easy, but I don't think it looks so good."

"Why do you say that?"

He sighed heavily. "I know that you have an impression of me as an upstanding sort of guy—" she forced herself to keep a straight face, given the situation he was in. "But I did time once."

"I know you did time," she said.

"You knew?" He looked up at her, a genuine look of surprise on his face. "And you still talked to me?"

"Of course, silly, you're my friend. Besides, everyone makes mistakes."

"Do you know what I hate about prison? More than anything?"

She waited.

"It's not very clean."

She gave him a blank stare and said, "I've got nothing."

"Is that why you won't go out with me? Because I'm a convicted felon?" he asked, changing the subject and taking another swig of his beer.

Kate laughed but she could see that his expression was very serious. She took a deep breath and placed her hand on his arm. "Vinnie, I care about you very much. You're my dear friend. But I don't have those types of feelings for you. Although sometimes I wish I did."

"You do?" he asked incredulously.

She nodded. "Yes. Because I know that you would be good to me. And God help me, things would never be dull."

He didn't say anything and she pressed on. "You deserve to be with someone who feels about you the same way that you feel about me. One hundred percent. If we were ever to get together, it wouldn't be fair to you. Don't settle."

"Can we at least try the bedroom thing out?"

She laughed, relieved to see shades of the old Vinnie returning.

"Now, is there anything I can do?" she asked.

"Nothing. Don't worry about it, babe, it'll sort itself out," he said with a faraway look in his eyes.

Kate stood up from the table and kissed him on his forehead. She put the empty beer can in the bin and went out through the front of the house, closing the door behind her, wondering what would become of him.

Lisa rang Kate the following morning at work.

"I spoke to my friend at the D.A.'s office," she said.

Kate heard her let out a big sigh and her heart sank. She sat up and paid close attention.

"They are charging him with criminal possession of stolen goods. It's a Class D felony and if convicted there is jail time," Lisa explained.

Kate gulped hard.

"The fact that he has a previous felony conviction does not bode well either," Lisa said.

"How strong is their case?"

Lisa sighed again and Kate's shoulders sagged.

"Well, they're going to look at all the circumstances relating to the case. They also have to prove that Vinnie knew the goods were stolen," Lisa explained.

"Can they prove that?" Kate asked, worriedly.

There was a moment's hesitation on Lisa's part. "Let me put it to you this way—if they didn't think they could prove it, they wouldn't have charged him."

Kate's stomach began to coil up.

"Look, Kate, don't worry about Vinnie. He may be an idiot, but somehow it seems to me that things tend to go his way."

There was a kernel of truth to that.

"Look, I have to go, I'll talk to you later," she said.

"Thanks, Lisa."

Debbie Cjaka approached Kate and Sherrie carrying a glass jar filled with strips of paper. The Christmas gift exchange was the last thing on Kate's mind. How could she even think of it when Vinnie might be going to prison to make license plates?

"Ladies, it's time to pick a name for the gift exchange," Debbie sang.

"Do I have to?" Kate whined.

Sherrie nudged her. "C'mon, be a sport." Sherrie drew a slip of paper from the jar.

"C'mon Kate. Pick one," Debbie said as she thrust the jar into her face. "Remember, the limit is fifty dollars."

Kate dipped her hand into the jar and pulled out a strip of paper. She read the name: Amy Mohr. Whew! That was an easy one. Amy was a voracious reader. A gift card from the bookstore should take care of it. She hoped and prayed that Mr. Cline wouldn't pick her name again this year.

Debbie took her jar and walked into Gavin's office.

After Debbie had left, Gavin buzzed Kate. "Can you ask Paul and Sherrie to come back here?"

She called them and they appeared within minutes. Paul didn't look too happy but she didn't particularly care. Gavin appeared in his doorway.

"Kate, do you have a minute to join us?" he asked her.

She smiled at him and stood up from her desk, aware that Paul was watching her. They all followed Gavin back into his office. He leaned against the front of his desk with his feet crossed at the ankles and the others gathered around.

"Sherrie, Paul, I called you back here to bring you up to speed on the campaign," he started. Paul raised his eyebrows. Gavin looked at Kate and smiled. "I've asked Kate here to have a go at some copywriting for the ads. She's come up with an idea that I think not only takes Alchemis in the direction I want it to go, but shows a lot of promise as well."

Sherrie grinned and reached over and squeezed Kate's hand. Paul was not smiling.

"Why was I not in the loop about this?" Paul demanded. "I am the Creative Director. I think it's up to me who writes copy for the campaign."

"Well, you're in the loop now," Gavin said evenly, not backing down. He then ignored Paul and said directly to

Sherrie, "Perhaps you and Kate can come up with some mock-ups for me in the meantime?"

They both nodded, delighted.

The following morning, the elevator door was just about to close and Kate yelled out, "Hold it, please." Suddenly it stopped, and she stepped in, all breathless, to see Gavin standing there. She'd felt bad about all the trouble she had caused him and decided that she should try to make it up to him. She hoped that she could redeem herself. She had put together a sampler of Christmas cookies for him. She had put them in a big round tin with a picture of a Christmas tree by a blazing hearth.

For a moment, neither of them said anything. They just stared straight ahead.

"These are for you." She handed him the tin.

"Me?" he asked, surprised, taking it from her.

"I wanted to apologize for barging into your office and giving you grief the other day," she explained.

He smiled. "Thank you, Kate. But to be honest, you're the only one in this office who doesn't give me grief."

They were both quiet again. Finally, she summoned up the courage and took a deep breath, ignoring her shakiness, and asked, "Um, do you have any plans for the weekend?"

"Just paperwork," he said, not looking at her.

"Are you up for another stop on the nickel tour?" she asked, trying to make light of her increasing anxiety.

"Pardon?"

She swallowed hard. "Would you like me to show you around tomorrow? Or Sunday if that's better for you? I could show you some more of the sights," she said. She hoped she didn't sound too eager. She felt foolish and embarrassed and stupid all at once.

"Look, Kate, I know that Ed forced you into this position and I appreciate your offer but it's not necessary."

She was surprised at her disappointment. "Really, I don't mind," she said quietly. It was true that Mr. Cline had initially forced her, but it hadn't turned out to be as bad as she thought it would be. Actually, she had enjoyed it. She liked being with Gavin.

The elevator door slid open and they stepped out.

"I won't impose on you anymore," he said as he walked beside her.

"What if I promise that there will be no more police or federal authorities involved?"

He laughed and opened the office door for her. Sherrie was right; he had impeccable manners. Kate liked it when he laughed. She wanted to see more of that.

"Well when you put it like that, I can hardly refuse."

When he smiled, she felt warm inside. She needed to keep herself in check and to prevent her thoughts from jumping on the runaway romance train.

"Will I pick you up at two?" she offered.

"I'll look forward to it." He smiled.

She was going to prove to him once and for all that she wasn't a honey trap for the law enforcement agencies.

Mr. Cline buzzed her right before she left Friday evening, summoning her to his office. Again. Kate wondered whether she should just move her desk back there, as it would save her the trips running back and forth. But then she would miss the eye candy that was Gavin Whyte.

She dragged her heels on the way, wondering all the time what kind of hare-brained idea he had cooked up now. By the time she neared his door she had decided that if he pushed her about this reality TV show one more time she would quit on the spot. She was formulating her resignation speech in her head when she tapped on his door.

Mr. Cline sat in his chair with his feet up on the desk.

"Listen, O'Connor, that idea we came up with—you with your own reality TV show, the diet drug, etcetera. The more I thought about it, the more I realized that it's not going to work. It's a direction that Cline and Company does not want to take at the moment."

Kate tried to show surprise and not give away the fact that she'd already heard Gavin giving him the verbal pistol-whipping he deserved. She had to admit to being disappointed at being robbed of the chance of telling him 'I quit.' *Geez, and I'd already made plans for the rest of the afternoon.* Gavin had kept his promise. He had taken care of it. She warmed inside.

"I know you're disappointed, kid," Mr. Cline said. "No hard feelings, I hope."

"None whatsoever," she replied. She turned to leave.

"One more thing, Kate," he said.

She turned back around to look at him, dreading what might come out of his mouth.

"It hasn't gone unnoticed around here what a team player you've been. Always helping everyone out," he started, tapping his pencil on his desk blotter.

She waited. She couldn't imagine what was coming next.

"Last year, when the company took a huge financial hit, you graciously agreed to give up your position and stay on as receptionist. That sacrifice on your part told me that you're an invaluable employee," he said.

Kate was speechless; Mr. Cline wasn't known for giving out compliments.

"We've all worked hard on this Alchemis account and again you stepped up to the plate and went above and beyond, taking Gavin Whyte around town on your days off. After the holidays are over, I would like you back on the copywriting team. There'll be a little pay raise—nothing big, as we're just getting back on our feet, but a token of my appreciation." Mr. Cline smiled. He almost looked...well, nice.

Kate smiled and said, "Thanks very much, Mr. Cline." She left his office perplexed. She should be elated but she wasn't. This is what she had been after since losing her copywriting position last year. So why wasn't she happy? She should be over the moon, but instead she felt hollow inside.

CHAPTER FIFTEEN

CHAPTER FIFTEEN

"So where are we going?" Gavin asked as he got into Kate's car the following afternoon.

He looked so much better than he had during the week. Fresh and rested. Kate told herself to stop mooning over him. He would be leaving in a few weeks and besides, he already had a girlfriend he missed and loved.

"Do you like to play sports?" she asked.

He shook his head. "I used to play sports a long time ago. Now I don't have the time."

"Well, we're going to play my favorite sport today," she said.

"Very well."

She headed out of the city and smiled to herself, secretly pleased. There would be no museums or art galleries today, nothing stuffy. It was going to be a relaxed day. The beauty of it was in its simplicity.

"Now, let's go bowling!" she said. She wouldn't tell him it was the only sport she played. How could you not love a sport where you got to sit down and drink alcohol?

Her father had been an avid bowler when she was growing up. He had played on a team every Monday night and had had a gold polyester bowling shirt with his name embroidered on it. She had that shirt now, hanging in her closet. He had taken her bowling every Saturday morning when she was a kid.

The bowling alley wasn't far from downtown. It was only a fifteen-minute ride. When they went inside, it all came back to her with its aromas of stale popcorn and smelly bowling shoes, with an underlying whiff of pine-scented disinfectant.

Gavin informed her that he had never bowled before and she responded, "Pay attention and learn at the knee of the master."

He laughed.

They each traded in their footwear for an ugly pair of bowling shoes and as Gavin laced his up, she had to shake her head. Never in a million years would she have guessed that she could be turned on by a man in bowling shoes, but somehow Gavin still managed to look sexy.

They picked out bowling balls and went to their assigned lane. She gave him a quick rundown of the scoring and he seemed to catch on. Overhead, a computer screen showed their frames. Kate told him that they couldn't even think of starting until they had their snacks. She made a quick run to the snack counter and came back with two bottles of beer, warmed-up pizza slices, and a couple of sweaty, rubbery hot dogs.

He was a little shaky to start but by the third frame, he'd nailed it and Kate realized that she had some serious competition on her hands. They ended up playing three games before calling it a day.

"That was fun," he said to her as they left the bowling alley. It was dark out. "I'm hungry."

"Yeah, me too," Kate said. "Get in the car."

"I love it when you give the orders," he said.

She hoped he wouldn't start flirting because the one beer had lowered her inhibitions and she couldn't be held responsible for her actions.

They went to a place noted for its beef on weck, a western New York specialty. The restaurant was an old house with the downstairs converted into a tavern. Walking through the door was like stepping into a time warp. It was wood-paneled with a big slate blackboard listing the menu. They sat at one of the many Formica-topped tables and ordered the famous roast beef sandwiches with mashed potatoes and gravy. Comfort food at its best.

Fortified, they carried on to the pub next door. Similar in style with its paneled walls, high tables, and barstools, it was separated from the restaurant by a loose gravel parking lot. They found two stools at the long bar and the bartender stopped wiping down the counter to take their drink orders. Christmas lights wound with silver garland twinkled across the bar. Somebody had put artificial frosted snow in the front window. Kate hadn't thought they made that stuff anymore. Once Christmas was over, they'd need a blowtorch to get it off. She headed for the jukebox in the corner, dumped a fiver into it, and selected some songs. She'd once come here a lot, way back when she'd had a life. It was a life she felt she was slowly reclaiming. She sat back down next to Gavin and they got into a friendly debate about the pros and cons of living in America and Ireland. Christmas music blared in the background.

"So," Gavin said. "What on earth are you doing working for Cline and Company?"

She giggled. "Tell me how you really feel."

He drank some of his beer, looked at her, and said softly, "Maybe someday, I will."

They were silent and she cursed the Christmas decorations and music for making her sappy.

"But seriously, Kate," he began again. "Surely, there's something better out there for you."

She laughed. "That's what I keep telling myself. But the truth of the matter is, since last year, jobs are very scarce on the ground."

He nodded. "It's the same all over. Ireland is awful, especially in the rural areas."

They were quiet for a minute, each lost in their own thoughts. "Don't settle, Kate. Get out of that place as soon you can."

"That's fair," she agreed. "But what about you?"

"Me? What do you mean?" he asked.

"You light up every time you talk about the farm in Tipperary," she said.

"I'm happy there," he said wistfully.

"Did you ever think of doing it full-time rather than what you're doing now?"

He looked at her like she had just grown a second head. He shifted on his barstool.

"No, really. Why not?" she pushed. "You could make a living, couldn't you?"

"Well, yes, of course, but I wouldn't make as much as I do now," he said. "I make an obscene amount of money at Alchemis."

"Does money make you happy?" she asked, signaling the bartender.

Gavin shook his head and drained his glass.

"Then what is it? What's holding you back?"

"I don't want to disappoint my parents," he said quietly. "They sacrificed a lot so I could get a good education and I'd hate to waste it."

"How long have you been working since you graduated from college?"

"A little more than fifteen years."

"Do you think your parents would want you to be happy?"

He laughed. "Of course!"

She went out on limb. She thought of her own mother and father. "I don't know anything about being a parent, but I do know about loving people, especially family. When you love someone, you want them to be happy. I bet if you went to your parents and told them you wanted to give up the high-powered job, move back to Tipperary, and join them on the farm, they'd be delighted."

He laughed again and she thought she saw a frisson of excitement crossing his face.

"Life is too short to be unhappy," she concluded.

He ran his fingers up and down his glass. He looked at her, smiled warmly, and leaned in, placing his hand on her arm. "Miss O'Connor, you are way too intelligent and way too good for the likes of Cline and Company."

She didn't say anything. His hand lingered for a moment, and she was sorry when he pulled it away.

It wasn't long before the place filled up and Kate was glad they had seats at the bar. After the fourth round, when she was feeling no pain, she thought she heard someone call out her name. Dismissing it, she sipped her beer, but then she felt a tap on her shoulder. She turned around and came face to face with Paul. Her smile quickly disappeared.

"What are you doing here?" he asked. He practically had to shout to be heard over the music and the noise of the crowd. His smiled vanished when he realized Gavin was sitting next to her.

"Just out and about," she answered vaguely.

Paul eyed up Gavin, who gave him a slight nod of acknowledgement.

The dislike between the two of them was palpable and Kate couldn't understand what had happened that there was so much tension between them. The atmosphere turned awkward and stilted.

"You said you weren't seeing anyone," Paul said, his hand around his beer bottle, jabbing his finger in the air at her.

"And I'm not," she said angrily. "Not that it's any of your business."

"Then what are you doing with him?" he asked, slurring his words and pointing rudely at Gavin. He was turning surly. She remembered how he used to be when they went out and he drank too much; she hadn't missed that. It dawned on her that she hadn't missed him so much as the *idea* of him. The idea of having someone to stumble through life with.

Gavin got up from his seat and stood face to face with Paul.

Kate had a bad feeling about this and sobered up quickly, realizing that she had to defuse the situation. "We're just out, that's all."

"Is this your idea of getting back at me? Sleeping with him? Rubbing my face in it?" Paul said angrily. "Boy, it doesn't take much for you to drop your panties."

Kate blinked. She felt as if she had been slapped. Before she could respond, Gavin's fist came out of nowhere and connected with Paul's face. He went reeling back into the crowd behind them. He quickly recovered and came back at Gavin, punching him on the cheek.

By now the other patrons had gotten involved. Any excuse to fight. The place was soon in an uproar. Gavin gave Paul a left hook and he went sailing across a table, clearing bottles and glasses from it. Somebody came at Gavin from behind and he landed on the floor on his back.

Mortified, Kate bent over and seized his hand, pulling him up and leading him out, grabbing her coat on the way. She pushed him outside and they stumbled down the steps, landing in the parking lot. In the distance, police sirens could be heard. She closed her eyes and groaned.

"We have to get out of here. The police are coming!" she said frantically.

He stood still, bent over with his hands on his thighs, trying to catch his breath. He burst out laughing. She stared at him. She couldn't see what was so funny. Finally, he said, "You promised there would be no police involved today."

"Well, I lied. Let's go," she said, trying to urge him on. The sirens were getting louder, wailing through the dark night. She didn't want to be dragged down to the police station again. She looked up at him and noticed that there was a cut along his cheekbone. "Oh my God—you're bleeding!" she cried. She dug through her purse for a tissue and dabbed gently at his cheek. He winced.

"Come on, we have to go," she said as a police car sped into the parking lot, sirens blaring, lights flashing, and gravel flying. She could still hear muted shouting and breaking glass from inside.

The officers jumped out of their squad car and headed toward them. Without thinking, Kate grabbed Gavin, pulled him into a tight embrace, and kissed him. Immediately, he responded, wrapping his arms around her and pulling her closer to him. His lips were soft and warm and quickly became more insistent. She got lost in his kiss. The two of them stood wrapped up in each other, illuminated by the lamppost overhead as the snow fell lightly around them.

"There's been a report of fighting," one of the officers called to them.

Kate tore herself away from Gavin, dizzy and breathless. "Do we look like we're fighting?" she responded.

A crash came from inside and the two police officers ran past them and into the pub.

She could not look at Gavin. She staggered to the car and it wasn't the booze that was making her legs weak. Once inside, she sank down into the seat and rang for a cab.

While they waited, Gavin finally spoke. "Boy, he's a piece of work!"

Her laugh was brittle. "Tell me about it." And she left it at that.

She saw the taxi pull into the parking lot and relief flooded her.

"You deserve better than him," Gavin observed. "I hope you know that."

She allowed him to get out of the car first and fell in behind him as they walked toward the cab. She didn't want him to see the tears in her eyes, or her fingers touching her lips where he had kissed her.

CHAPTER SIXTEEN

On Sunday morning, Kate dragged herself out of bed with the mother of all hangovers and tried, unsuccessfully, to shove all memories of the previous night out of her mind. Except, of course, for the kiss. It tormented her because she wanted more like it, and she knew she couldn't have them.

She spent the morning on her sofa, staring at the Christmas tree. Presents wrapped in shiny paper with big bows were strewn underneath it. The house was quiet in an awful way, as if suspended and waiting for something to happen. The bright winter day filtered through the sheer panels at the window, bathing the room in a pale blue light.

At noon, she padded into the bathroom and stepped into the shower, getting ready for dinner at her mother's that afternoon.

Her mother had suggested casually that they might have a small pre-Christmas dinner at her house with Hank and her best friend, Gladys. Kate regretted agreeing to it, wishing instead that she could just stay holed up at home with a hot cocoa and marathon Christmas movies. She really felt like she needed a pajama day.

But she couldn't let her mother down. And she had to face the fact that her mother was rebuilding her life without her father. It had taken her a good number of years, but she was doing it. She was moving on with her life.

Kate went through the motions of hair, make-up and clothes, forcing herself to wear color but secretly wishing for the safe haven of navy and black. She forced herself to perk up. She wasn't going to drag anybody down with a sour puss.

She arrived at her mother's house with a platter of homemade Christmas cookies, and couldn't help but get into the swing of things. The Ray Conniff singers sang Christmas harmonies from the CD player, the artificial white Christmas tree was ablaze in red lights and ornaments, and something smelled good coming from the kitchen.

"No curry tonight, Kate." Hank winked at her, taking her coat.

Kate laughed. As hard as she tried, she couldn't find any fault with him. He was nice and seemed genuinely fond of her mother. Gladys, her mother's single friend, seemed to approve of him, too, and that said a lot, as she disapproved of most members of the male species.

There was a standing rib roast and twice-baked potatoes for dinner, followed by Christmas cake. Kate got caught up in the bonhomie and began to cheer up. The refills on the vodka-and-tonics helped as well.

Hank and Gladys insisted on doing the cleanup after dinner and that left Kate alone with her mother. She poured an after-dinner Baileys for each of them and they parked themselves on the sofa in the living room. They listened to the amiable chatter that floated in from the kitchen, the tap running, and the occasional, "Where do you think this goes?"

"Kate, are you all right?" her mother asked, her face full of concern.

Kate would have loved to unload everything onto her mother: the dead-end job, another Christmas alone, Paul, and most of all, her growing feelings for Gavin. Her list was endless and she wanted her mother to take it all on so she could just have a moment's peace. But the sound of Hank's voice in the kitchen convinced Kate that she would not dump her troubles on her mother. This was her first Christmas with Hank, and Kate was determined not to rain on her parade.

"I'm fine, Mom, just out a little too late last night," she said. *And starting to fall hopelessly in love with a hot Irishman.*

"Are you sure?" her mother pressed.

Kate nodded quickly. She changed the subject. "Hank is really nice."

Her mother took a sip of her drink. "Kate, you have no idea what it's like to lose your spouse." She looked quickly at her daughter. "I'm not talking about what Paul did to you. What he did was appalling and that's a different kind of pain. What I'm talking about is spending your whole life with one person, and then it's over."

Kate waited, swirling the Baileys around in her cordial glass.

"You wake up one day and not only do you realize that a major part of your life is over, but the best and happiest part of it is gone, as well."

Kate downed the last of her liqueur.

"When Hank first asked me out, I said no. In fact, I said no for months."

Kate smiled. Her mother had played hard to get. She really needed to get a hold of that playbook.

"Do you know why I said no, Kate?" she asked. She didn't wait for an answer. "I said no because I was afraid. I will admit that at first, it was very uncomfortable for me to be going out with someone other than your father. But then I realized that I still had a lot of living to do."

She picked up the bottle of Baileys and refilled their glasses.

"I'm in no hurry to get married again, but it is nice to have a companion." She sipped from her glass. "But that doesn't mean that I don't miss your father. Because I do. And it doesn't mean that I've stopped loving him. Because I haven't."

Kate smiled at her, happy for her. Now if she could just sort out her own life.

Mrs. O'Connor winked at her and slapped Kate on her knee. "C'mon, let's go see what they're getting up to."

On Monday, embarrassed, Kate avoided Gavin and spent most of the day hiding out in the break room or the restroom. She noticed his cheek was bruised and slightly swollen and Paul was sporting a black eye.

There would be no more sightseeing, she decided. The Christmas party was Wednesday night and Christmas was Friday. She just had to hang on until then. And he was flying back to Ireland for Christmas. She had no idea when he'd be back. And then things would wrap up for the Alchemis campaign and she would never see him again. And somehow, she would have to manage to get on with her life.

The awkward silences were beginning to take their toll. Neither Kate nor Gavin mentioned the Saturday-night kiss, or anything else, for that matter.

Gavin emerged from his office Monday afternoon, carrying his laptop and wearing his coat.

"I'm off, Kate," he said, hesitating. He looked as if he wanted to say something.

She looked up at him, expectant. "I'll see you in the morning, then."

"No, I'm actually flying out to Ireland this afternoon," he said.

"Oh." It was all she could manage. She felt hollow inside, but she made a stab at humor. "It's a shame—you'll miss the Christmas party."

He gave her a small smile. "Yes, it is a sacrifice."

There was a long silence between them and Kate didn't know what to say, but she knew she didn't want him to leave. She couldn't confess that she had a crush on him. No, that wouldn't do. Silence was the only answer.

"I really do have to get back home. I need to be there for Christmas."

She nodded knowingly, thinking about the girlfriend that waited for him. She pictured a Kate Moss lookalike with fabulous dress sense and a pout, to boot.

He turned to walk away.

"Wait a minute," she said, standing up and coming out from behind her desk. She faced him and twisted her hands in front of her. "I am really sorry about all the trouble the other night."

He laughed. "What is that all about with you? It's like you have your own police detail and they follow you wherever you go."

She winced. "It does seem that way."

"Despite all of that, I did enjoy myself," he said quietly.

She wanted to reach out and touch his face. To kiss him just one more time. To feel his lips on hers and to be in his arms again. She blinked, staving off the tears, and silently scolded herself for being so foolish. It was all those romances she read. No good was going to come of it.

"Well, Miss O'Connor, have a happy Christmas," he said.

"You too," she said. "When will you be back?"

"Sometime after the New Year. I don't have a definite return date yet."

"Okay."

"Please give my best to your mother," he said.

"I will."

"You have my number if you need me."

She wondered if that included her need to hear his voice, that delicious accent of his. Probably not. He probably wouldn't be too keen on a call in the middle of the night.

"Well, I better get going to the airport—the snow is coming down pretty heavy," he said.

"Really?" She had no windows anywhere near her desk.

"It looks like you'll have a white Christmas after all," he said, and nodded toward his office. "Take a look for yourself."

He stood there for a moment looking at her, and she wished she was courageous enough to say or do something that would let him know how she felt. She wished she could live on the edge a little. She wanted to be brave, but she wasn't. She swallowed hard and smiled at him, then turned away.

"I better go," he said and his voice trailed off.

She watched him walk out the door, sorry to see him go and sorrier that she didn't have the courage to say the things she wanted to say.

After he departed, Kate went straight to his office to take a peek out the window. The snow was indeed falling in the form of fat, heavy snowflakes. The wind had picked up and the sky had turned almost black. She looked at the clock: it was almost two. She wondered if it would let up or get worse by quitting time. Tonight was going to be a great night for a mug of cocoa and a Christmas movie. She was going to need the distraction; she didn't want to think about missing Gavin Whyte.

By four o'clock, Kate couldn't see out the window. It was a complete blanket of white. By now, various employees were walking back and forth to the conference room to keep an eye on the worsening situation.

"They've closed the Skyway and Route 5," Ben Davidson said to her as they passed in the corridor.

Oh great, that was her route home. She'd have to take the alternate route, which was all side streets and would take forever.

At five o'clock, everyone hurried out the office.

She stepped from the lobby into the middle of a blizzard. She could not see across the street. The sky was very dark and the wind whipped the heavy snow around. The traffic was bumper to bumper. Looking up and down the street, she could see only the indistinct red blur of taillights. It was gridlock; most of the cars appeared to be at a standstill.

She considered the mile-long walk to her car. And for what? To sit in traffic? Sighing heavily, she resigned herself to the situation and turned around and walked back into the building.

She took the elevator back up to the sixth floor. Outside the door of the office of Cline & Co., she fished around the bottom of her purse for the keys. She unlocked the doors, turned off the alarm, and flipped on the light switches.

She removed her coat and hung it on the back of her chair. She'd go back down and assess the situation in an hour. Maybe then she would be able to get home. In the meantime, she settled down at her desk and after rooting around in the bottom drawer of her desk found some Sudoku puzzles and started working on them.

An hour later, she rode the elevator back down to the lobby and stepped outside, hoping against hope for some improvement. But in fact it was much worse. Abandoned cars littered the street. The heavy snow continued to fall quickly and the wind blew in fiercely from the lake. She turned around and headed back inside, her heart sinking.

Security had changed shifts and an unfamiliar guard sat at the desk. As she approached, heading to the bank of elevators, the young man said to her, "Not a good night out there."

"It certainly is not," she agreed.

"It's supposed to be like this until after midnight," he volunteered.

"Oh terrific," she grumbled.

Kate hit the button for the elevator and the door immediately opened for her.

Back in the office, she made a few phone calls from her desk. She spoke to her mother, relieved that she was at home. Hank was with her. *At least she's not alone*, Kate thought grudgingly. She called Lisa. Nate had gotten her home and was cooking her dinner. Kate didn't keep her long. She wished someone had gotten her home. Everybody else seemed to have made it home but her.

Dread filled her at the thought of spending the night alone in the office. During the day, it was just a plain old office. But at night, all quiet, it was creepy. She turned on the lights on her desktop Christmas tree, hoping it would cheer her up. Boy, how she wished she were home. Tomorrow would be a snow day. She wondered if the Christmas party would be cancelled. She hated to get her hopes up. It was still two days away and if the storm didn't last too long the city would be cleaned up in no time.

Bored with the Sudoku puzzles, she found a women's magazine lying around and began to read the recipes inside, trying to decide if any interested her. At about seven, she went to the restroom and from there she headed to the break room and searched for something to eat. She found one stale glazed donut in the box on the table but decided against it. In the fridge she found creamer and a bottle of water. She grabbed the water. It would do. She headed back to her desk. Settling back down, she flipped the magazine back open.

It was then she heard movement behind her and gave a little shriek when she turned around to see Gavin coming out of his office.

"You scared me!" She let out a short burst of laughter and held her hand over her heart. "Where did you come from?"

"I'm sorry, I didn't know if anyone was still here. The door was open."

"I was in the break room. What are you doing here, anyway? I thought you were going to Dublin." Secretly, she was happy to see him.

"They closed the airport right before my flight was to take off, so I cabbed it back to the city," he said. He had his suit jacket off. Five o'clock shadow looked good on him.

"Did it take long?"

"Almost two hours. It was bumper to bumper heading out of the city and no one was moving. There were a lot of stranded vehicles," he said.

The airport would normally be only a twenty-minute ride to or from downtown. With no traffic and a heavy foot, you could do it in fifteen. But two hours to get back? Oh crap. She wondered what she could use in the office to make a bed for herself for the night.

"Is this your first blizzard?" she asked.

"Yes, it is," he said. The cut on his cheek was beginning to heal but he had dark circles under his eyes. She'd have loved to take him home and comfort him.

"Welcome to western New York."

"I thought I'd come back to the office and get a little work done," he said.

"You are devoted," Kate said. "I'm just hanging out until the storm dies down."

"You're not going home?" he asked.

"No, I don't want to chance it. I'll stay here until things clear up." She was glad he was here. She thought he seemed a little distant. She couldn't really blame him. After all, he always seemed to get hurt or nearly arrested when she was around. He needed her like he needed a rash on his face.

He disappeared into his office.

Gavin sat at his desk in front of his laptop, with several file folders open beside him. He was in no hurry to get started, though, and picked up the phone. He dialed his parents' house. His father answered.

"Hi, Dad."

"Gavin! Are you at the airport?"

"That's why I'm calling. I'm stranded in Buffalo. Blizzard."

"Oh no," his father said. "Do you know when you'll be able to get out?"

"That's anyone's guess. But I'll keep you posted."

"But you'll be home for Christmas, Son, won't you?"

Gavin couldn't imagine not spending Christmas with his family. "If I have to walk, Dad. Hey, how's Mom?"

"Hold on, let me put her on." Gavin could hear his parents talking in the background.

His mother came on the line. "Gavin, I hear you're stuck there."

"Hopefully not for long," he said, trying to allay her fears. "Any word yet on the biopsy?"

"Yes, it was negative," his mother said. He didn't miss the relief in her voice. He himself felt unburdened. "So that is my Christmas present for this year."

"Mine, too." he smiled. He promised to call them as soon as he knew anything, and hung up. His mood had elevated considerably with his mother's good news. He had thought a lot about what Kate had said to him. This lifestyle wasn't for him. He'd had a good long think in the back of the cab to and from the airport and he had come to the conclusion that he really didn't want to market this drug for Alchemis anymore. In fact, he no longer wanted to work for Alchemis. He was almost forty and it was time for a career change. Climbing the corporate ladder didn't seem as important as it once had. He realized that he just wanted to be back in County Tipperary, working the land. He had a lot of ideas for the farm. And he had Kate O'Connor to thank for that epiphany. It was as if his world had been in black and white and this girl had come along and made it explode into blazing color.

He had been delighted to see her there in the office. Things had been awkward between them since she had kissed him in the parking lot. He had thought he was at an age where he couldn't be surprised anymore, but she had surprised him. And then she had excited him. It was all he had thought about the rest of the weekend, but when he had arrived back at work Monday morning, she had seemed distant and aloof. He'd wondered if perhaps she had regretted it. So he'd stood back.

All he wanted was to be alone with her. And now he was. He put the paperwork away and stood up from his desk.

"You're still here, Kate," Gavin said, more as a statement of fact than a question.

"There's no change outside and now they have a driving ban in effect. No driving allowed until further notice," she said miserably.

She noticed he had his coat on—she envied him. His hotel was only four blocks away, so he'd be able to walk. It wouldn't be pleasant, but it would be doable.

"Look, I'm heading back to my hotel. Why don't you come with me and we'll get you a room? It would be better than staying here overnight," he offered.

Kate thought about it for a moment and had to admit that there was a lot of appeal to his idea. The hotel was a little more expensive than she would have liked, but the thought of a nice luxury room, a hot bath, and room service during a bona fide blizzard excited her. And she did have her credit card on her. After all, it was an emergency.

She bundled up in her winter coat, gloves, and scarf. "I think that's a great idea."

The boots she wore were not ideal for the four-block trek to the hotel. For one thing, they had no traction in the greasy, new-fallen snow, and although they looked great, they were not waterproof. At the end of the first block she had to grab onto Gavin's arm for stability. The snow whipped against her face and snowflakes clung to her hair, scarf, and coat.

The warmth that enveloped them when they stepped inside the hotel lobby was almost intoxicating. They stamped their feet to remove the packed snow from the bottom of their shoes. Kate felt her nose threatening to drip and she pulled a tissue from her coat pocket to wipe it. The tips of her fingers were red and numb. Her legs and feet were damp with snow and cold. There were quite a few people settled on the sofas and wingback chairs in the carpeted lobby. Coffee tables were laden with coffee pots, cups, and sugar and creamer.

They approached the reception desk together.

"Good evening, Mr. Whyte. Terrible weather," the young male clerk said. He wore a serious expression and a navy blazer with his name, 'David,' in black on a gold badge.

They made small talk for a few moments and Gavin said, "This lady needs a room for the night. She won't be able to make it home."

The clerk scrunched up his face. "Oh I'm sorry, we're all booked up. With the storm, a lot of people decided to remain downtown."

Kate piped in, disappointed as she saw her dream of a hot bath and room service blown to smithereens. "I'm not fussy. Anything at all—the broom closet will do."

The clerk threw her a sympathetic smile.

"What about the hotel across the street?" Gavin asked.

"They're booked as well. We started referring people over to them as soon as we were full. They called half an hour ago and asked us to stop sending people over as they have no more vacancies."

Kate didn't know what to do. The thought of walking back to the office in this weather was disheartening. She really didn't want to spend the night in the office all alone. But then she might have no choice in the matter. If there were no rooms, there were no rooms. It was as simple as that.

"Okay, thanks," Gavin said, and they stepped away from the desk to let the couple behind them in line attend to their business.

Kate wrapped her scarf around her neck again, gearing up for the trek back to the office. She shook the wet off her gloves.

"What are you doing?" he asked.

"Well, there are no rooms here, so I'll head back to the office and hang out."

"Kate, don't be ridiculous. It's too dangerous out there," he said. He sounded concerned. About her. And that sounded real sexy. "C'mon, let's go to the bar. I'm starving. How about you? We could have some dinner. The food is good."

How could she refuse a hot plate of food, especially when the alternative was a four-block walk in blinding snow?

"Okay," she said. She smiled at him, unraveling her scarf once again.

The hotel boasted a formal dining room done up in pale blue and gold damask and cream table linens. They bypassed this for the in-house bar, which reminded her more of a pub or even a library. It was mostly dark with only minimal lighting. The room was heavily paneled, with a green-and-burgundy mosaic-tile floor around the bar itself. The remainder of the room was furnished with a burgundy floral carpet, booths with wood-paneled backs, and low upholstered stools. A couple stood up from their booth to leave, and Kate and Gavin grabbed it, settling down promptly and with great relief. A special edition of the local news played on the big-screen TV, covering the storm. People stood two to three deep at the bar, their faces bathed in the blue light from the television and their glasses sweating in their hands.

The waitress handed them menus and took their drink orders. They removed their coats and Kate watched as Gavin lifted his chin to get at his tie and loosen it, just as he had in her kitchen the night of the purse party. She practically shuddered at the sight—she found the gesture so appealing. She wanted to slide under the table. She shook her head, thinking that she really had to get a hobby.

The waitress came back with beers for them both.

They scanned the menus. Kate realized that she was starving. Gavin ordered a plate of chicken wings to start as well as a bacon cheeseburger. She decided on a burger and fries.

His wings were brought out first. He leaned back against the booth as the waitress set the plate of wings in front of him. The hot sauce wafted off the wings and made Kate's nose tingle.

"Do you know that I am addicted to these things?"

Kate smiled, thinking that so was everyone else in western New York.

"Help yourself," he said, indicating the wings.

She picked one up, dipped it lightly in the blue cheese dressing, and tried to be as ladylike as she could with this finger food, which was just about impossible. She loved chicken wings, but they were messy. She thought it best that she just to stick to one. She noticed that he apparently had no problems with hygiene and seemed to be enjoying them.

They ordered another round of drinks before their dinners were brought out. By the end of dinner and the end of her third drink, Kate was feeling much looser and she knew if she stayed any longer or drank any more she'd do something foolish—like confess her feelings for him.

Finished and with no excuse to stay, she stood up from the table.

"I really have to go," she said, fumbling around for her things. She had to get out of there, blizzard or no blizzard. *C'mon*, she thought. *I'm a western New Yorker for Pete's sake—I could shovel my way out with my bare hands if I had to.*

He stood up and caught her wrist. "Don't leave, Kate."

She thought she saw warmth and kindness in his eyes, but that could just have been a reflection of the ambient lighting in the bar.

Against her better judgement, she stayed. He ordered another round of drinks.

"Do you think you'll be able to get out tomorrow?" she asked.

"I hope so," he said. "I was trying to get a lot done before Christmas as I'd hoped to take some time off and go down to Tipperary for a while."

She smiled. "Of course. I'm sure your parents will be happy to see you."

"I've decided to take your advice," he said, taking a sip from his drink.

Kate startled and choked on her own drink. "My advice?" She was lost. She was hardly in any position to be giving him advice, or anyone else for that matter.

He continued. "You were right. I love the farm. Being outdoors. When I return to Ireland, I'm handing in my resignation."

"No way!" she said, but something went flat inside her with the realization that she would never see him again.

She wanted to cry. She finished the rest of her drink in one gulp.

He nodded and smiled. "It's true. The corporate world has burned me out after fifteen years and 'life is too short to be unhappy,'" he said, echoing her words.

"Are you unhappy?" she asked tentatively, wanting to kick herself in the pants for not keeping her big mouth shut.

"I think I was, but I didn't realize it until very recently," he said. "But I don't intend to be for much longer. I can't thank you enough for pointing out the obvious."

Yeah, that's me, she thought. Sadness flooded her, making her tired.

The waitress set the bill, enclosed in a leather folder, on the table. Gavin picked it up. Kate dug in her purse for her wallet.

"Kate, put your money away. Dinner is on me," he said.

"Oh no," she protested. "I can't let you pay for dinner. In fact, due to all the trouble I've caused you, I should really buy you dinner." She actually felt she should buy his dinners for the rest of his natural life.

He laughed. "Absolutely not."

"Oh please—" she started.

"No, really, Kate, I would be offended if you didn't let me treat you," he said. She remembered how her father had always told her to think more of a man who got offended if you offered to pay.

"Well, I wouldn't want that." She laughed nervously. "All right then," she added graciously. "Thank you very much for dinner. I enjoyed it."

"My pleasure." He smiled and reached into his pocket for his wallet. "Besides, I have had a lot of laughs with you."

Not to mention run-ins with law enforcement agencies, she thought, but said nothing.

With the bill paid, they stood up from the table and picked up their coats. Her legs felt a little shaky, but her belly was comfortably full, so all in all she was good.

She followed him over to the bar, where they ordered another round of drinks.

"Look, Kate, I don't want to offend you, but you could stay in my room tonight," he said easily, glancing away. "I have a sofa that I could sleep on."

Kate's face reddened at his invitation and all the possible things it implied.

CHAPTER SEVENTEEN

"You can see much better if you turn out the light," Kate suggested. She flipped off the light switch on the wall near the door. The room was instantly bathed in a grey glow from outside. Gavin appeared as a silhouette at the window. She walked to the window and stood at his side, deciding that she really had to practice the art of thinking before speaking. Here she was in a hotel room with an incredibly gorgeous man, with the lights out at her insistence. She felt vulnerable. He said nothing; he was still.

She pulled back the sheer curtain panel and they looked out the window. The snow, thick and heavy, swirled madly in the light cast by the street lamps. Kate pressed her hand to the window, feeling the cold. The glass pane muted the howl of the wind outside. Cars were littered in a haphazard fashion all over Delaware Avenue. The snow had begun to pile up heavily on them, leaving only their bulky outlines as identifying factors. There was no traffic. There wasn't a soul to be seen. A few seconds passed before they saw a lone police cruiser cross one of the side streets, its flashing red light blurred in the falling snow.

They stood there for a long time. Neither of them said a word.

She leaned forward, her forehead pressing against the window. She tucked her hair behind her ear, thinking how she should turn the lights on. Gavin stood next to her, his shoulder almost brushing against hers. Her heart thumped wildly. She closed her eyes.

"Kate..." he said softly, his voice trailing off. With his accent, he made her name sound almost lyrical.

She looked at him, seeing an intensity in his eyes that even the darkness of the room could not mask.

"Come here, love," he whispered.

And with those three words, she was his.

He reached for her and in one movement that was both fluid and natural, she was in his arms. He cradled her face and his lips came down on hers, warm and insistent. They kissed for what could have been hours or minutes. His hand cupped the side of her neck and his thumb grazed the skin underneath her chin.

He pulled away and whispered, "I have wanted to kiss you for a very long time."

In his eyes, she saw unabashed desire. She put her arms around him and pulled him back to her. He began to pull his jacket off. With his jacket half off, he looked at her and hesitated. Then he pulled his jacket back on. Kate frowned at him.

"All right, Kate," he said, without looking at her. "I'm going to insist you sleep in the bed and I'll sleep out here on the sofa."

Kate looked around the room, her gaze bouncing off everything: the suite, the bedroom off of this room, the big television. Anything, so she wouldn't have to look at him. Wordlessly, she followed him to the bedroom. There was a king-sized bed in the middle of it. She swallowed hard.

"There's a bathroom right off there and I'll be out here if you need anything," Gavin said. He pulled the door shut behind him.

Kate didn't move for a few minutes, trying to figure out what had just happened. Or more specifically, what hadn't happened. She bit her lip. She had enjoyed the kissing and had thought he must have as well. But he ended it abruptly.

And Kate knew why.

The girlfriend back home. And she had to admit that she did admire that about him. He could have easily cheated on her and with her being in another country, she'd be none the wiser.

But she wondered what did it say about her that she hadn't pulled away?

Something woke Kate in the darkness. Looking for her bedside alarm clock and not finding it, she was momentarily confused. Then it dawned on her that she was in a bed. In Gavin's hotel room.

How will I face him in broad daylight? What will I say to him? And how will he feel when he wakes up in the morning and finds me in his bed?

Unable to go back to sleep, she watched as the light streamed from a gap in the drapes at the window gradually brightened and the room went from black to grey.

As quietly as she could, she slipped out from beneath the blankets and straightened them out as best as she could. Hurriedly, she dressed, her main aim to exit his room. She opened the door slowly. The outer room was bathed in semi-darkness. A light snore came from the direction of the sofa. Kate tip-toed over to the back of the sofa and peered over. She sighed at the sight of him. He looked at ease and his chest rose and fell in a rhythm. His blanket had slipped down. With a smile, Kate reached over and gently pulled up the blanket so that it covered his shoulders.

Without looking back, she slipped out of his hotel room, closing the door gently behind her.

Kate stepped out onto Delaware Avenue into the aftermath of the storm. Everything was calm. It felt like a major holiday with the lack of traffic and pedestrians. She was alone on the street. The new-fallen snow glittered in the bright morning sunshine. The sky was blue and cloudless. Trucks from the National Guard swept by her, their trailers loaded with mounds of snow. Some people had returned to their cars and were in the process of digging them out with shovels, snowbrushes and brooms. Other cars were being towed away to prepare for the snowplows, which had begun to make some headway in clearing the roads.

She walked in the direction of her car, parked about a mile away in a parking garage. The fresh-packed snow crunched beneath her feet as she walked. Her boots were still damp from last night, and still unsuitable.

She took her time. The office would be closed today. By the looks of traffic, or the lack of it, it appeared there was still a driving ban. The sun warmed her face and she felt a lump form in her throat.

Last night had been a close call. And despite the fact that he had chosen to remain faithful to his girlfriend—which was admirable, Kate couldn't help but feel rejected. Did she really believe someone like him would choose someone like her? And how would it affect their work relationship? Would things be awkward? Most likely. Would this lose the account for Cline & Co.? Not that she really cared any more—her loyalty to the company had plummeted in recent weeks. And after everything that had happened with Paul and knowing how it felt when the man you loved cheated on you, how could she possibly almost become the other woman? Had she learned nothing?

She reached the ramp and retrieved her car. She had a permanent parking pass that allowed her in and out without the need of an attendant. She nosed her car slowly out of the ramp, waiting for a snowplow to pass and then falling in line behind it.

She headed south on Delaware to the McKinley monument at the circle, yielded, then traveled partway around the circle and turned off onto Court Street on the City Hall side. She cut over to lower Elmwood and proceeded to the Skyway that would take her out of the city and away from Gavin Whyte.

A police cruiser with its lights flashing blocked the entrance to the Skyway, indicating it was still closed. It was an elevated highway and it would be nasty up there with blowing snow. She cut over to lower Terrace, swung around to where the old Aud once stood, where her father had taken her to hockey games as a girl before the new arena was built, and headed along South Park Avenue toward home.

Gavin woke and yawned. He sat up on the sofa and looked around the suite.

"Kate?" he called out. Noticing the door to the bedroom was ajar, he stood up, stretched and walked over to the bedroom. He knocked gently on the door and said, "Kate?" When there was no answer, he pushed open the door slowly and saw the made bed.

He sighed. Why had she left? And what he was going to do about the fact that he was returning to Ireland, resigning from his job, and potentially seeing her no more? He groaned out loud.

Once he opened the drapes, he looked down to the street below, squinting against the bright morning sun. The plows were out, clearing the streets, but cars were still buried under snow and it was relatively quiet. There'd be no going into the office today. He padded to the bathroom to shower and dress.

After breakfast, he pulled out his briefcase and booted up his laptop to get to work, his default mode. After ten minutes of being unable to concentrate, he gave up. His heart just wasn't in it. He had already mentally quit the job—he no longer cared about Alchemis, Cline & Co., or any diet drug. His thoughts were solely preoccupied with Kate O'Connor. Last night would have led to something more if he had not stopped it. It had taken a Herculean effort on his part to stop kissing her. Going forward, he was going to do things right by her. He leaned back against the sofa. He'd rescheduled his flight for Wednesday. The Cline & Co. Christmas party was Wednesday night.

He was making big changes in his life, and he wanted Kate O'Connor to be one of them. He wasn't going to look back on his life and say about her that she was the one who got away. He had to tell her how he felt before he left.

He pulled out his phone and called the airline.

A ride that normally took half an hour took two.

By the time Kate arrived home, she was stiff, tired, and hungry.

She jumped in the shower and turned the handle over to red, needing the water as hot as she could stand it. Standing under the hot spray, she closed her eyes and tried not to think about how her life had taken a complete turn in the last twelve hours.

She was glad she'd left before he had woken up. She was terrified that once the morning dawned, there would be an awkwardness between them. And that would have crushed her.

Reinvigorated after the shower, she threw on her flannel pajamas, made herself a cup of cocoa, and turned up the heat. She plopped down on the sofa and watched the local news at noon, and of course most of the broadcast was dedicated to the snowstorm. The snow had fallen at a rate of four to five inches an hour starting at midday yesterday, paralyzing the city, if only for a little while. They hoped to lift the driving ban by evening and the plan was for the airport to be opened by morning.

Gavin would be gone and she would never see him again.

She sat on the sofa, hugged her knees, and thought about Gavin. She tried pushing him out of her mind, but she couldn't. Tears streamed down her face.

Perhaps it was just as well that he'd be getting on a plane back to Ireland. There would soon be a whole ocean between her, him, and what had almost happened last night.

She took a good look at herself and realized that she was in a rut. She'd finally got her copywriting job back, and now she didn't think she wanted it. Well, at least not at Cline & Co. She needed a change of scenery. As much as she hated change, she knew it was time to move on. She could take some time over the holidays to think about what she would do next. She had some savings she could live off of for a while if it came to that. She spent the next few hours crafting her resignation letter.

Later that afternoon, she threw on a track suit and trudged through the calf-deep snow on the sidewalk over to Vinnie's house, determined to stop thinking about Gavin Whyte.

She climbed up the porch steps, covered in drifts of snow. She knocked on the door and when there was no answer, she rang the bell. A gust of wind picked up some loose snow and it swirled around her feet. Except for the low howl of the wind, all was silent. After a few minutes, she peered in the front window but there was no sign of Vinnie. She hoped he was all right.

She headed back home, the sun still bright, and got comfortable on her couch, settling in for some marathon television.

Kate was flustered when she saw Mr. Cline's name come up on her cell phone. What was he doing calling her at home? She muted the television.

"Hello," she asked tentatively.

"Kate? It's Ed Cline," he said.

"Yes?"

"The boiler has broken down and there is no heat in the building," he explained. "Please call all the employees and let them know the office will be closed tomorrow."

She wished for tap shoes to do a happy dance.

"What about the Christmas party?" she asked, crossing her fingers.

"What about it?" he asked irritably. "That's still going on. I expect to see you there tomorrow night." Before she could respond, he hung up.

She was not going to ring all the employees at Cline & Co. so she just wrote a text and sent it in a group message to her co-workers.

CHAPTER EIGHTEEN

Kate met up with Lisa later that evening for dinner. The driving ban had finally been lifted.

They went to a steak house where there were black leather booths with white linen tablecloths and the walls were painted a dark red.

As soon as the wine was poured into their glasses, Kate was tempted to tell Lisa what had almost happened last night. But the more she thought about it, the more she decided to keep that to herself. She didn't want to share it with anyone.

"I'm quitting my job," Kate announced.

Lisa had just put her wine glass to her scarlet-coated lips, but raised her eyebrows and set her glass back on the table. "It's about time."

Kate nodded in agreement. "I know it is. It's been a long time coming. I'm undervalued there."

"Yes, you are. Don't waste your talents there anymore." Lisa smiled. "Do you have another job lined up?"

Kate shook her head. "No. I want to think about things over the holidays. I'll start looking for something right after the New Year."

"Sounds like a plan," Lisa said. "Don't forget to use me as a reference."

The waiter brought their entrees. Lisa had ordered the queen's cut prime rib and Kate had chosen the seafood linguini.

Kate changed the subject. "Enough talk about me—how are things going with Nate?"

Lisa drew in a sharp breath. "Well, I already told him that we could never get married."

Kate laughed at her bluntness. "Why not?"

"Because his last name is Beane. Nate Beane," she explained, waving her fork in the air. "And if I marry him, my name will be Lisa Green Beane."

Kate winced at that and Lisa caught it.

"See what I mean?" she said between bites. "And it's a shame, because I really like him and he's marriage material."

Kate laughed and added, "Not to mention if you had children—"

Lisa cut her off. "I've been through it. They'd have a life of misery being called lima bean, string bean, and kidney bean."

They kept the rest of the meal light-hearted. They hugged when they parted and wished each other a merry Christmas.

In light of the fact that Kate didn't have to go to work on Wednesday, she decided to go to the spa in preparation for the Christmas party. She still dreaded going to the party alone, but at least Gavin wouldn't be there. She couldn't face him. The airport had reopened and he was surely en route to Ireland.

A facial was the first thing on her agenda. The technician had Kate lie flat on a bed and then she covered her up to her chest in warm, thick blankets. She rolled some warm goo on Kate's face and began to circulate and massage it. Kate began to relax and had to control her yawning. She chose to ignore the tech's comments about her large pores and her *obvious* tendency toward blackheads.

Kate stood up from the facial so drowsy she wanted to dive for the nearest sofa.

During her manicure and pedicure, she poured out her entire life story, outlining all the main players and how she was now quitting her job. The nail tech nodded sympathetically and even made some appropriate comments, however Kate suspected the girl thought she was in dire need of an inpatient psychiatric stay.

Eager for more self-improvement, she allowed herself to be talked into buying all sorts of lotions and potions. In fact, she'd spent so much money on product that she had none left for a tanning session.

She left the salon with her hair piled high on top of her head in an updo, strategically dotted with the tiniest of rhinestones.

Once home, she left her bag of spa products in the hall and got the mail from the mailbox on the front porch. She stood just inside the front door, leafing through numerous bills and stopping at a postcard that showed a picture of a white sandy beach, a cloudless blue sky, turquoise water, and one lone palm tree. Kate flipped it over and read, 'Hey babe—hot, sunny, and great poolside drinks. Wish you were here.' The last part was underlined. She closed her eyes. *Oh, Vinnie.*

She slipped on her dress. It was a dream dress she'd found online, and it seemed to be made just for her. It was a glittering, platinum-colored floor-length gown with a deep V-neck. Somehow it hugged her curves in just the right way. She thought that if moonlight and stars were a dress, then this would be it.

She took one final look, pleased with herself.

The doorbell rang. It was the cab she had ordered. She'd decided to treat herself and not drive alone.

She shut off the lights and locked the door. Unbidden, the thought of Gavin crept to the forefront of her mind. She kept trying to sink it into the recesses of her mind, but it kept popping back up. It was always there, tapping her on the shoulder. She bit her lip. *No crying,* she told herself. *You'll ruin your perfect makeup.*

It had snowed all day and a lovely, heavy blanket of it covered everything. The world glistened like crystal under the streetlights.

The Towne Royale was magnificent. The two-story lobby was all marble and gilt-covered, suggesting opulence from a previous era. A large chandelier with heavy crystal teardrops hung suspended in the main lobby. Directly beneath it stood a marble-topped gilded-leg table, on which sat a huge display of white poinsettias. French provincial furniture was positioned throughout the lobby on the gold floral-patterned carpet. A large white Christmas tree with gold decorations flanked the fireplace.

Kate checked her coat and threw a few dollars into the basket on the counter. She found the marquee for the Cline & Co. Christmas party and headed toward the ballroom.

It was breathtaking. It was a high-ceilinged room done up in salmon, maroon, and gold. In the center of the room was a parquet dance floor, surrounded by clusters of round tables covered in cream-colored linens. Every table had eight upholstered chairs around it. In the middle of each table stood a tall silver pedestal bedecked with white flowers and candles.

Sherrie and her husband, Nick, were sitting at a table with Amy Mohr and her fiancé, Brian. Sherrie waved to her when she saw her and motioned to the empty seat at their table.

"Oh, Kate, you look gorgeous," Sherrie gushed when she saw her. Sherrie looked radiant herself in a black strapless evening gown. She stood up and hugged Kate.

Sherrie's husband kissed her hello.

Kate sat down next to Sherrie and laid her purse on the table.

Sherrie leaned into her and whispered, "Guess what happened at work?"

Kate looked at her with raised eyebrows.

"Remember that brilliant brainstorm that Alexis and Mr. Cline had about you and the reality TV show?" Sherrie looked at her pointedly.

Kate interrupted her. "Mr. Cline told me that they weren't pursuing that anymore."

"No wonder," her friend answered. "Do you know why?"

Kate did know, but shook her head, as she didn't want to have to explain that she had stormed into Gavin's office, made of fool of herself, and then cried all over his shirt. She nodded to the waiter who appeared and he poured some wine into her glass.

"Gavin Whyte put the kibosh on it," Sherrie beamed. "Now what do you think of that?"

"Well, I'm not surprised. He said he would take care of it," Kate said.

"You knew?" Sherrie quizzed.

"He may have mentioned it in passing," Kate said, evasively.

Sherrie talked on. "Well, whatever you said to him, it must have worked, because he was absolutely livid. He walked into a meeting with creative and account services and told Alexis very calmly that he didn't want the ad campaign turning into a three-ring circus. Let me tell you, Kate, he was contained white-hot fury. Then I heard he went into Mr. Cline's office and went ballistic and told him that if he forced you to do this reality TV show he would pull the Alchemis account immediately."

"Really?" Kate thought of what she had overheard in the break room, when Irish had given her boss a good tongue-lashing— it had been one of the highlights of her year.

"I wish you could have been there. Alexis practically got down on her hands and knees, begging him not to pull the account." Sherrie was giggling.

"Speak of the devil," Kate whispered as Alexis appeared at their table. She was annoyed at Alexis' arrival. She wanted to digest everything Sherrie had just told her and figure out how it fell into the whole scheme of things.

Alexis wore a very revealing red halter dress.

"No date tonight, Alexis?" Sherrie asked.

She shook her head. "I'm on my own tonight, open to all possibilities." She threw her head back and laughed.

Kate sipped her wine and sat a little straighter in her chair.

"Sherrie, do you think Gavin Whyte is gay?" Alexis asked.

Kate coughed and sputtered, almost spitting the wine out of her mouth.

"Absolutely not," Sherrie said with conviction.

Kate felt she had nothing to offer on the subject, so she said nothing.

"Why do you ask that?" Sherrie questioned Alexis.

"I don't know—he just doesn't seem interested..." Alexis said, her voice trailing off.

Sherrie had less patience with Alexis than Kate did. "Interested in what? Women? The weather? You?"

This was enough of a prompt for Alexis. "You know, I've asked him to dinner and other things a few times—in fact I even asked him to be my date for this party, but he always has an excuse."

A real woman would never admit to other women the constant rejection at the hands of her object of interest. Especially other women she wasn't particularly chummy with. However, Alexis' ego was so big and deformed that she didn't view this so much as a rejection of her, but as an aberration on his part.

"He never talks about a girlfriend or anything," she whined.

"Maybe he doesn't have one," Sherrie said. "Move on with your life, Alexis. Find another man."

"You're absolutely right, Sherrie." Alexis smiled and then scanned the chairs at their table. She honed in on two vacant ones.

"Any room at this table for me?"

"No!" Sherrie and Kate said in unison.

Alexis walked off in a huff toward the bar. Kate watched as she approached Paul and soon the two of them were deep in conversation. She'd forgotten about Paul. He had kept a low profile since Saturday night, refusing to enlighten anyone in the office as to how he'd gotten his black eye. Kate had said nothing either, not wanting to give the gossips anything to speculate about. From where she sat, it looked like his eye was starting to heal. She hoped that he would leave her alone tonight. She wanted no dramatics that evening. She planned on eating her dinner and staying long enough for her Kris Kringle, and then she would head home. She hoped to be home in time to curl up with a DVD and a mug of cocoa. She was counting the days until after Christmas when she would march into work and hand in her resignation letter.

After a fabulous dinner and dessert, Mr. Cline threw his linen napkin down on his table, stood up, and walked to the center of the room where hotel staff appeared out of nowhere and deftly handed him a microphone. (The brochure did say they would anticipate your every need.) He made a surprise announcement that there would be significant bonuses in their end-of-year checks. Everyone clapped, including Kate.

Kate noticed that Mrs. Cline was bedecked in a lot of black hair dye, black mascara, and black velvet. Her eyes were at half-mast, probably due to the pitcher of martinis in front of her. Kate sympathized; if she were married to Mr. Cline, she'd self-medicate, too.

"Hmm, no verbal abuse for a change," Sherrie said, leaning over to her. "It must be a New Year's resolution for him."

"It's not that at all," Kate said. "It's his black tie—it's cutting off the circulation to his head."

The dancing soon commenced. Kate watched Nick and Sherrie together on the dance floor. Fifteen years of being together and their rhythms were completely attuned to one another. She watched Amy and Brian together. Brian hadn't taken his eyes off of Amy all evening; he was clearly smitten.

Feeling alone and not wanting to wallow in it, Kate stood up from the table, retrieved her purse, and headed for the lobby, needing some fresh air and a change of scenery.

As she exited the ballroom, she came face to face with Gavin.

He looked stunning in a black tuxedo. His dark hair curled just above his collar.

He came to an abrupt halt in front of her, smiling.

"Kate, you look incredible," he said.

"Thank you." She smiled. She felt awkward, and fingered her purse nervously. Anxious to break the silence between them, she said, "I thought you were heading out to Ireland."

"I am, but I changed my flight," he said.

"Oh." It was the only response she could manage.

He stared at her, taking in her hair, her face, her dress. She loved the way he looked at her.

"Why did you leave the other night?" he asked. He stepped in closer to her and touched her arm.

She felt her face go red. "I had to," she said, looking away.

"Why?" he asked.

"You were gracious enough to let me stay in your room that night and I really appreciate it," she started. "But I didn't want it to be awkward in the morning."

Gavin frowned. "Why would it have been awkward?"

She saw Debbie Cjaka making her way toward them and Kate lowered her voice. "Gavin, you have a girlfriend. And having been cheated on myself in the past, I could not do that to another woman, no matter how I felt about you."

A look of surprise washed over his face. There it was out in the open; now he knew that she knew.

"Hold on, Kate—" he started, but Debbie Cjaka had come between them.

"Come, you two, they're doing the Kris Kringle. You don't want to miss that." She was beaming. It was the highlight of Debbie's year. She winked at Kate.

"No, I wouldn't miss that for the world," Kate said, and she turned her back on Gavin, her eyes wet with tears, and followed Debbie back into the grand ballroom. Gavin remained in the lobby.

She stood at the bar, ordered a drink, and watched as Mr. Cline, now dressed in a Santa Claus suit with microphone in hand, stood in front of a small table laden with gifts and began to call out individual names. She felt shaky; she hadn't expected Gavin to make an appearance. She thought for sure he'd be back in Ireland at this point. Why had he changed his flight?

One by one, Kate's work colleagues marched up to get their Christmas gifts, and there were small shrieks of delight when gifts were opened and a wave and a smile directed to the buyer. The pile gradually dwindled and Kate was just beginning to wonder if this would be another year where she was forgotten, when her name was called out. She walked up to Mr. Cline in his ridiculous Santa suit, and he handed her a tiny square box wrapped in heavy gold paper.

"Merry Christmas, Kate," he said. The way he winked at her, she prayed that he hadn't gotten her name in the exchange again.

She made her way back to the table and took her seat next to Sherrie. She tossed the gift carelessly onto the table.

"Open it, silly," Sherrie prodded.

"Who's yours from?" Kate asked, nodding toward the cellophane-wrapped wicker basket on the table in front of Sherrie. It was full of gourmet coffee and chocolate, and tied with a big, red bow. She picked up her own gift again, noting the expensive, heavy wrapping paper.

"Ben Davidson. Not bad, huh?" Sherrie said.

"That's a great gift," Kate said.

"C'mon. Open yours."

Kate tore off the gold-foiled Christmas paper to reveal a small black box embossed in gold lettering. She read it aloud. "Mr. Cavanaugh & Sons, Jewelers since 1875."

Sherrie looked at her quizzically. Kate shrugged and let out a nervous giggle. "It's probably a gag gift." Other than her parents and Paul, no one had ever bought her jewelry, and the little box looked suspiciously like a jewelry box. She opened it. Inside was a smaller black velvet box. She took this out and opened the top. Her eyes grew wide. Inside was a pair of diamond stud earrings. They were small, delicate, and absolutely gorgeous.

"Geez, these look real," she managed to say.

"They are. They're beautiful!" Sherrie enthused.

"It looks like someone spent a lot more than fifty dollars," Kate said, examining the earrings closely. They caught the light and dazzled. She thought there must be some mistake. "These can't be for me. Maybe Mr. Cline gave me the wrong gift. I wouldn't put it past him."

Sherrie picked up the box. "Look, there's a note inside."

Kate removed the note, unfolded it and read it aloud. "To Kate, the girl who put stars in my eyes. Gavin."

"Holy cow!" Sherrie said, grinning and clapping her hands.

Kate said nothing. She couldn't think straight.

"What does this mean?" Kate finally asked.

Sherrie laughed. "What does it mean? It means he likes you. A lot."

"What's going on here?" Debbie asked, as she leaned over their huddled shoulders.

"Kate just got a fantastic gift from the gift exchange," Sherrie told her.

"What did Gavin get you?" Debbie asked.

"How did you know he picked me?" Kate asked, turning around in her seat to look up at her.

"Do you think it was a coincidence that he drew your name?" Debbie asked, smiling.

"It wasn't?" Kate asked, dumbfounded.

Debbie shook her head.

"Do tell," Sherrie said.

Debbie explained. "I approached Gavin about our gift exchange. I didn't want him to feel excluded. I was surprised when he asked if he could have Kate's name—I told him that rules were rules and he had to pick randomly like everyone else. He then told me it would be the only excuse he would have to buy Kate a Christmas present. I asked him what was so special about Kate." Debbie paused and smiled. "And he said, 'Everything.'"

"Oh, wow, Kate, how romantic," Sherrie cooed, putting her hand up to her heart.

"What can I say, girls? He appealed to my sense of Christmas magic and romance," Debbie said.

"When did this happen?" Kate asked Debbie.

"Oh, weeks ago," Debbie said, shrugging her shoulders casually.

"But he has a girlfriend back home," Kate protested.

Debbie looked at her like she'd just grown a third eye. "No he doesn't. I asked him."

Kate was trying to process all of this. A little seed of horror was beginning to take root and grow as she realized she had made a false accusation against him. She was pretty sure there was a commandment about that and obviously, it was one she needed brushing up on.

"Show her the gift," Sherrie said, nudging her.

Debbie took a long look at the earrings and let out a low whistle. "He must think an awful lot of you, Kate. I'd say he parted with a few coins for these. I was surprised to see him here, as I know he's catching a plane back to Ireland first thing in the morning."

"I'd say," Sherrie agreed.

"Now girls, keep this to yourselves. Don't let anyone know that this year's gift exchange was compromised or next year's exchange will be a nightmare of requests and impositions," Debbie said.

Kate was not listening; she was too overwhelmed. Gavin actually had feelings for her? Mr. Tall, Dark, and Handsome? He didn't have a girlfriend. And pretty soon, he'd be leaving on a plane to Ireland and she'd miss her chance. She had to find him. She didn't know what she'd say to him, but she'd figure that out as she went. She couldn't let him leave without telling him how she felt. She'd never forgive herself.

"What's wrong?" Sherrie asked.

Kate stood up from the table.

"Where are you going?"

Absentmindedly, she responded, "I'll be right back. Will you watch my purse?"

Before Sherrie could answer, Kate headed off in the direction of the lobby. That's where she had left Gavin and where she had last seen him. She'd lost track of him during the gift exchange.

She clutched the earrings in her hand, thinking that she had to find him and not only thank him for the gift, but apologize as well. Again. She apologized to him a lot. And if he wouldn't accept her apology, she thought that it might be time to join the cloistered nuns up on Hertel Avenue.

There was no sign of him in the lobby. She checked the men's room surreptitiously and even the ladies' room in the off-chance he'd wandered in there by mistake. But there was no sign of him anywhere. Her heart began to sink. She went down a corridor off the main lobby and began opening doors to conference rooms in the slim hope that he was in one of them, contemplating his very being. There was no sign of Gavin. He was gone.

CHAPTER NINETEEN

Dejected, she made her way back into the ballroom in search of her purse. She tucked the earrings safely into her bag, dug out her cell phone, and rang for a cab. Sherrie tried to talk her into staying but she explained that she had had enough and just wanted to get home.

She waited alone in the lobby, just inside the entrance, willing her taxi to get there faster. She couldn't believe how much she had made a mess of things. Gavin had practically handed himself over on a platter and she kept handing him back! What on earth was wrong with her? And now, it was too late.

Her cab pulled up in front of the hotel and she climbed in, giving the driver her home address.

As they pulled away, she spotted Gavin standing in front of the hotel's water fountain, hands in his pockets. The water gushed high into the air with red and green spotlights shining on it, giving it a seasonal look. But he didn't seem to notice—he was staring at the sky. The moon was a pale orb in the middle of the navy sky.

"Stop the car," she told the driver. "I need to get out."

She climbed out and asked the driver to wait a minute.

Kate walked gingerly up the sidewalk, tottering in her high heels, on the lookout for black ice. The last thing she needed was to do a header in front of God and everybody.

Gavin noticed her and watched with interest as she approached him.

She tried to read his expression but she wasn't near enough to him. Butterflies flew around like kamikaze pilots in her stomach and she still had no idea what she was going to say. She bit her lip, wondering if he thought she'd come back for another round of false accusations. The truth was she was flying by the seat of her pants, as usual. *Note to self: in the future, try to think things through.*

Oops! Her shoe caught on something and almost tripped her up. An image of her sprawled out on the front lawn of the hotel appeared in her mind and she shuddered at the thought of it. The way things were going lately, nothing would surprise her anymore.

She attempted to take a step forward, but her foot was truly stuck. She glanced down to see that her stiletto heel was entangled in the grate on the sidewalk. She tried twisting her foot in the opposite direction but it wouldn't budge.

Gavin was at her side. "Problem?"

She let out a nervous laugh. "My shoe is stuck."

Without a word, he hitched up his trousers at the thigh and bent down, lifting the hem of her dress and placing his hand around her ankle. His grip was warm and firm. His touch made her breathless. She had to put her hand on his back to steady herself. She looked down at the top of his head, admiring his thick dark hair and the way it curled slightly at the collar of his tuxedo jacket. She almost gasped; she wanted so badly to reach out and touch it. And touch him. She closed her eyes and a sob caught in her throat.

He looked up at her. "Are you all right?"

She could only nod.

With a firm but careful twist, he freed her shoe from the grate. He stood up and gave her a small smile. She was sorry that his hand was no longer on her ankle.

"I wanted to thank you for the earrings. I love them!" she said. "They're the most beautiful thing anyone has ever given me. Thank you so much."

He bent his head in a slight nod of acknowledgement but said nothing. Despite her coat, the air was cold and damp.

"Gavin, I owe you an apology." Again.

When he didn't say anything, she soldiered on. "I am truly sorry."

She didn't know whether to laugh or cry. "I'm utterly hopeless."

"Well, I wouldn't say utterly," he smiled.

She laughed, a little relieved.

"Can I ask what made you think I had a girlfriend?"

He was beautiful in the moonlight!

"I overheard you on the phone telling someone that you loved them." She was embarrassed that she had basically just admitted to eavesdropping on his conversation. But it had to be done. Everything needed to be out in the open. "And then you were so quiet at the hockey game later that night, I just assumed you were missing your girlfriend."

"All this time, you thought I had a girlfriend?" he asked. "Why didn't you just ask me?"

She stared at the water fountain, unable to meet his gaze. She felt foolish. It had been easier to make assumptions. Jumping to conclusions was the only exercise she got. She looked up to find him watching her intently.

She struggled to find the words and when she spoke, she didn't look at him. "Had I asked you if you had a girlfriend, then you would have known how I felt about you, and I wasn't ready to put that out there. Yet."

"I see. I was talking on the phone that day to my mother. She'd had a big health scare."

Instinctively, Kate put her hand on his arm. "I'm sorry to hear that. Is she all right?"

He nodded, looking relieved. Kate knew how he felt. "She is now. It didn't look so good for a while but she'll be fine."

Neither one of them said anything for a few moments and the awkward silence stretched out between them.

"Tell me, how *do* you feel about me?" he asked.

Kate blushed. "I like you." She looked away. "A lot."

He smiled. "I will consider that your Christmas present to me this year."

"So you don't have a girlfriend?" she asked.

He shook his head. "But I'm in the market for one." He paused and added, "And I know exactly what I want."

He took a step closer and reached over and unbuttoned the top button of her coat. "Someone who does nothing without police involvement."

She laughed. He took another step closer and undid the middle button. "Someone who is funny and kind and a great baker."

She raised her eyebrows and smiled. He opened the bottom button and her coat fell open. "And most importantly, a girl whose beautiful blue eyes turn purple when she cries."

She blushed. He reached out and traced his finger from her neck down to her shoulder, making her shudder. "I love it when you blush like that. It's so beautiful." He slid his arms inside her coat and around her waist.

She wished she could DVR this moment so she could play it over and over for the rest of her life.

His face was inches from hers. "I've never met anyone like you. I can't stop thinking about you."

"Really?" she asked incredulously.

"Why do you have such a hard time believing this?" he asked softly.

Kate looked away. He pulled her closer to him and whispered in her ear, "Don't judge me by the actions of other men."

She could only nod, for his closeness, his scent, and the sound of his voice with that delicious accent had robbed her of the power of speech.

"Do you know what I realized yesterday morning when I woke up and found you gone?" he asked.

She shook her head and waited.

"That I want to spend the rest of my life waking up next to you."

His lips were mere inches from hers and the only sound was the sound of their breathing.

He kissed her tentatively at first, as if he wasn't sure if she felt the same way about him. She threw her arms around his neck and kissed him with urgency, letting him know in no uncertain terms precisely how she felt. His kiss became more demanding and she felt as if she couldn't get enough of it. She wanted to drink him in.

The cab driver was yelling something and Kate reluctantly pulled away from Gavin, breathless. Despite it being a snowy December evening, she no longer felt cold.

"Hey lady, do you want this cab or not?"

She giggled and Gavin held her tight. She shook her head and waved the driver on.

Looking back at Gavin, she asked, "Now where were we before we were so rudely interrupted?"

"I do believe that we were right here," he said as his lips came down on hers.

He wrapped her up in his arms and Kate O'Connor began her best Christmas ever.

ALSO BY MICHELE BROUDER

Happy Holidays Series
A Whyte Christmas
This Christmas
A Wish for Christmas
One Kiss for Christmas
A Wedding for Christmas

Escape to Ireland Series
A Match Made in Ireland
Her Fake Irish Husband
Her Irish Inheritance
A Match for the Matchmaker
Home, Sweet Irish Home
An Irish Christmas

Hideaway Bay Series
Coming Home to Hideaway Bay

Meet Me at Sunrise
Moonlight and Promises
When We Were Young
One Last Thing Before I Go

Printed in Great Britain
by Amazon

40161961R00192